ghostgirl

by Tonya Hurley

L B

Little, Brown and Company

New York Boston

Little, Brown and Company

Hachette Book Group • 237 Park Avenue, New York, NY 10017
Visit our website at www.lb-teens.com

Little, Brown and Company is a division of Hachette Book Group, Inc.
The Little, Brown name and logo are trademarks of Hachette Book Group, Inc.

First Paperback Edition: May 2010
First paper-over-board edition published in August 2008 by Little, Brown and Company

Library of Congress Cataloging-in-Publication Data
Hurley, Tonya.
  Ghostgirl / by Tonya Hurley. — 1st ed.
    p. cm.
  Summary: After dying, high school senior Charlotte Usher is as invisible to nearly everyone as she always felt, but despite what she learns in a sort of alternative high school for dead teens, she clings to life while seeking a way to go to the Fall Ball with the boy of her dreams.
  ISBN: 978-0-316-11357-1 (POB) / ISBN: 978-0-316-03635-1 (PB)
  [1. Future life—Fiction. 2. Popularity—Fiction. 3. High schools—Fiction. 4. Schools—Fiction. 5. Death—Fiction. 6. Ghosts—Fiction. 7. Friendship—Fiction.] I. Title.
PZ7.H95667Gho 2008
[Fic]—dc22   2007031541

10 9 8 7 6 5 4 3 2

RRD-C

Book design by Alison Impey

Printed in the United States

For Isabelle & Oscar

Acknowledgments

To my beloved, Michael Pagnotta — thank you for believing.

Thanks and love to my mother Beverly Hurley and to my twin sister and best friend Tracy Hurley Martin — your lifelong encouragement and support have made this book possible. Special thanks to my grandparents Anthony & Martha Kolencik — may you rest in peace until we are together again — and to Mary Nemchik, Tom Hurley, Mary Pagnotta, and Vincent Martin.

My heartfelt gratitude to all who helped bring *ghostgirl* to life: Nancy Conescu, Craig Phillips, Megan Tingley, Hardy Justice, Jane Rosenthal, Lawrence Mattis, Andy McNicol, Chuck Googe, Jr., Zack Zeiler, Andrew Smith, Tina McIntyre, Lisa Laginestra, Andrea Spooner, Christine Cuccio, Van Partible, Stephanie Voros, Alison Impey, Jonathan Lopes, Melanie Chang, Shawn Foster, and Chris Murphy.

ghostgirl

1

Ever Feel Invisible?

The only thing worse than being talked about
is not being talked about.
—Oscar Wilde

You never think it will happen to you.

You think about what it would be like. You go through it over and over in your mind, changing the scenario slightly each time, but deep down, you don't really believe it would ever happen, because it's something that happens to someone else, not to you.

harlotte Usher headed purposefully across the parking lot to the front doors of Hawthorne High, repeating her positive mantra — "This year is different. This is my year." Instead of being forever etched in her classmates' high school memories as the girl who just took up space, the seat filler, the one who sucked up precious air that could be put to better use, she was going to start off this year on the other foot, a foot with the hottest, most uncomfortable shoes that money could buy.

She'd wasted last year feeling like the unwanted stepchild of the Hawthorne High student body, and she wasn't about to go out like that. This year, the first day of school was going to be the first day of her new life.

Approaching the front steps, she could see the last flashes from the school yearbook staff's cameras sparking in the doorway, as Petula Kensington and her crew strutted farther and

farther down the hallway. They were always the last to arrive and then they'd suck everyone in behind them in some kind of super-popular undertow. With their entrance, the school year had officially begun. And Charlotte was alone outside and falling behind schedule. Same as always. So far.

The janitor manning the doorway peeked outside and looked around to see if anyone was coming. There wasn't. Well, there was, but, as usual, he had overlooked Charlotte, who was picking up speed as he began to close the massive metal door. To her, it looked like the door to a bank vault. But undaunted for a change, Charlotte reached the doors and found just enough room to squeeze in her new shoe and keep it from closing.

"Sorry, I didn't see you," the janitor mumbled indifferently.

She wasn't seen, which was expected, but she did get some acknowledgment and an apology. Her "Popular Plan" — a to-do list that she had meticulously crafted in hopes of snagging the object of her desire, Damen Dylan — must have been working.

Like many of her peers, Charlotte spent all summer working, but, unlike most, she was self-employed in the remodeling business, you could say. She had pored over last year's yearbook as if her life depended on it.

She'd studied Petula, the most popular girl in school, and her two ass-kissing best friends, the Wendys — Wendy Anderson and Wendy Thomas — the way some fangirls study their favorite celebrity. She wanted to get it perfect. Just like them.

She approached the first destination on her agenda with confidence: the sign-up sheet for cheerleader tryouts. Cheerleader. *The* most prized and exclusive "sorority" of all and her

Golden Ticket to being not only noticed but envied. Charlotte grabbed the old pen that was dangling from the clipboard by a frayed string held together with masking tape and started to sign her name in the last open spot.

As she started writing the "C," she was tapped harshly on the shoulder. Charlotte stopped writing and turned to see who was interrupting her first task of the day — no, of her new life — and then saw a line of girls who had been "camped out" all night waiting to sign up. The gathering resembled less of a tryout than a casting call.

The obnoxious candidate looked her over from head to toe, grabbed the pen, and simultaneously wrote her name in and Charlotte off. She then opened her hand and let the pen mercilessly drop the length of the string.

Charlotte watched the pen sway against the wall like a hanged man.

She heard the pack of aspiring cheerleaders giggling behind her as she walked away. Charlotte had experienced this kind of cruelty before — to her face and behind her back — and had always tried not to care about what other people thought or said about her. But even in makeover mode, she hadn't developed a skin so thick it could withstand total mortification.

Charlotte shook it off, refusing to lose her temper or her dignity. She consulted her planner and muttered, "Locker Assignments," to herself as she crossed it off the list and headed quickly to her next destination.

As she walked, her mind raced through her itinerary this past summer. If she was being honest, she had to admit that

ghostgirl

she had gone to a ridiculous amount of effort to get his attention. Some might say too much. There was no "nipping" or "tucking," nothing that extreme, but the hair, the diet, the wardrobe, the grooming, and the styling had pretty much taken up her entire vacation. After all, she'd taken a chance on herself, and when all was said and done, what real harm could come from a massive dose of self-improvement anyway?

Sure, she knew it was mainly . . . okay, *totally,* surface stuff, but so what. If her life so far was any indication, all that pat "inner beauty" sermonizing was a load of crap anyway. "Inner Beauty" does not get you invited to the greatest parties with the coolest people. It certainly doesn't get you invited to the Fall Ball with Damen Dylan.

Bottom line, Damen was a priority, and deadlines like the dance had a way of motivating Charlotte. Life was a series of choices, and she'd made hers.

She was able to justify her detour into superficiality as a strategic move. The way she saw it, there were only two ways to Damen. One was through Petula and her posse. But given Charlotte's reputation, or lack of one, the odds were not good. Those girls had always been popular. They always would be. In fact, the whole essence of popularity was its very unattainability. It wasn't something to be worked at or achieved. It was conferred — by what or whom, Charlotte thought, remained a mystery.

But — and this is where Charlotte's game plan took a much more subtle turn — if she could manage to *look* enough like Petula and the Wendys, *act* enough like them, *think* like them, "fit in" with the people Damen fit in with, she just might have

a chance with him. There was a lot to be said for looking the part, and she thought she had gotten at least that much right.

This led her to the other way to Damen. The better option. Her preferred option: bypass the girls completely and go straight for Damen himself. This was a risky move, for sure, since she wasn't much of a flirt. The makeover was the necessary first step, but the next phase was make or break. She'd signed up for classes she knew he would be in and planned to hang around his locker, which she was on her way to locate now.

Like everyone else, Damen never had given Charlotte a moment's notice before, and some makeup and a professional blowout were unlikely to change that. Still, Charlotte held out hope. Hope that if she could just spend some quality time with him, especially now that she had upgraded her exterior, things might yet work out.

This wasn't just wishful thinking on her part but rather a conclusion Charlotte had drawn from intensive observation of Damen. In the hundreds of pictures she had secretly taken of him during the years, Charlotte believed that she had detected a certain, well, decency in him. It was in his eyes, in his smile.

Damen was gorgeous and athletic and behaved exactly as an authentically handsome guy was supposed to behave — superior — but he was nice about it. Unsurprisingly, his decency was the thing about Damen that Petula liked the least. Maybe it was the quality she most disliked because it was the one she and all her friends lacked the most.

With the laughter from the cheerleading candidates still echoing in her ears, Charlotte was needing a little luck as she

approached the gym. The locker assignments were posted on the double doors, and Charlotte made a beeline for them. She ran her finger slowly down the alphabetized column of students, the P–Z page, glancing at their locker numbers as she searched for her own.

Each name was familiar; they were kids she'd grown up with, known since preschool or from elementary school or middle school. Their faces flashed through her mind like a slide show. Then she came to her name:

USHER, CHARLES. Locker: 7

"Seven is a lucky number!" she said, taking it as a good omen. "Biblical, in fact." She reached into her backpack and took out a pencil, threw it back in, and fished out a pen. She changed her name permanently from "Charles" to "Charlotte." She wanted it to be right — especially today.

Another finger-hunt down the list revealed that Damen's locker was on the other side of the building. She headed to her locker, giving herself a pep talk the whole way.

"No big deal," Charlotte reassured herself as she tested the combination on her lock a few times, opening and closing the door, before setting off to find Damen's.

She continued to walk and talk to herself, gesturing like some theater geek rehearsing a monologue, when she suddenly started to choke.

Preoccupied, she'd come to the skywalk, which was filled with smokers taking their last drags before class. The synchronous exhaling of carbon monoxide produced a dense, acrid fog, and it was already too late to hold her breath. So she walked faster. Conversations ended one by one as Charlotte passed

through. Lit cigarette butts were drowned in venti coffee cups or pounded out into the concrete as swirly traces of smoke escaped upward all around her.

As she emerged from the haze and approached the doors at the other end of the walkway, Charlotte could see a bunch of kids gathering and backing their way down the hall like autograph hounds at the stage door of a sold-out show.

"Damen!" she gasped with awe.

Above the throng, all she could see was his thick, beautiful hair, but that was all she needed. She knew it was *his* hair. No shapers, no wax, no putty, no gum, gel, volumizer, goop, or hint of metrosexuality of any kind. Just a simply gorgeous head of wavy hair. Charlotte kept her eyes on the prize as she broke into that weirdly desperate kind of run-walk that she'd used to get to the bus stop earlier, and sped breathlessly toward the locker next to his. She arrived just before Damen and the adoring crowd that had parted to let him through.

It had been a while since she had been this close to him in person, and it affected her more than she thought it would. She'd viewed him, or at least pictures of him, all summer, but this was the real thing.

She was starstruck. As he approached, the crowd converged. The closer he got, the less of him she could actually see. She stepped into the whirl of activity around him, trying to get closer still, but she was drowned in the vortex each time. On this, her first day, Charlotte found herself in an all-too-familiar place — on the outside looking in.

2

Dying To Be Popular

*I was one to the world,
But my dream was to be the world to one.*

—JJ

If it's meant to be,
then it will be.

——◆◆◆——

Believing this can be a good or not-so-good thing. "Meant to be" can comfort you if something happens that is hard to deal with or understand. But it can also take away all your power by relieving you of responsibility. If things do work out, then all your hard work was for nothing because it was bound to happen with or without your intervention. Charlotte was trying to decide if she had more faith in herself than she had in Fate.

he warning bell for first period rang, and the crowd around Damen dispersed. The hallway chatter thinned as students headed for class, and the only sound to be heard was the metallic echo of slamming lockers and the marching band tuning up with a ridiculous arrangement of what sounded like The Cure's "Why Can't I Be You?"

Despite the morning's setbacks, Charlotte tried to remain positive. Her first class, after all, was Physics with Mr. Widget. And Damen. And Petula too, for that matter. Physics would be like an episode of Wild Kingdom for Charlotte. She could get to study the exotic behavior of the popular girls like Petula, the Wendys and their friends and embark on the big game hunt to bag Damen.

Charlotte slipped through the classroom doorway and looked left at the students circling their preferred seats, dropping book

bags, zipping and unzipping backpacks searching for notebooks, pens, pencils, calculators. She could tell it was the first day of school because everybody was so . . . prepared, if not totally happy to be there.

The only empty seats she could see were in the back, behind Petula and the Wendys. One of them was probably being saved for Damen, she thought as she let out an involuntary squeal. She'd be spending first period for the whole year in really close proximity to the Hawthorne A-List. Perfect placement. But as she walked back, Charlotte realized that she was not exactly welcome.

There were no hi-fives, "how was your summer?" or even hellos from the other kids she passed. No acknowledgment of all her hard work or even the barest modicum of courtesy whatsoever. Just a disapproving scowl from both Wendys and a "who farted?" face from Petula as she approached the open desk behind them.

Charlotte sat down and stared blankly toward the front of the room counting heads. No Damen! Maybe he wasn't in this class after all! But he had to be. At least that's what it said when she steamed open his pre-registration envelope. Securing that little piece of intelligence had been the entire goal of her summer internship in the principal's office. She found herself feeling a little sick.

"BONDING AND MAGNETISM" was written on the blackboard in huge block letters and beneath was the comb-over of the seemingly decrepit and balding Mr. Widget. He was hunched over, wearing the PHYSICS IS PHUN tee that he wore to begin each year.

"Good morning, people. I'm Mr. Widget," he said, jumping

to his feet in response to the bell. His demeanor had changed entirely. From decaying mad scientist to game-show host. Widget's name never failed to produce a few snickers when he introduced himself, and this year was no exception. Just as quickly, however, the chuckles gave way to squinty eyes and tilted heads. Everyone had heard the rumors, but few had actually seen him this close before.

It wasn't totally obvious at first, but as Mr. Widget continued to speak, his gaze wandered without his head turning. In fact, he seemed able to stare at all of the students at the same time. Quite a useful tool for a teacher, Charlotte thought, except it wasn't a skill at all. He had a glass eye.

"You've all had some basic grounding in biology, chemistry, and science or you wouldn't be here, would you?" he said somewhat sarcastically.

"So, our first topic for the semester will be" — and for this he turned sideways with unexpected flair and gestured, palm up, to the blackboard — "bonding and magnetism — the laws of attraction.

"You all are interested in 'attraction,' *correct*?" he continued, rolling his *r*'s. Charlotte had to hold her right arm down to keep from raising it in agreement.

"And since I've always believed that the best way to learn anything is to *experiment* . . . our first order of business will be to choose lab partners. Everybody please stand and pair up."

The classmates turned toward each other, pointing to friends across the room, some were screaming and jumping up and down as if they'd "made it through to Hollywood" on *American Idol*. The Wendys were already a combo and Petula

surely would want Damen, but not enough to wait for him for very long. After just a few impatient seconds, she yanked the closest Wendy — Wendy Thomas — to her side, not wanting to get stuck with a loser.

Likewise, Wendy Anderson snapped up the last jock she could find with lightning speed while the other kids frantically made their choices. Charlotte was left standing solo, the only one not chosen. She'd been so distracted by Damen's absence that she really hadn't been paying attention to anyone. But now, standing knee-deep in humiliation, her entire school career came flooding back.

Is it really possible to feel so alone in a crowded room? she wondered as she felt her ears getting hot.

Widget scanned the room and caught a few last-minute stragglers arriving late, and made a halfhearted plea on Charlotte's behalf.

"C'mon people, she seems quite . . . capable."

Charlotte was waiting for him to bust out in an auctioneer voice, but he didn't, thank the Lord.

"Nobody for . . . ," Widget pointed and fumbled for Charlotte's name, but couldn't recall it, "ah . . . her?"

Before he could even get the words out, everyone had paired up. The sounds of the marching band rehearsal outside seemed much louder to Charlotte now. And the laughs that she'd left at the cheerleader sign-ups made a roaring comeback.

Just when it couldn't get any more embarrassing, the door flung open.

"Sorry I'm late," Damen said hurriedly to Mr. Widget.

There he was! The clouds had parted and the sun was shining through.

"Ah, you're just the *somebody* we were looking for," Widget responded, knowing that being paired up with Charlotte would be sufficient punishment for his tardiness. He continued, "Meet your lab partner for the semester."

"I have a note," Damen pleaded, wide-eyed.

Charlotte looked like she wanted to burst. She was happy enough that he was in her class, let alone her very own lab partner. Was this happening? She somehow managed to maintain her composure as Damen walked over, resignedly.

Mr. Widget approached them for a word with Damen, but, given his glass eye, Charlotte thought he might be addressing her. They were both unsure and neither wanted to get off on the wrong foot, so they both paid attention.

"I think you should take advantage of this coupling. It looks like Fate to me," Widget said with a wink of his real eye.

Charlotte was over the moon and in total agreement, while Damen looked somewhat miserable and a little confused, both by the statement and by Widget's glass eye, which he was getting a good look at for the first time. Mr. Widget then leaned into Damen, as was his habit.

"You know, they're really cracking down on student athletes this year. There's a new policy. You have to maintain a C average in all of your subjects or you'll be kicked off the team," he warned.

Charlotte, seeing an opening to advance her strategy, smiled and blurted out, "I love Physics!"

Mr. Widget and Damen looked at Charlotte oddly, as if they were studying a trained parakeet screeching out nonsense words from a cage. Widget walked away with a slight smirk on his face as he packed up his things. Damen leaned into Charlotte, trying to be discreet.

"Hey . . . ," Damen whispered, "uh . . ." He stuttered, fumbling for her name.

". . . Charlotte," she responded helpfully, pointing to herself.

"You're smart . . . ," he continued, matter-of-factly.

"Thank you," she replied, clasping her hands behind her back modestly, as if he were paying her a flirtatious compliment.

"I was wondering . . . ," he continued.

"Yes???" Charlotte eagerly responded, as if he were going to ask her out right then and there!

"Would you maybe be into, you know, tutoring me or whatever?" he asked.

Charlotte wasn't so naïve to believe this was a romantic gesture, or even a friendly one. She knew he had a major ulterior motive. Still, she dismissed all that and put the best spin on it. It wasn't an invitation to the dance, but it was an opportunity to spend time alone with him, and she couldn't have been more thrilled.

She stifled the quiver in her voice and consciously tightened up her knees, which had been slowly buckling ever since Damen walked in the classroom. She tried to play it cool for a second as she kept him waiting for a response to his offer. Her wish was coming true, not the way she had intended, but coming true just the same. It was Fate, like Widget said. It had to be.

Just as she was about to agree, Petula, with one Wendy on each side, walked over to Damen and interrupted.

"Where were you?" she asked Damen angrily.

"Time's up," Wendy Anderson said snidely to Charlotte, hip-checking her to the outskirts of the conversation.

Charlotte stuck around anyway and started popping gummy bears in her mouth as she put her laptop and books away. She decided to try and "hang" like she was one of the group while she waited to get a last word with Damen.

"I was sooooo worried," Petula cooed.

The idea of Petula caring that much about anyone else's well-being, even Damen's, was so ludicrous that even the Wendys had to turn away and bite their lips to keep from laughing.

"Not worried enough to wait for me though," Damen said sarcastically, looking back at Charlotte and making it clear to Petula he knew she was more worried about getting stuck with a D-List lab partner than his whereabouts.

"You didn't expect me to wait, like, forever, did you?" Petula said selfishly. Petula's choice of words surprised Charlotte, since she would have waited forever and a day for him.

"Forever?" Damen jibed. "I told you I might be a little late."

"Oh, really? I didn't get your text," Petula replied, only half-listening by this point.

"How'd you know it was a text, then?" Damen said as he shook his head and zipped up his backpack.

Stalling until she could come up with a plausible excuse, Petula rambled, "My phone was in my bag, and my bag is —"

"Right here," a snotty voice interrupted from outside the classroom. Petula turned to the familiar but unwelcome

sound to see a girl holding her bag as if it were radioactive. She rolled her eyes in disdain and walked to the doorway.

"Didn't I tell you never to touch my things!" Petula said firmly in a loud whisper.

"You left it in Dad's car and I didn't want you to get textually frustrated, God forbid," the girl said, holding the super-expensive designer satchel at arm's length. "Besides, I know how hard it is for you to get through a day without lip plump."

"I don't plump!" Petula snapped.

Charlotte was as shocked by the young girl's brashness as her darkwave-meets-burlesque outfit: pink and black Plasmatics tee peeking out from under a long fitted V-neck, an enormous vintage pink-stoned ring to emphasize her overused middle finger, short black skirt, black fishnets, silver studded flats, and flaming matte red lipstick. She recognized her immediately as Scarlet Kensington, Petula's younger sister. And from the looks of things, the only thing they had in common was DNA.

Petula snatched the purse away with a scowl and rifled through the bag to make sure nothing was missing. Confirming that all was indeed intact, she pulled out a razor blade that she used to shave her silky-smooth legs.

"This is for you," Petula offered sarcastically. "A little gesture of appreciation. Maybe you can use it to relieve some stress later?"

The Wendys laughed out loud at the dis while Damen just shook his head as if to say, "Here we go again."

"The only way to relieve my stress is if I cut your throat with it, but then what would you vomit your meals through?" Scarlet said with a phony smile.

Charlotte could not believe Scarlet's audacity and let out a single gasp ignored by everyone but Scarlet.

"What are you looking at?" Scarlet groused, her dyed black bob flying around her face like a dark curtain as she turned to stare daggers at Charlotte. She was totally intimidated as Scarlet's hazel eyes burned into her.

Before Charlotte could get out a "Who, me?" in response, Scarlet turned and bolted, the jiggling sound from the chains on her leather jacket fading as she turned away.

Petula, her attention span rapidly shrinking, reached for her lip gloss and spackled her lips with her signature shade of pink. She held the compact up, turned her face to each side, pouted seductively, decided she looked great, and kissed the mirror, leaving, as always, a perfect pink lipstick trace.

Charlotte, who was close enough behind Petula to see her own reflection in the compact, lined up her lips with Petula's mirror kiss, pretending for a second they were her own.

Sam Wolfe, a "slow" student affectionately nicknamed A/V Retard by Petula and her friends, startled Petula and Charlotte from their respective daydreams as he awkwardly moved the video monitor in front of the room, next to them. Petula, still stressing over the shade of her ball gown, snapped the compact shut and turned to Sam without warning.

"You're so lucky you're retarded," Petula said at Sam.

Sam smiled indifferently, but Damen looked at Petula in disgust. Charlotte made a mental note — she was liking him more and more.

"What?" Petula replied to Damen's look of disapproval with genuine confusion.

She then turned to Sam again, and in her own pseudosensitive way attempted an apology.

"Oh, I'm sorry . . . MENTALLY retarded," she said to him, now thinking she was PC.

The bell rang and everyone started frantically filing out of the room. Everyone except for the Wendys, Damen, and Petula, who always took their time leaving and getting to the next class. Charlotte, too, slowed down, remaining at her desk, nervously popping more gummy bears as she became increasingly preoccupied by Damen and Petula's conversation and increasingly hopeful that she and Damen might be able to finish theirs.

She watched Petula give him a perfunctory air kiss as they prepared to go their separate ways. Damen left first, and as he passed by the teacher's desk, Mr. Widget also stood to leave, but took a second to caution Damen.

"Remember the new policy, Mr. Dylan," Widget warned as he closed his briefcase and walked out.

With that, Damen was reminded of his encounter with Charlotte a few minutes before. He looked back nonchalantly and held up his Physics book in Charlotte's direction. He opened his eyes wide and shrugged his shoulders, as if he was asking for Charlotte to give him an answer.

"Will you help me?" Damen mouthed to Charlotte, backing slowly out the doorway and followed closely by Petula and crew.

Charlotte popped a last gummy bear into her mouth, and as she started to walk forward and mouth her response, she accidentally sucked in the candy, lodging it in her throat.

She started to walk faster to the doorway, making desperate hand signals, but there was such a big crowd around Damen

already, as soon as he stepped out into the hallway, he couldn't even see her. Charlotte was doing her best to cough up the gummy bear so that she could yell out to him, but just as it was about to dislodge, Petula abruptly slammed the classroom door shut in Charlotte's face.

Charlotte smacked right into it, lodging the candy even deeper in her airway. She tried futilely to give herself the Heimlich, sputtering around like a balloon losing air. She was gagging badly now and the room was totally empty. There was no one to notice her. No one to help.

She put one hand around her throat and the other up on the glass window in the door to steady herself. Unable to breathe, she desperately tried to get Damen's attention by pounding her hand on the window, but Damen thought she was just waving to him.

He waved back at her briefly, put his arm around Petula, and headed for the next class.

She pressed her face against the glass like Tiny Tim outside the toy shop, and, unable to keep herself up, ever so slowly slid down the door. She could still see the students laughing and talking on their way to their next class as she fell, keeping Damen and Petula in her sights as they walked away.

Her hand, which she hoped someone would see, slowly lost its clammy grasp on the long rectangular window as her faint handprint smeared its way down to the ground, joining the rest of her body on the floor.

3

A Wake

How can you see into my eyes like open doors

Leading you down into my core

Where I've become so numb without a soul

My spirit sleeping somewhere cold

Until you find it there and lead it back home.

—Evanescence

How do you know?

———❖———

How do you know that it's not just some crazy fantasy or dream, a delusion you've created in your own mind? There are no dress rehearsals in life and there certainly aren't any in love. That much Charlotte now knew.

houghts of Damen were swirling manically through Charlotte's mind as she woke to the gentle buzzing from the fluorescent bulbs that lined the classroom ceiling. As she slowly opened one eye, and then the other, she couldn't help but notice the cool white light was bright, but it didn't hurt to stare at it.

She blinked a few times and then jacked herself into a semi-seated position, propping herself up on her elbows. She could see the dingy, brownish water stains and the spitballs stuck to the foam board ceiling squares above her. She felt a little dizzy but blamed it on all the excitement.

"Great, he asks me to help him. ME. And what do I do? I pass out," she chastised herself.

All those changes she'd struggled to make, Charlotte reasoned, hadn't changed who she was on the inside. What was it that Horace said? "We can change our skies but not our nature"

or something like that? You are who and what you are. The sad reality that a 2,000-year-old Roman poet probably had a better grasp of her life than she did was . . . disappointing to say the least. Even weirder was why this, of all things, was occurring to her just now. And then a much less demoralizing scenario sunk in.

It must have been low blood sugar! she thought, remembering that she forgot to eat breakfast in her anxiety to make the bus and amid all her premeditated brushes with Damen at school.

As Charlotte turned her head from side to side, she noticed that she was totally alone. No surprise, since she didn't really expect that anyone would be looking for her. Then, looking down, she realized she was not as alone as she thought. There it was — The Gummy Bear — lying there innocent and lifeless, almost taunting her like the Talking Tina doll in that old *Twilight Zone* episode. It wasn't the slightly opaque color red, but rather the transparent bright red that they turn when they are sucked on a little.

She stared at the candy for quite sometime — oddly suspicious of it — reached for her throat, and coughed. It was there on the floor but she still felt it in her larynx.

"That's . . . peculiar," Charlotte said, completely perplexed.

Just as she began forming a recollection of what happened, an announcement came over the PA system.

"Charlotte Usher, please report to room 1313," the muffled voice requested.

She gathered her stuff and walked out the door into the empty hallway, in a pretty good mood, all things considered. Expecting to be heckled on her way to the office, she was al-

most disappointed that her summoning had gone unnoticed, but then again, everyone was in class, so she marched on.

"Room 1313?" she asked herself, still reeling from her brush with both Damen and the gummy bear.

Turning down a long corridor, a reading of Edgar Allan Poe's "Annabel Lee" seeped into the hall from a distant classroom. It was her second period Lit class, a place she was supposed to be, already in progress. The words echoed through the vacant hallway, bouncing off the newly waxed and buffed first-day-of-school floors.

> *But our love it was stronger by far than the love*
> *Of those who were older than we —*
> *Of many far wiser than we —*
> *And neither the angels in Heaven above,*
> *Nor the demons down under the sea,*
> *Can ever dissever my soul from the soul*
> *Of the beautiful Annabel Lee.*

For some reason, she seemed to know the way to the strange room, though she'd never been there. She was drawn to an unmarked door at the end of the hallway. As she opened it, she looked down the stairwell into a basement area, still more disoriented than scared. Descending, she could see the chipped, exposed pipes on the ceiling above her and a cement floor below as she stepped down. Charlotte took a breath and held her nose as a precautionary measure thinking she'd sucked in enough pollutants for one day on the skywalk.

"Walk this way," she whined to herself, nose pinched,

channeling her best *Young Frankenstein,* and headed down. Her footsteps fell silently.

The pipes looked slick from condensation, but oddly, they weren't dripping, and there was no smell of mildew or mold. She let go her nose to take a second breath and quickly realized there was no need to go on holding it.

As she walked on through the narrow corridor of plumbing, air ducts, and wiring, she saw a light shining into her path and stopped. It was bright, but pale, like moonlight. It seemed to come from behind the old boiler, which was cold from not running. She peeked behind and saw a room in the corner. Etched in the glass on the door was 1313.

Charlotte was starting to get nervous, not so much from the ominous office and chilly beams that emanated from it, but because she was falling behind her self-imposed schedule. This little detour had taken up so much of the time she planned to use stalking, er, "getting to know" Damen. Still, she was more curious then irritated when it hit her.

"This must be where the sign-ups are for AP classes! Could this day get any better?" she asked herself obliviously, bolting through the doorway and up to the counter with all the exuberance of Tracy Flick in *Election.*

The first thing she saw was an old transistor radio and a few vases of wilted flowers at the reception desk. The first thing she heard was the Terry Jacks song "Seasons in the Sun" playing at low volume. She didn't know the song well, but hearing it now, wafting through the humid air, in such a quiet, dank, and empty room, it was hard to imagine it was ever a hit. Even in the seventies.

Bummer, Charlotte thought as she looked around and drummed her fingers on the counter, hoping someone might hear.

"Hi, ah, I got called to this office? Charlotte Usher!" she finally yelled to the back of the office, hoping to get someone's attention.

A secretary with a messy bun and wearing a high-neck, lace Victorian blouse popped up from below the desk.

"Oh, sorry, I didn't mean to yell. I didn't think to look down," Charlotte said.

"No one ever does, sweetheart," the secretary quipped.

Without making eye contact, the secretary handed her a clipboard with a bunch of paperwork.

"Here, fill these out, and remember . . ." the secretary stopped mid-sentence and pulled Charlotte close to her, as if she were about to impart some invaluable advice. ". . . to give me back my PEN."

Charlotte was taken aback by the secretary's strange behavior, but then she thought that if the woman was a "people person," she wouldn't be stuck in a high school basement, working by herself, in virtual isolation.

Before Charlotte could get her first question out, the secretary slammed the window shut. Charlotte organized the papers on the clipboard and headed over to take a seat next to a girl sporting long, curly orange-red locks and a bright Kelly green majorette outfit. Charlotte didn't think the girl was there when she first came in, but she'd been so preoccupied she couldn't be sure.

As she shuffled through the paperwork for a second, she

turned her head and tried to make eye contact with her —
without success.

"Hi. I'm Charlotte," she said tentatively, her hand thrust
forward for a shake. And . . . nothing.

The greeting seemed to fall on deaf, or at least disinterested, ears as the girl kept looking downward, her nose in her
book. Charlotte was all too used to this kind of dismissive
treatment, but from a NEW girl? Were things actually worse
than she imagined?

She decided to overcompensate, thrusting her hand out
even farther, but the girl continued reading, not even acknowledging the Charlotte Usher welcome wagon. Maybe this girl
was already friends with someone else in school, Charlotte
thought. Maybe she moved here over the summer and this
"friend in school" told her about Charlotte. No, that couldn't
be right; she couldn't imagine anyone talking about her over
the summer — even to say bad stuff.

Charlotte was awakened from her daydream by a faint whistling sound. Kind of like a solo flute warming up in the band
room. Looking around, Charlotte could not tell for the life of
her where the sound originated. She put her finger in her ear,
twirled it around, and hoped the noise would stop. It didn't, so
she tried her best to ignore it, turning her attention back to the
forms. The top of the first page read "New Student."

"Ah, so I guess this *does* mean that I got A.P. classes for next
year!" She trumpeted proudly, hoping to impress the girl.

In her excitement, she started filling out the paperwork
quickly, barely reading the questions.

As her slender fingers glided over the questions at a light-

ning pace, she became increasingly leery as she read them out loud:

"'Full Name, Date of Birth, Place of Birth, Sex . . .'"

"Sex? . . . Yes, please!" Charlotte said out loud, trying yet again to get the girl's attention, but to no avail.

"'*Organ donor*'?" Charlotte read, just a little less giddily. "Wow, they need to know everything."

She continued to fill out the sheet as best she could, arriving at the end of the form and her patience at just about the same time. The last box read "C.O.D."

"C.O.D.?" Charlotte said aloud, now totally exasperated. "Cash On Delivery? I shouldn't have to pay for A.P. classes. This is public school."

She left that space blank and returned the paperwork and the pen to the secretary, who handed back a tag with Charlotte's name on it, attached to a very small elastic band.

"Here's your ID," the secretary snapped.

"Ah, thanks," Charlotte replied, not quite sure why she needed a new ID, but way too intimidated to ask.

Charlotte pulled the tag out of the secretary's cold, clenching grasp and put it on her wrist. Although it was super-tight, she kept it on and didn't say a word.

The secretary stamped Charlotte's papers as "received" and then approached a jumbo stainless steel filing cabinet.

"Okay. One more thing . . . I need you to confirm . . ." She paused, turned, and nonchalantly opened a large drawer. ". . . That this is YOU, and initial here."

Charlotte was stunned. She could not believe what she was seeing. There it was. Her silent and graying corpse, still wearing

her first-day-of-school outfit, lying still on the metal slab right before her very eyes. She wanted to faint, but she was paralyzed.

For the first time, she began to feel the cold in the room creep along her skin. She grabbed her wrist and pressed for her pulse. Nothing. She brought both palms to her chest to feel for her heart, which should have been pounding by now. But there was no beat. Freaked and shuddering, she moved closer to the cadaver and poked it gingerly in each limb, hoping for a reaction. Again, nothing. The final straw: an opened package of GUMMY BEARS protruding from her pocket with the culprit, the murderer, in a ziplock bag pinned to her chest. It wasn't a trick. This *WAS* her!

"C.O.D . . . Cause Of Death," the secretary instructed, pointing to the candy as she broke out in a grin.

Charlotte recoiled in an effort to distance herself from the corpse and tripped, hitting a huge industrial metal fan on the desk. It fell directly on her forearm, catching her hand in the blades.

Helpless, she watched as, one by one, her fingers were chopped off right at the middle knuckle by the twirling scythes. Her digits went flying off in every direction, spraying the room. She clenched her eyes shut and waited for the pain and the nauseating warmth of spurting blood to arrive. But it never came.

Confused, she mustered all her courage and opened both eyes ever so slowly and looked. Her hand, which should have been mangled, gnarled, and torn to pieces, was completely unscathed. She held it up and examined it over and over, mesmerized.

The girl in the waiting room approached just as Charlotte desperately tried to digest the reality of the surreal moment.

"Nothing can hurt you anymore," the girl said matter-of-factly. "I'm Pam . . . and you're, well, you're . . ." Pam said as she bent down to help Charlotte up.

"No, please don't say . . ." Charlotte begged.

". . . Dead," Pam whispered, directly into Charlotte's ear.

Her words blew through Charlotte's ear and into her mind like a blustery winter wind, and as they did, the haze of her own obliviousness began to clear. Looking around the room now, it was as if someone had hit the "rewind" button on her day. She saw everything from a different, almost third-person perspective, noting things that she hadn't before.

It was all so obvious. The loudspeaker announcement, the cold basement, the "waiting" room. She looked around and started to notice things that she hadn't before, like the unnatural blue tint of the secretary's nails, the morgue-like filing cabinets in the back, the examination lights. And, of course, the gummy bear.

Charlotte screamed with such intensity that no sound came from her mouth. It was an otherworldly scream, one that can only be produced through sheer and utter terror.

"You're dead," echoed through her mind and rattled her soul as she ran out of the room and into the stairwell.

4

Why Me?

All that we see or seem
Is but a dream within a dream.
—Edgar Allan Poe

Destiny is the best
defense mechanism.

⸺ ◆ ⸺

It offers solace that there is order in the
Universe and saves a lot of time and effort
explaining the unexplainable — especially to
yourself. Charlotte was gradually becoming
less of a skeptic and more of a believer. It
was definitely easier — and more importantly,
it worked to her advantage. She believed
because she had to.

hy me? Why me?" Charlotte repeated, not really expecting an answer, but hoping that the more times she uttered the question, the clearer her situation would become, and just maybe she could find the solution. That's how she approached her Trig homework, by repeating the problem out loud to herself, and it always produced results. She prided herself on her self-reliance.

She recalled a fact that most people had heart attacks on Monday, the first day of the week. She died on the first day of school, when everything was on the brink of going her way. Why was this happening? Why did it happen after Fate paired her and Damen as lab partners? She needed answers.

Charlotte raced up the staircase, still screaming, burst through the unmarked door into the hallway, and screeched to a stop at the sight of Pam directly in front of her. She thought

that if she ran fast enough, she could escape from the nightmare she was living, or not living, as the case might be.

"You can't run from this . . . ," Pam said calmly as Charlotte, spooked beyond words, turned completely around and tried. Rounding the corner of the newly waxed hallway, she noticed there was no echo to her footsteps, no squeaking from the rubber on the bottoms of her shoes.

With each turn, *BAM!* — there was Pam. Charlotte grabbed her heart, but then remembered that there was nothing to clench. Her heart was not beating. Her chest felt like it was a hollow cavity encasing a cold, hard rock.

"You can't run from this . . . ," Pam repeated as Charlotte scurried away.

Trying desperately to escape the wraith, and the reality closing in on her, Charlotte headed instinctively for the Physics classroom. What better place to find answers than the scene of the crime? As she entered, Charlotte noticed she'd stepped over something, but wasn't quite sure what it was. She turned around and looked down to see a chalk outline of a body. Her body.

"An empty shell. *That's* how they'll remember me now," she said despondently, considering that this generic, sexless, roughly drawn, gingerbread cookie–like figure was now to be her last, as well as lasting, impression on the Hawthorne student body.

It was the scene of the crime, all right. The crime against all that is unjust in society. The crime against humanity. The societal ranking system laid out right there on the ground for all to walk over.

Dying was horrible enough, but to die in such a pathetic and stupid way . . . choking on a bear-shaped semisoft gelatinous candy was an indignity almost too much for Charlotte to bear. It would validate everything they'd always thought about her and confirm her worst fears about herself. She couldn't even chew right.

What was left to do other than punish herself a little bit more? So she lay down on her back, arms and legs splayed, configuring herself exactly to the outline, in a gesture of surrender. A sort of morbid snow angel, if you will.

And for just a second, everything seemed just a little bit funny. Cruelly, ironically funny. The final and most appropriate in a series of embarrassing pranks ever to be played on her, and she was in on the joke. Mr. Widget was right. Fate had intervened in her day, her life, but not exactly as she had hoped. Not nearly.

"God must really have quite a sense of humor," she thought, staring upward.

Then, speaking of "God," something not so funny crossed her mind. She hadn't seen or heard anything from the Big Guy, or Big Gal, as the case might be. Best to remain PC, she cautiously thought, as now, everything counted.

She'd spent a lifetime being judged. How bad could this be? The fleeting thought of her luck getting worse was more than enough motivation, however, to get her up from the classroom floor.

Charlotte straightened herself up, paused mournfully over the outline as one might at a grave, and walked slowly toward the door. Stepping back into the hallway, she could see Pam

pointing ominously at something — kind of like one of those Ghosts of Christmas Whatever. It was her locker. Number Seven.

"Yeah, *what a lucky number,*" Charlotte said, dripping sarcasm.

The locker was shut tightly by caution tape. No evidence of tampering by the other kids, which was pretty insulting, actually. It meant that no one was even curious enough about her stuff — *about her* — to steal anything. She walked away, a strand of the caution tape stuck to her foot like a piece of wayward toilet paper.

"This is NOT happening," Charlotte moaned, closing her eyes to wish it all away. As she opened them again, Pam reappeared, but Charlotte was a little less startled than before. "How long have I been . . . gone?" she asked tentatively.

"I don't know exactly," Pam answered matter-of-factly. "Time doesn't really mean anything here."

"You mean I could be . . . gone . . . for, like, a thousand years already?" Charlotte pondered.

"Probably not," Pam said, and pointed silently again, this time toward a window. "Look."

Charlotte looked out toward the parking lot in front of the school, where a group of classmates were gathering around a minibus as yet another announcement came over the loud-speaker.

"Attention, students! Any of you who would like to attend the Charlotte Usher Memorial, please report to the courtyard. The bus will be departing shortly."

Charlotte could not believe what she was seeing. If it were still possible, a tear might have come to her eye. There was a small group of people waiting to board the bus for *her* memorial.

Could it be that dying had made her more popular than she ever imagined? Her mind started swimming wild with possibilities. What would they say about her at the memorial? Would anyone, dare she even hope, weep? Might there even be an outpouring of emotion in the community? Official Days of Mourning. She was filled with anticipation. This was suddenly really . . . exciting.

Charlotte was shaken from her reverie by an even more baffling development. There, in the middle of the throng, was Petula and the Wendys — crying! Charlotte could not believe it. Was this heaven after all? Maybe she was now the same as all those writers and artists who were ignored during their lifetimes but revered in the end. She had become perfect in death. Canonized, by even her greatest detractors. Maybe even Damen would miss her now.

These comforting thoughts lasted for about as long as it took Charlotte to puff out her flat chest in pride. It wasn't collective grief that attracted Petula and the Wendys after all, but the cameras and notepads of the school press corps, and the promise of an early dismissal for the day. Charlotte braced herself and listened through the open window to the reporter's questions . . . and Petula's answers.

"I ate half a gummy bear for lunch just yesterday," Petula said as she "sobbed," studiously wiping at her eyeliner with

the French-manicured tip on her index finger, all the while sneaking a peek at her makeup in Sam's A/V video monitor. "It could have been me!"

"She's a gummy bear survivor!" Wendy Anderson chirped to the reporters like a junior publicist as both Wendys held Petula, trying desperately to comfort her.

Leave it to Petula to jockey for face time by selfishly playing victim and sucking the air out of her memorial! And as much as Charlotte hated it, she admired it. Envied it, even. It was hard for Charlotte to sort out whether Petula just found it impossible to give up the limelight to anyone else or that she just couldn't let a great opportunity to promote herself go by. The end result was the same either way, she guessed. It was all about Petula.

As the press opportunity ended, camera crews packed up their equipment, and Petula commanded the Wendys to TiVo the local cable access channel, Charlotte noticed the rest of the slackers swinging their arms through backpacks like parachutes, high-fiving each other, a sure sign the day was over. Yes, they cared. They cared about skipping school.

"Let's see now," Charlotte recounted, turning away from the window, "I'm dead AND forgotten."

Pam watched her meltdown begin and said nothing. Charlotte was grieving for herself, which was normal, but was also becoming unusually unstable. At least Pam didn't have to worry about Charlotte missing her family. Dead teens didn't. They were *way* too self-involved.

Charlotte's "Why me?" mantra now changed to "Why not me?" as glimpses of her geeky and loser-ish self began to

re-emerge. There was no point repressing it any longer. Summer was over and everything, literally everything, was lost.

"Why couldn't something bad have happened to Petula?" Charlotte ranted spitefully. "Maybe it will," she hoped. "But, then," she continued, catching herself mid-argument, "if something like this happened to someone like Petula, it would make national news, wouldn't it? Gummy bears would be pulled off every shelf. There would be national hearings on gummy bear safety. CNN would declare gummy bears the new bird flu. There would be 'team coverage' on the gummy bear crisis. Not to mention the televised memorials every year. Damen would send red roses to her grave anonymously on a weekly basis for the rest of his life. Hawthorne High would be re-named in her honor. Church bells would toll commemorating the exact moment of her passing. Not for what she ever did in her life, but for who she was. She would be a hero."

Charlotte continued to babble at Pam and complain self-pityingly.

". . . And me?" Charlotte pondered. "I'm a chalk outline that people stepped *on,* not over. An inconvenience for the authorities. A lot of paperwork, not even worth a moment of silence."

She felt cheated.

"Are you through?" Pam asked.

"Almost," Charlotte said.

"Take your time," Pam replied, the first notes of sympathy sounding in her voice.

But it was the other notes Charlotte was hearing that really got her attention. A faint whistling. The kind she'd heard in

the office. This time there was no doubt about the source of the melancholy tones.

"What the heck is that noise coming out of your mouth?" Charlotte asked.

"Let me officially introduce myself," she said, extending her hand to Charlotte. "I'm Piccolo Pam."

"Piccolo?" Charlotte giggled.

"It's my death name," Pam answered.

"*Death* name?" Charlotte asked, realizing she didn't have one and feeling excluded once again.

"Yeah, it's like a nickname that some of us acquire, only it usually has to do with the way we died," Pam said. "You don't always get one right away. Don't take it personally."

How could she not? Charlotte thought what her "death name" might be and was becoming increasingly dismayed at the potential for perpetual humiliation a stupid death name might hold.

"I'm Piccolo Pam because I tripped while showboating, allegedly, at the all-county band parade and swallowed my piccolo."

"Oh, I'm so sorry," Charlotte said.

"Yeah, me too, but at least I went out doing something I loved and that I was really good at," Piccolo Pam replied.

"Yeah . . . ," Charlotte said softly.

"And I died during my solo, so no one will ever forget it. That's what matters," Piccolo Pam added proudly.

"Yeah . . . ," Charlotte repeated blankly. She was clearly overwhelmed, trying desperately to make sense of everything.

Piccolo Pam smiled and put her arm around Charlotte. She squeezed her a few times, trying to cheer her up.

"It's not all bad," Pam joked. "Look at it this way, at least you don't have to shave anymore!"

Charlotte still wasn't sure if God had a sense of humor, but Pam sure did.

"Not that bad?" Charlotte said, bug-eyed with indignation. "I'm going to be known as a 'choker' for all eternity!"

As she grew more upset at the thought, Charlotte's throat tightened and she coughed a few times, as if on cue.

"Don't stress about the name thing," Pam said, attempting to ease Charlotte's insecurity. "Right now, you need to get oriented."

Pam grabbed Charlotte's hand and led her away.

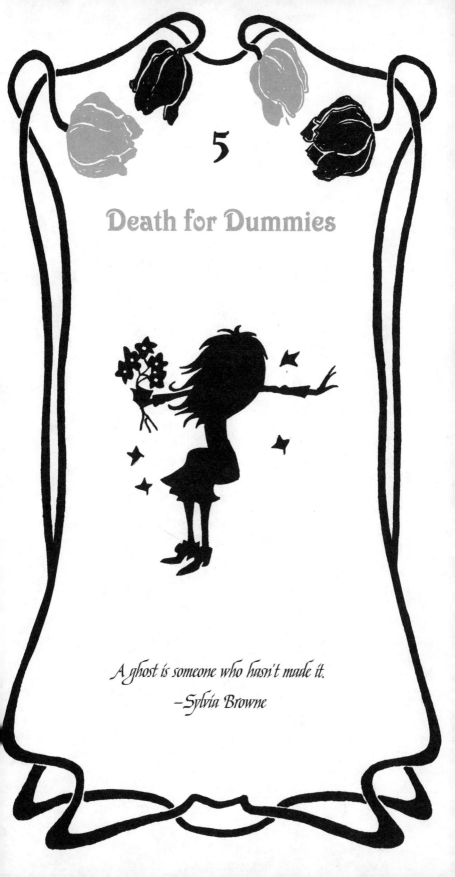

5

Death for Dummies

A ghost is someone who hasn't made it.

—Sylvia Browne

Time will tell all things.

The past was pretty much irrelevant now —
a closed door — other than the fact that it
had led her to the present. The present was
terribly uncertain, a place of fear and doubt —
restless. But the future existed to allay those
fears, and to make both the past and the
present bearable. The future was a place
where all Charlotte's hopes and dreams lived.
And now she was all out of future.

here was so much that Charlotte still wanted to do, so much she wanted to accomplish. She wanted to see one more snowfall, see Damen's rosy cheeks after a pick-up game of football after school, get another report card. But then, everyone dies with a to-do list, she reckoned. It's never enough.

One more snowfall wouldn't be enough, and seeing Damen one more time, well, that would never suffice either. All this sadness and more was buzzing around in her mind as she followed Pam down the hall.

"Who are you — really?" Charlotte pressed.

Pam looked normal enough, but what if she were some kind of shape-shifting demon sent to escort her to the Netherworld. Then she might have to face an eternity of pushing a stone up a hill or something.

"I'm here to help you," Pam clarified. "We all need help adjusting at first, and the transition, from 'there' to 'here,' is the most difficult time."

"What or where is *here*?" Charlotte asked.

"You'll find out everything you want to know at orientation," Pam confided.

"Orientation?" Charlotte asked testily, throwing up her hands in frustration.

Before Charlotte could get a follow-up in, Pam stopped and motioned with her head, answering Charlotte with the gesture. She signaled toward a faint glow radiating from behind a classroom door, but said nothing.

Pam started toward it, but Charlotte was just frozen in place. She stared wide-eyed as Pam gradually disappeared into the aura, turning her head back toward Charlotte and smiling sympathetically just before she was swallowed entirely by the glare, leaving Charlotte completely alone.

"Pam!" she called nervously. "What do I do . . . ?" Charlotte's voice trembled, trailing off.

Face-to-face with insurmountable odds, Charlotte became, as she often did, entirely rational. Delaying the pain by keeping things in perspective. It was the instinctively self-protective math and science geek in her.

This is IT, Charlotte thought, staring down the hall.

THE moment had come. She was D-E-A-D for sure — still not quite able to let the word escape her lips. She'd seen the evidence on the slab in the office and through the window in the courtyard. She'd met Pam, her spirit guide or guardian

angel or whatever you want to call it. And now the most tell-tale sign of all — the Bright Light. It was all pretty much as she'd been taught it would be, which was oddly comforting. She was scared, but no longer surprised, which helped tamp down the fear factor considerably.

In fact, she was even beginning to feel a little self-satisfied. Everyone always wants to know what happens after you die, and now she knew. Finally, a member of an exclusive, well, semi-exclusive club. Everyone dies, but rarely do they die this young, she rationalized, still trying to feel special. This was her time.

Unfortunately, though, there was nobody to tell. No way to exchange the information for hot gossip, a party invite, or even a fake ID. The secret would now be kept with her for all time, as it must have been with all who went before her. There was no one who faced what she was about to face and lived to tell about it, well, except for all those Near-Death Experience people who never shut up about "the Afterlife," and whom she was suddenly more than a little pissed off at.

If it was so great being dead, why didn't they just kill themselves and stop talking about it? she thought. What she wouldn't give for a return ticket courtesy of some defibrillator paddles and an overzealous paramedic or ER doctor.

"Lightweights!" Charlotte laughed snidely to herself, figuring it was the last laugh she'd ever have.

"Thanks, folks," Charlotte muttered. "I'll be here . . . forever."

And with that cheap attempt at a one-liner, more loneliness

ghostgirl

than she had ever felt rushed through her. Pam had been gone for just an instant, but it was more than enough time for Charlotte to relive every disappointment, every mistake, every failure, every missed opportunity, she'd ever experienced. Suddenly, all those cliché TV movie-of-the-week deathbed montages she'd laughed through appeared a little less cliché.

Of course the final frame was the biggest, hardest loss of all: Damen. "The End" might as well have superimposed itself on her consciousness. It was clear to her now how it could have all been different, but it was far too late to change what had been. One thing she wasn't feeling was "peaceful."

"Life is wasted on the Living," she quoted, and started down the hallway, slowly, tentatively, her knees knocking, toward "the Light."

As Charlotte approached, she was bathed in the brilliance of the Light, its pureness. She felt like an envelope held up to sunlight on a bright summer's day. Translucent. She was completely blinded, and she could swear she heard a choir of heavenly voices singing just for her. The bitterness faded.

It's so beautiful . . . so peaceful, she thought, luxuriating in the nirvana moment.

She could see dust particles sparkling like tiny specs of glitter, floating softly in the rays. As she continued to move closer, she was able to see more clearly. She could discern the outline of a door, slightly ajar. She closed one eye tight but left the other partially open, squinting as if she were watching a horror movie, and walked through, afraid, but curious nevertheless.

Her Zen moment was suddenly interrupted when she tripped over a cord of some kind and hit the floor, flat on her back. As she fell, the Light that was so magically beckoning her was knocked to the ground as well. It was shining on the ceiling, no longer blinding her.

There she was again, lying on the floor looking up, taking it all in. She slowly opened her eyes and blinked a few times, trying to focus.

Turning her head sideways, she could now see that the Light was emanating from an old 16mm film projector bolted to a steel cart. Charlotte had seen such a relic only once before, when she was assigned to help Sam Wolfe clean out the old A/V Club storage room in the Hawthorne basement.

She tilted her head up slightly above ground level to a most unexpected sight: a sea of feet adorned with toe tags. Charlotte's eyes widened as she noticed that the tag she got in the office, the one she force-fitted around her wrist, was actually *her* "toe tag." She was in a classroom filled with fellow dead students.

Before she could officially freak, an adult male voice distracted her.

"Mike, hit the lights," it requested.

A guy near the door turned on the lights, not that it mattered much because she could see pretty decently without the light, but now she could focus on other things. The classroom, for example. With the lights up, she could see it in all its . . . obsolescence.

It was old-fashioned — literally — drab and outdated, like

a cross between a thrift shop and a VFW hall. The white-oak desks and chairs looked hand-carved and rock solid but were mismatched. Maps of ancient lands long since redrawn hung above the blackboard. Bookshelves, partially concealed by threadbare velvet drapes, lined the back wall from floor to ceiling, teeming with outmoded texts and incomplete sets of encyclopedias. Fossil fragments and extinct creatures preserved in formaldehyde were displayed on long black marble countertops.

Fountain pens, inkwells, sealing wax, and parchment littered the scuffed maple wood floors. A glass-sided typewriter with cloth ribbon, slide rule, letter scale, compass, and abacus lay on a counter next to a wind-up Victrola and stacks of scratched 78 speed records.

She looked behind her, above the doorway, where a clock should be, but saw none. The only instrument she could see that measured time was the hourglass on the front desk, but the sand did not run through it. Charlotte recalled Pam saying that time had no meaning "here" and she wasn't kidding. It seemed that nothing in the room had any meaning — anymore. This classroom was decorated as if the past century or so had never happened.

What, no sundial? Charlotte thought.

It wasn't just that the décor was old — which it was — but that it was . . . defunct, that struck her. All of the items she'd taken note of, including the projector, were state-of-the-art at one time or another, vital even, but had long since been upgraded, replaced, or just plain *forgotten*. She'd only seen such things on PBS or at some dead grandma's garage sale.

It all made a weird kind of horrible sense. All the detritus of daily living that had been discarded seemed to be on display here. The poetic way to describe the place was probably "timeless," but everything and everyone could more accurately be described as "out of time," painfully, obviously, totally "out of time." Including her.

"Thank you, Mike," the male voice said sincerely, only this time, Charlotte turned around to see who it was. A pale hand extended to greet her and help her to her feet. She reached out tentatively and grabbed it.

"Ah, the new student," he said, gently grasping her fingers with his as she stood up, transfixed. "Welcome. I am Mr. Brain," he articulated with considerable pride. "We've been waiting for you."

Before "student" could register in her mind, Charlotte became completely distracted by Brain's appearance. As with the classroom, there was a timelessness about Brain too that was both disorienting and comforting. He was tall, thin, polite, and meticulously turned out, as if he were about to be off to a dinner party rather than to teach school. In fact, there seemed a touch of funeral director in him, dressed as he was in a tailored black suit, crisp white shirt, and burgundy necktie.

"Have a seat." He motioned hospitably to Charlotte. Charlotte looked at Brain quizzically and perused the room for someplace to sit. The sole empty chair and desk was at the back of the room. And, unlike the cheerleader sign-up sheet, this space seemed reserved for her alone.

"Sure," Charlotte said excitedly, remembering that only the

most popular people sat in the back. She walked to the back proudly and took her seat.

"Now, class, permit me to introduce Charlotte Usher. Please welcome her to Dead Ed, or as I like to call it, Special Ed for the Dead," he joked.

"Welcome, Charlotte," the class recited a bit mechanically.

Brain laughed so hard at his own joke, even through the class's greeting, that his "toupee" — make that a large portion of his scalp and cranium — detached and flopped down from his head, dangling by the most fragile piece of skin and exposing the spongy outer ridges of his brain to the entire class. Embarrassed, he quickly stifled his giggle and flipped it back into place (sort of), pressed down his suit jacket nervously, straightened his tie, and cleared his throat as if nothing had happened. And judging from the non-reaction by the other kids, Brain's head-toss was not uncommon.

"Of course . . . *Mr. Brain* . . . ," Charlotte whispered to herself, having solved at least one piece of this postmortem puzzle.

Brain walked over to the chalkboard like a praying mantis, light-footed but slightly hunched — around his C-5 and 6 vertebrae, Charlotte noted specifically — and began his lecture, manically writing a phrase on the chalkboard.

Non sum qualis eram. (I am not what I once was.)

Completing the phrase, Mr. Brain underscored it with the chalk and then motioned to the class like a symphony conductor at the start of a piece. On command, once again, all of the students chanted in unison:

"Non sum qualis eram."

Charlotte had never taken Latin, and, though she couldn't explain how, she knew it. Horace again.

"Dead teacher. Dead kids. Dead poet. Dead language," she mumbled. "Makes sense."

She tried to make eye contact with her fellow classmates, but almost all the students remained focused on Brain — even Pam. All except one: an angry-looking girl who sported a black bob and perfectly poker-straight bangs, faded lipstick, a rumpled and stained red dress, seated right in front of her. Charlotte could have sworn she heard the girl say "Loser," but everyone was still facing forward, lips sealed.

Who, me? Charlotte thought silently, looking around for the source of the diss.

"Yes, YOU," a reply echoed thunderously in Charlotte's head. To make the point even clearer, the girl spun her head completely around and shot Charlotte the nastiest look she'd ever seen, and she had seen some nasty ones.

Charlotte, petrified, looked down at the girl's feet to check her toe tag for her name, which read PRUDENCE, but much more noticeable was that she was wearing just one shoe. She gazed at the worn-out Mary Jane and recalled all the horrible news stories she'd seen in her short life. When, in the aftermath of any fatal hit-and-run, the only image shown would be one solitary shoe lying in the street while a reporter relayed the horrific details of the accident. That shoe — "the shoe" — was the visual that haunted people. That brought it all home. That shoe belonged to someone. They chose that shoe to wear for the day. They put it on themselves that

morning. They were going somewhere in that shoe, that shoe was going to get them to where they needed to go, and now, now it was orphaned in the middle of the road. A temporary tombstone.

"Well, as you can see, I was preparing the film projector for your arrival — a little "orientation" film for your edification, shall we say?" Mr. Brain explained.

As he walked toward the projector to lift it from the floor and finish threading the film, the school fire alarm went off.

The piercing buzzer prompted Charlotte to instinctively run for the door, but everyone else just stayed in their seats, unaffected. Mike, who was randomly playing rapid-fire air guitar, reached out and grabbed Charlotte's wrist before she could split. She was startled, but immediately sensed it was more to protect than to restrain her. Ear buds were jammed deep in his ears, but they weren't attached to anything.

"You've already left the building," Mike said, bouncing his legs in time as if he were manning double kick drums.

"Force of habit," Charlotte responded. "You can hear me with those things blasting in your ears?"

"Yeah," Mike answered, just a little too loudly.

Mike held Charlotte back, but nothing could keep the painful memories suddenly flooding through her mind at bay. Maybe it was the fire alarm, the reminiscence of a tiny part of her daily life, but the twinges of hurt, like the phantom pain of an amputee, remained.

Piccolo Pam walked over and introduced her formally to Mike.

"That's Metal Mike. He had his stereo up way too loud

while taking his driver's test," Pam explained. "He got . . . distracted. It didn't end well."

"Oh, so he got his dead name from listening to heavy metal music?" Charlotte asked.

"No," Pam corrected her, "he got his name because listening to it killed him . . . and the fact that he also has actual metal shards in his head from the accident," she added.

"Did I pass?" Mike asked Piccolo Pam, pretend-fingering his imaginary double neck electric bass.

"He asks that all the time. He's stuck there, so I just tell him that he did," Piccolo Pam whispered to Charlotte.

"Yes, Mike, you *passed*," Piccolo Pam said in her most sympathetic voice, which seemed to have the desired effect on Mike and Charlotte as well.

Mike released Charlotte's wrist and Piccolo Pam escorted her back to her desk. As she walked, she looked down at the kid's feet for names and learned more than she cared to about them from their footwear.

"Mike" wore worn work boots, of course — with his big toes peeking out. "Jerry" wore hippie-style Birkenstocks. "Abigail," dripping murky water, wore flip-flops — the bluish-green veins emerging from the tops of her feet and her naked, pale legs; Charlotte couldn't help but look up slightly to see that the girl was wearing a school-issued swimsuit. "Suzy" was barefoot and covered in deep scratches from head to toe; she checked nervously to see if any of the other kids were looking before plunging a sharpened fingernail into her scars. Charlotte pretended not to see.

Each one was creepier than the next, but in that classroom

setting, each fit in. *How do I look to them?* she wondered. *Do I "fit in" too?*

She didn't feel any different, really, since she "arrived," except for the "frog" in her throat. Was she still the same tall, thin, awkward geek she'd been all her life? With the same unruly mop of hair she'd only been able to tame with an entire drugstore shelf of conditioners, detanglers, and spray-holds?

"As I was saying, you must have a lot of questions . . . ," Mr. Brain said, seeming to have read her mind, as he turned the projector light back on.

"Yeah, I have one," Jerry interrupted before Charlotte could get hers out. "Do we have to watch this movie again?"

"Yes, you do, burnout," Prudence snapped. "Have you got something better to do? We are going to watch it over and over until it sinks in to your — and everyone else's — brain-dead heads."

Prudence, or Prue as she seemed to be known by her classmates, pretty much put an end to the subject, not just for Jerry but for the entire class. Except Charlotte, of course. Charlotte had a specific question on her one-track mind, and before she could edit herself, it spilled out.

"Do you know how this will affect my Physics class?" she asked. "I just got my lab partner today, and I'd hate to leave him hangin'."

The whole class busted out into unbridled laughter at Charlotte's naïveté — all except Prue, who could barely contain her disgust.

"Oh God . . . we got a 'live' one here," Prue quipped, rolling her eyes.

Charlotte sank down in her seat, realizing that what she just said must have sounded ignorant to everyone. But so what? They didn't know her. They didn't know her situation. She still wanted to know about Damen. Strangely, that's all she wanted to know.

"I tell you what, let's get this film going and whatever cremains" — he stopped to giggle and acknowledge his wit yet again — "I mean, 'remains' unclear, we can discuss afterward. . . ."

Mr. Brain passed a book back to her. It was titled *Deadiquette*.

"This one is for you, Charlotte," Brain said helpfully. "To catch up on your studies."

"Studies?" she asked.

Charlotte opened her book and began to peruse the Contents page. She read the chapter titles out loud to herself as Mr. Brain started the projector.

"'Levitation'? 'Telekinesis'? 'Phase-shifting'? 'Teleportation'?" She couldn't believe what she was reading, but she was definitely intrigued, and fresh out of shock by this point. She skimmed the book quickly as Mike dimmed the lights and the movie, a flickering 1950s-style industrial film, complete with 5-4-3-2-1 countdown and the moralistic voice-over narration, began.

Deadhead Jerry — the guy in Birkenstocks — was already sleeping, only with his eyes opened. As he snored, Charlotte could see Piccolo Pam out of the corner of her eye reach over

gently and close his eyes as one would do for a person who had just died.

How sweet, Charlotte thought, acknowledging Pam's kindness.

As the room went completely dark, Charlotte was startled once again by Prue's angry rasp.

"You'd better pay attention, Usher," Prue warned, tapping her shoe loudly on the floor. "We're watching this again for your sake."

"I got that," Charlotte answered, and coughed. Asking to go to the nurse's office crossed her mind, but there didn't seem to be much point.

Pam looked over at Charlotte with total seriousness, as if to caution her not to rub Prue the wrong way. From the looks of things, it was already too late. It was crystal clear that "here" Prue was the queen bee, or worse yet, wasp, of Dead Ed, and Charlotte had already felt her sting.

The mystery that still remained for Charlotte was the *reason* why Prue hated her so much. Prue had barely had time to notice her, let alone to loathe her. At Hawthorne, it had taken some kids a whole semester to really shun her. She was proud of that little statistic. But with Prue, the hatred was instant and seemed to go much deeper than just the way she looked or the things she said.

Up on the movie screen, a Coronet insignia appeared with some old-school signature theme music.

A 1950s-looking teen girl, with short curly hair wearing a navy skirt, flats, and starched white blouse appeared.

A male narrator's voice called out to get her attention, "Susan Jane? Susan Jane?"

Susan Jane looked around for the source of the voice and appeared disoriented by the classroom setting and the books in her hand.

"Susan Jane will soon find out that even though she is dead, she still has to graduate," the narrator said.

Susan Jane looked disappointed.

Charlotte couldn't help but react the same way.

"School?" Charlotte asked. "Great, life sucks and then you die and then it sucks again."

"I'm dead, not deaf," Mr. Brain said, admonishing her to be quiet.

Charlotte slumped down in her seat and continued watching the movie.

"How are you feeling, Susan Jane?" the narrator asked.

"Okay, I guess? But now that you mention it, I do feel a little funny," she responded.

"There's a reason for that, Susan Jane," the narrator said.

Next, a split screen of two Susan Janes appeared: one alive and one dead. She looked exactly the same in both states.

"Here are two pictures of Susan Jane," the narrator pointed out, and as he did, a tiny red arrow pointed to her "before" and "after."

"Not much of a difference on the outside, you might say, but on the inside her body has gone through a lot of changes," the narrator continued.

Suddenly, on the screen, the bodies were replaced by

outlines, one showing circulation and internal movement with hundreds of tiny red arrows, and one not.

"The most obvious change is that Susan Jane's physical body doesn't work anymore, but just because her body doesn't work doesn't mean that she doesn't have work to do," he announced.

The camera zoomed in on a *Deadiquette* handbook as the cover was flipping open to the first few pages. The chapter heading "Introduction to Death" came into focus. There were pictures of two simply drawn boys in the book. Billy, who appeared to be a polite, well-dressed, obedient 1950s teen with Bryl creemed hair and then Butch, a more rebellious, disheveled, slightly dimwitted and disobedient '50s teen.

"This is Billy," the narrator said as he introduced the "fellows." "And this, well, this is Butch."

"In life, Butch and Billy were 'ball hogs.' They had to score the winning run, be the coach's favorite, and be the superstar of their teams. Now, they must learn to be 'team players,' and that transition is a hard one to make, especially since they're dead."

The film showed the two "fellows" on a school playground. There were two separate groups playing kickball, one living and one dead. The camera closed in on the living game, and the scoreboard revealed the game tied in the final inning.

"Today, Butch and Billy are learning to master telekinesis" — as the narrator announced this, a dictionary entry of *telekinesis* appeared on the screen — "one of the essential spirit skills, through a simple game of kickball."

The ball rolled toward the kicker's box and was struck hard to the outfield. Butch telekinetically propelled the ball over the head of the outfielder so that he could make the catch, but instead he caused the other team to score the winning run. The losing team, angry at the outfielder, ran off the field bitter and sad while Butch was left holding the ball and feeling bad. Butch threw the ball and sped off on his motorcycle, angry and ashamed.

"What's the matter, Butch? Looks like you were way 'off base' out there," the narrator taunted, as Butch sped away.

Meanwhile, the outfielder who missed the play sat on the bench alone, sobbing.

"Now watch Billy. He's playing with other Dead kids," the narrator announced with enthusiasm.

On the Dead field everyone was in the same game situation. Billy was playing third base. The ball rolled toward the kicker's box and was struck hard toward the infield gap between third base and the shortstop. Billy motioned toward the ball, using his powers to guide the ball into the shortstop's hands rather than to make the play himself. The shortstop made a double play! The game was over and Billy's team won! The crowd roared. His jubilant teammates formed a victory circle of raised hands and cheering, with Billy propped high above the crowd.

"That's it, Billy! That's the RIGHT way," the narrator said.

"Why didn't it work for Butch and why did it work for Billy? Well, Butch was up to his old tricks and using his powers to try and stay connected to the living, but Billy, well, Billy

overcame his selfishness and used his powers to lead his team to victory.

The two "fellows" were replaced once again by Susan Jane seated at her old wooden desk.

"Well, Susan Jane, are you a Butch or a Billy?" the narrator asked.

Susan Jane shrugged her shoulders as the "fellows" appeared to the side of her. Billy graduated while Butch held a report card with an big fat F on it.

"Remember, these special abilities must be used only to seek resolution so that you can cross over. Your teacher will 'coach' you on the skills, but it is your responsibility to use them the right way," he said.

The music swelled as the *Deadiquette* book closed. THE END was written on the back.

Mike switched the lights back on as the film strip flapped against the metal on the projector.

"Questions?" Mr. Brain asked, singling out Charlotte.

"How do we know what our goal is?" Charlotte asked.

"Everyone in this class is here for a reason," Mr. Brain said. "You've all got an unresolved issue you need to deal with before you move on."

The bell rang, and Charlotte just sat in her seat. She wasn't sure if she should get up and risk embarrassing herself as she had during the fire drill. Once all the other students started exiting the room, she gathered her things and began to follow while reflecting on what Brain had just said.

"People! Homework. There's a dorm meeting tonight at Hawthorne Manor. It is at seven sharp and it is not optional!" Mr. Brain yelled after them as they all scurried to freedom.

Homework? Charlotte thought.

6

Death and Dating

And there was a beautiful view
But nobody could see.
'Cause everybody on the island
Was saying: Look at me! Look at me.
—Laurie Anderson

Identify yourself.

———◆———

Charlotte was never really sure who she was, not before and certainly not now. But she was always sure who she wanted to be. The thing is, in high school, no one wants to know who you are, they want to know who you aren't. It is much easier to categorize and file you that way. She had been filed under "Nobody," but that was all about to change if she had any say in it. She was ready to see the world though someone else's eyes. Anyone's but hers.

carlet, Petula's younger sister, was summoned unexpectedly to the school newspaper office to write an obituary, her first ever, on "some girl who died in school." She headed to the room as nervous about the assignment as about dealing with Mr. Filosa, a hard-bitten old-timer who ran the school pamphlet, ah, newspaper, like it was the *Daily Planet*.

"Where the heck have you been, Kensington?" Mr. Filosa remarked impatiently. "We're on deadline to publish this obituary."

"I know there is a joke in there somewhere," Scarlet cracked. "Deadline . . . obituary . . ."

Filosa wasn't impressed with Scarlet's sense of humor or her stalling. "You don't really want to do this, do you?"

"Well, now that you mention it, what am I doing on the deadbeat?" Scarlet asked. "I'm supposed to be the music critic."

"You've got to be kidding," he chided, looking her over, "You're a natural."

"I've never had to do one before," Scarlet said with surprising diffidence. "Besides, I'm not really good at praising people I didn't know, or people I *do* know for that matter."

"Suck it up, Kensington, and do something nice for somebody for a change," Filosa barked. "Here are the photos from the . . . ah . . . what was her name . . . Usher, that's it, the Usher memorial this morning. The layout is on the computer." He grabbed his straw hat and tweed jacket and slammed the door on his way out.

Scarlet sat at her computer, staring at the blinking cursor. Not a thing occurred to her. She put on her fedora, which had piercings all around the rim, for inspiration, then opened the jpeg folder of the photos from the memorial and noticed not a soul in any of the pictures.

"Where is everybody?" Scarlet said, the tiniest trace of sympathy in her voice.

Scarlet pulled up the police report and reviewed what little information there was in the official file. She was startled when she came to her class portrait.

"Oh no," Scarlet blurted. "It's that girl I was mean to the other day."

Scarlet pored over the picture for a minute, as if to acknowledge the person she'd treated so dismissively before. She decided the best apology would be a nice obituary, even if it might be more of a listing.

"I guess your life is in my hands now," she said as she began to write.

It was comforting for Charlotte to know that if there had to be school, there was cafeteria time too. A time to leave the classroom setting and take a breather. A time to "pause" everything and digest the first part of the day, everything except the universal pecking order that was nowhere more evident than at the school lunch tables.

This did not escape Charlotte's notice as she and Piccolo Pam entered the room. Charlotte could barely contain herself when she saw all the Living kids fluttering about as they usually did, enjoying their semi-freedom.

The Hawthorne cafeteria had always reminded her of a Wal-Mart or Sears, broken up into specific departments. It was easy to navigate. Not a lot of crossover. Populars here, Brains there, Jocks over here, Potheads over there. In class, integration was pretty much unavoidable, mandatory even, thanks to alphabetized seating plans. But in the cafeteria, you had a choice — and what more definitive statement could you make than where you sat and who sat with you.

Once you decided who you were, or more likely, who Petula decided you were, it was easy to find your place. Looking at it now, what had seemed so intentional and cruel to her before, seemed completely natural. Maybe "like attracts like" after all. Or maybe death had dulled her envy.

"People aren't magnets," Charlotte said out loud, and then, realizing her absent-mindedness, grabbed quickly for her mouth to shove the words back in.

"Don't worry," Pam said. "They can't hear you."

"Never could," Charlotte replied sarcastically.

As she scoured the room, she noticed that everyone in there was assigned seventh-period lunch. This was unbelievable to her. When she was alive, she had sixth-period lunch, now she had seventh-period lunch. Lucky seventh-period lunch. This was Damen's lunch period. Oh, sweet death! At least something good had come out of it.

Distracted by her thoughts, Charlotte accidentally "bumped" into a kid walking with his tray. Actually, it was more like she passed right through him. Piccolo Pam wasted no time in grabbing Charlotte's arm and trying to stop the interaction.

"NO!" Pam cried. But it was too late.

A look of sheer terror crossed the kid's face as he froze for a moment, looked around like a scared rabbit, dropped his tray, and bolted for the exit. His face was twisted up so badly that it was almost funny. At the site of the tray hitting the floor everyone in the cafeteria laughed and clapped, making sure that he was totally humiliated in a way that only high school students can.

"Don't EVER go through the living!" Pam said, scolding Charlotte.

"Sorry?" Charlotte replied, not quite getting it.

"Interacting with the Living in any way is strictly forbidden," Pam warned. "*Most* of us know it instinctively when we arrive."

Charlotte was wounded by Pam's unexpected dig.

"Why?" she asked innocently. "We can see *them*. We can hear *them*. Why shouldn't they *feel* us?"

"We coexist with them, but in different realities," Pam explained curtly. "They mean nothing to us, and vice versa."

"They mean something to me," Charlotte said.

"Didn't you see what just happened?" Pam asked. "Keep your *feelings* to yourself, Charlotte."

"Okay," Charlotte said timidly.

Tugging Charlotte away from the lunch tables, Pam continued, "We're over *here*."

"Here" was a different cafeteria line that she had never waited in before. A line that was set up only for the Dead students. Invisible to the Living.

"Isn't this segregation of some sort?" she asked. But Pam didn't respond. She was too busy filling up her tray with junk food.

Suddenly, a girl tried to jump the line. "Sorry, Kim," she muttered.

"Cuts," Kim said in an aggressive tone. An uptight girl with long shiny hair and a beautiful profile, Kim sported an arsenal of PDAs. She looked and sounded like she was preoccupied and in a rush, which was really weird, given the circumstances. When Charlotte didn't move fast enough, Kim became more agitated.

"Can you move it?" Kim explained curtly. "I'm in a hurry and I'm expecting an important call!"

As she shoved her way in, Charlotte noticed something fall into her tray. This was no stray hair — it was flesh. Burnt, decayed flesh. Charlotte stepped back and allowed Kim to have as much room as she needed, all with the kind of forced, big-toothed smile you might use to hold back vomit.

Charlotte's queasiness was calmed when, out of nowhere, a cell phone started ringing. She looked around and reached for

her pockets reflexively, surprised that such a sound was even possible here.

"Somebody gonna get that?" Charlotte asked jokingly.

"It's for me," Kim said as she turned her head to the other side, revealing a cell phone protruding from her gaping head wound, which measured from her temple to her lower jaw. Radiation had apparently eaten a big hole out of her head and neck area, leaving it raw and exposed.

"Talk about having a 'bad' side," Charlotte whispered to Pam.

"To Call Me Kim, every call is urgent," Piccolo Pam whispered to Charlotte. "She ignored the warnings about obsessively using her cell phone and look where it got her. Her unresolved issue is to listen when she's told something and to try to suppress her impulsivity."

"I thought that the 'cell phone radiation' thing was a myth," Charlotte said, trying her best not to look at Kim directly.

"Apparently not," Pam said, pointing and shaking her head sympathetically at Kim, who was gabbing away.

Charlotte tried to change the subject but couldn't stop staring at Kim.

"Hold on," Kim commanded her phone friend abruptly as she turned to Charlotte and shot her a look. "Can I *help you*?"

"No, I don't think you can," Charlotte answered with total seriousness.

"New students . . . ," Kim said, rolling her eye and resuming her one-way conversation.

"I can't figure out this whole 'unresolved issue' thing. Maybe I don't have one?" Charlotte asked Pam.

"Issues are like assholes, we've all got one," Pam snipped.

"Everyone?" Charlotte asked, wondering to herself what Petula or the Wendys might have to resolve except conflicting waxing appointments.

"Look at DJ, for example" Pam motioned over to the "Dead Boys" table. "He seems really cool and together. You wouldn't think he's got much to resolve."

"Right." Charlotte said in agreement.

"Wrong," Pam explained. "He considered himself an 'artiste' and refused to spin popular songs at this gang house party he was hired to play."

"So no one was dancing and . . . ," Charlotte said haltingly.

"Somebody got mad. A fight broke out, and DJ was caught in the crossfire," Pam continued. "He took ten bullets, one more than 50 Cent."

"That's not a contest you want to win, is it?" Charlotte said sympathetically.

"No, it's not," Pam concurred. "His arrogance got him killed."

"No more breakdancing for DJ," Charlotte concluded, getting Pam's point.

As they continued down the line, Charlotte scanned the smorgasbord of sweet, fried, and trans-fatty goodies on display. French fries and gravy, pepperoni pizza, mac & cheese, pancakes, burgers, corn dogs, petrified Jell-O Squares and whipped cream, potato chips, corn chips, deep fried Twinkies, Marshmallow Fluff, vats of chocolate sauce, maple syrup, and melted Velveeta. All the good stuff. It was McWilly Wonka Hut. Basically anything that caused fat around the middle was fryin' on the griddle.

The Dead lunch ladies wore full body nets, instead of the standard-issue hair nets that the Living lunch ladies wore, in order to "keep it together," she assumed, so that no flesh would fall into the food while doling out these decadent dishes. All of the drinks were carbonated sodas: Fresca, Shasta, brands that were rarely found anymore except on hipster T-shirts. Perfectly good, just . . . forgotten. Definitely a far cry from the whole-wheat pita wrap and salad bar on the Living side of the lunchroom.

Charlotte loaded up on food and guilt. What would her anorexic role models, Petula and the Wendys, think? They obsessed over their BMI index the way some people obsess over SAT scores.

Besides, who even cared anymore? What was it going to do? Kill her? Portion control was not exactly top of the list any longer.

A wave of post-mortem depression swept over her once again. Did anything matter now? She threw caution to the wind and accepted all the lunch ladies had to plop. Her whole reason for self-improvement, diet, exercise, blah, blah — everything — was Damen, and he was literally a lost cause. After all, what good was a hot bod on a dead girl?

"It's not that nothing matters, Charlotte. It's that you have different priorities now. A different purpose," Pam, who was well ahead of her in line, explained telepathically.

"Which IS . . . ?" asked Charlotte out loud, freaking out and spinning around to locate her friend.

Charlotte began thinking that she wanted all of this to stop, especially the mind-reading stuff. It was such an invasion.

First Prue, then Brain, now Pam. She tried desperately not to think about it, because she didn't want to offend Pam, and Pam's commonsense take on the situation was welcome. But the more she thought about it, the more she couldn't help but think that she hated Pam and all of them intruding on her private thoughts like that. Sensing Charlotte's discomfort, Pam waved her over and lightened the mood.

"Hey, it's your first lunch as a dead girl. My treat!" Pam joked, stopping the paralyzing, obsessive thought cycle spinning through Charlotte's brain as Pam led her to a table in the corner. Pam took a seat, but Charlotte hesitated.

"Anybody sitting there? " Charlotte asked of the seat next to Pam.

"Yes," Pam said smiling. "*Somebody* is."

Actually, Charlotte wasn't used to such a welcoming response. She often found herself needing somewhere to sit, standing up for an uncomfortable amount of time, tray in hand, searching for a place. Pam sensed Charlotte's struggle as she tried to take it all in and come to grips with everything. She decided the best way to help was to be a friend.

"Don't worry. Eventually you'll fit in," Pam said as they circled the table.

"I tried that once and I ended up dying from it," Charlotte replied.

As the girls nodded in agreement and looked up from their conversation, they noticed a girl sitting alone at the next table, hunched over and pulling up the cuff on each arm of her long-sleeve turtleneck sweater to inspect the cuts on her wrists and forearms.

"What happened to her," Charlotte asked sarcastically. "Did she itch herself to death?"

"Suzy?" Pam explained, "She was a *scratcher*. You know, she'd cut herself but not deep enough to do any real damage."

"Or so she thought, I guess," Charlotte said.

"Yeah. A 'cry for help' thing that went really wrong," Pam continued. "She gave herself too many little cuts and wound up in the hospital anyway. She died from one of those drug-resistant staph infections."

"She seems so secretive," Charlotte said. "And sad."

"She's here to learn to commit," Pam said. "Doing things halfway can be just as dangerous."

Both girls returned to their meals, barely noticing another girl standing in front of them. It was a stick-thin, overaccessorized "Hollypop" who wore huge dark sunglasses, a vintage dress, and a Chanel necklace. On her tray was a child-sized cup of mixed nuts and a grande espresso.

"Hey, CoCo," said Pam. "'Fashionably late' as usual, I see."

"It's my brand," CoCo reminded. "Room for a third?" she asked rhetorically, with clenched-toothed affectation.

"A true fashion victim," Pam whispered to Charlotte.

"What? Did she get trampled at a sample sale or something?" Charlotte asked.

"Hey, that's a good one, but no, it's much worse," Pam said, leaning in closer to Charlotte. "She got drunk at a party, threw up in her oversized handbag, passed out in it, and drowned in her own vomit. Sometimes bigger is not better.

"Rest in Prada," Pam said mockingly as CoCo took a seat.

CoCo immediately started devouring her daily printout of

online gossip blogs as she cracked open a Red Bull and refilled her espresso cup.

"So what exactly happened to you?" Pam asked Charlotte.

CoCo appeared disinterested, hiding behind her shades, but couldn't resist the temptation to eavesdrop on some juicy gossip, nonetheless. It had been a while.

"What happened to me was that my dreams were starting to all come true. . . ." Charlotte began.

"And?" Pam replied.

"I got paired up with Damen Dylan, the hottest boy in school, for labs. I had this fantasy . . . that if he got to know me, he might, well . . ." Charlotte paused, feeling an urgent need to clear her throat.

"Go on!" CoCo blurted, earning stares from both Pam and Charlotte.

". . . ask me to the Fall Ball instead of his girlfriend, Petula," Charlotte continued, coughing a little.

"Oh, is that all?" CoCo said, disappointed, as she got up, leaving her tray behind for others to clean up.

Pam also gave Charlotte a "there's gotta be more" look. But there wasn't.

"So this dude has a girlfriend? I guess it wasn't meant to be," Pam said matter-of-factly.

Just as Pam spoke, Damen walked past Charlotte to dump his tray, not giving her enough time to feel the slightest bit disappointed by Pam's crushing blow. Charlotte was immediately drawn in by the laugh that he so generously gave to his friend's joke.

"You know, Pam, I never bought that meant-to-be crap,"

Charlotte said, her voice rising with each word. "It's just self-rationalizing BS. You couldn't possibly be wrong either way!"

"Not exactly," Pam replied. "Fate is not totally circumstantial. It's pre-determined. The outcome cannot be changed. Period. That's why it's called . . . Fate."

"That's it!" Charlotte exclaimed, fighting to get words out between coughs.

"It is?" Pam asked, utterly confused.

"He smiled at me right before I died . . . we were about to connect. That was my chance for him to get to know me, and then, eventually . . . maybe even . . . ask *me* to the dance," Charlotte rambled. "Fate," she declared.

"What are you saying?" Pam asked, completely confused but still trying to understand what she was getting at.

"I'm saying that . . . Damen . . . and me . . . ," Charlotte said, now breaking out into a full-fledged choking fit. Pam whacked her square on the back, desperate to hear the big reveal. ". . . are meant to be," Charlotte said, barely able to get the words out.

"I thought you said that meant-to-be's were crap?" Pam reminded, trying to digest Charlotte's outlandish revelation.

"I thought you said they weren't," Charlotte said, one-upping her.

Damen walked past them again on the way back to his table, Charlotte keeping him in her sights like a determined bidder watching a Chloé bag on eBay.

"Did you ever think that maybe Fate actually intervened to keep you *apart* by letting you die?" Pam interjected. "That *this* is your Destiny?"

Charlotte didn't answer; she was lost in thought. Pam was

becoming increasingly concerned about Charlotte's denial of her circumstances and decided to take action.

"Besides, Charlotte, you've got another major problem," Pam said, suddenly standing on her seat, and started yelling, making faces, and waving her arms in Damen's direction.

"DAMEN!!!" Pam screamed with all her might.

Charlotte was mortified and tried to get her to sit down.

"Pam! Please!" Charlotte begged.

The more Charlotte begged her to stop, the more she carried on. The more excited she got, the more the piccolo sound radiated from her throat.

"BLOW ME!!!" Pam yelled to Damen, pointing at her larynx.

Charlotte waited for Damen to walk over in a huff, but he didn't. In fact, he didn't react at all. No one did.

"Things are different now, Charlotte," Pam said as she sat back down in her seat. "It's not about him dating you. He can't even see you."

With that, the frustration in Pam's voice morphed into a more soothing tone.

"You'll just have to accept it," she said as she reached for her friend's shoulder. "There's a reason why they call it a love *life*. Love is for the living."

Instead of being disappointed or deflated, Charlotte got a wild look in her eye, as if Pam had just solved the Riddle of the Sphinx.

"You're right . . . ," Charlotte proclaimed as she grabbed Pam and kissed her on the cheek in sheer gratitude. "He can't even see me!"

7

He Doesn't Even Know I'm Alive

This is going to take a long time...
Can't take no more
Wonder if you'll understand
it's just the touch of your hand
Behind a closed door.
—Vince Clarke

Being in love with someone who doesn't even know you exist isn't the worst thing in the world.

In fact, it's quite the opposite. Almost like passing in a term paper that you know sucked, but having that period of time where you haven't gotten your grade back yet — that kind of exhale where you haven't been rejected, although you pretty much know how it's going to turn out. When it came to Damen, Charlotte wanted to wait as long as possible for that paper to come back. But waiting until you've just died is, well, maybe waiting a little too long...or maybe not.

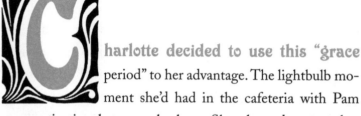harlotte decided to use this "grace period" to her advantage. The lightbulb moment she'd had in the cafeteria with Pam was motivational, to say the least. She planned to turn her greatest disadvantage — being dead — into a positive and use it to get closer to Damen. If he couldn't actually see her, he couldn't object to her invading his personal space. She could basically go and do whatever she wanted without being detected. She could "get into" Damen in the most literal sense of the word.

"His classes, his locker, his car, his drawers!" she shouted, and then stopped suddenly. "Well, not his *drawers* . . . as in his underwear . . . but his *actual* drawers . . . in his bedroom dresser . . . or somewhere." She blushed, as much as a dead girl could, surprised and the tiniest bit ashamed to find how

calculating she could be. She was bursting to tell someone about her ingenious plan, but she couldn't.

Charlotte was feeling powerful in a way she never had before. She felt "reborn." In fact, the endless, albeit stalker-ish, possibilities were almost overwhelming, *almost* being the operative word. She beat back the momentary crisis of conscience over the creepiness of this invasion of his privacy, and decided selfishly, shamelessly, to work her plan as Damen turned the corner in the hallway.

Everywhere that Damen went, Charlotte was sure to go: to his locker, where she was perched inside (not as uncomfortable as one might think); to study hall, where she watched him drift off to sleep from the next seat, resting her head on his shoulder until he was awakened suddenly by the slight chill he felt at her touch; to the locker room — the inner sanctum for all guys. She knew this was how he finished each day, with a football practice and a workout and, God willing, a shower. She made sure to get there before him, to get a good seat. Death was definitely looking up in terms of instant gratification.

Charlotte waited patiently outside the gym for reasons she couldn't quite explain. She could have floated in through the metal vent, or even passed right through the locker room door for that matter, but she didn't. Instead, she followed close behind a few jocks who had turned up early for practice. She stepped in the locker room with a mixture of fear and curiosity. This was, after all, virgin territory for her.

She didn't necessarily want to see him stark naked, per se,

but she did want to see more of him. Damen arrived and plunked down his black-and-white Adidas gym bag on the bench. Charlotte sat next to it, waiting like a first-timer at a rock concert for the show to begin. She wanted to see his arms, his shoulders, his chest, up close.

The cringe factor was almost off the chart by now, but she stayed put. She just wanted to experience him in a less formal and more intimate way.

"What's wrong with that, anyway?" she wondered aloud. "It's not like he would ever know." And they had already "slept together" in Study Hall. "Sort of . . . ," she felt obliged to note for the record.

Not even the smell of steamy mildew, dirty socks, and sweaty pits was enough to deter her, though it came pretty close.

Damen unzipped his gym bag, reached over for his combination lock, spun the dial around a few times, and pulled it open. Maybe it was the sound of the zipper opening, but she suddenly got extremely nervous as he proceeded to cross his arms in front of his body and lift his hoodie over his head, revealing the wifebeater underneath. The tee was so fitted she could see every fold of his beautifully sculpted six-pack abs.

He was tall, slim, and tight, with a chest and shoulders just wide enough to make a girl swoon. His arms were strong but not bulky, the kind you could feel safe and comfortable in. She wanted more than anything just to lay her head on his chest, but she was afraid that if she did, he might feel her chill again and put his hoodie back on prematurely. Damen, unaware, continued undressing, much to Charlotte's wide-eyed delight.

She'd been so used to fantasizing about him, she almost needed to close her eyes to experience what was going on right in front of them.

Damen took off his shoes, and as he bent over, his shoulder muscles flexed in a way that made her want to be wrapped up by them. He took his track pants out of his bag and undid his button-flys. Charlotte was totally gone.

"Boxers or briefs?" she wondered, anxiously bouncing her legs up and down rapidly from the balls of her feet.

It didn't take long for her to get her answer. As his pants dropped to the floor and he lifted his left leg and then the right out of the crumpled loose-fit denim that collected around his ankles, his tartan plaid boxer shorts were revealed. Slightly oversize but thankfully not hip-hop big. They were unpretentious and modest, conservative even. Just like Damen.

The mood was broken when she saw a couple of jocks approach the locker next to Damen's and heard a loud groan.

"Cup check," she heard Bradley Grayson, an arrogant freshman lacrosse player, yell as he slammed his forearm, without warning, into Sam Wolfe's groin.

Sam, naked, bent over and clutched himself, thrusting his large, pale, Sasquatch-like hairy, pimply ass right in her face.

This was every girl's greatest fear come to life. The Gates of Hell had opened. She would never, she thought, be allowed to enjoy even a moment's pleasure without an eternity of pain in exchange. For a little Damen, she'd have to endure a LOT of Sam. The metaphor was not lost on Charlotte.

And it got worse. As Sam clenched, a tiny, involuntary puff of sulphurous gas escaped. For the first time ever, she was glad

to be dead, for no other reason than his butt smelled as bad as it looked. . . . Was it even possible to die twice?

She felt really bad for Sam; so did Damen from the look on his face, but Brad just kept on walking and laughing. Charlotte, gagging, bolted out the open window above Damen's locker, disturbing the humid vapors in the room just enough for Damen to notice. Slightly spooked for a second, he blinked, shook his head, and figured the apparition he thought he saw was just the after-burn of Sam's gas. He grabbed his mouthpiece and headed for the gym.

Charlotte was disgusted, but not discouraged. She waited outside for practice to end, hoping to catch a lift home with Damen. His home. Damen walked out of the gym toward the parking lot, slung his bag over his shoulder, and reached into his pocket for the keys to his bright red Viper Convertible. Before he could get his door unlocked, Charlotte had jumped right into the passenger seat. She began to put her seatbelt on, realized that she didn't need one anymore, and flicked it back with total abandon.

"The upside of mortality," she reasoned. "So, my place or yours?" Charlotte asked Damen sarcastically as he buckled himself in.

Damen obviously couldn't hear her, but the fact that he didn't answer still stung a little. Regardless, she was having fun with the whole thing. She was riding shotgun in Damen's sports car, and under any circumstance, the jealousy quotient among the other girls would have been astronomical. In Petula's case, quite possibly homicidal.

Yes, any girl would die to be sitting where she was — the

only difference was, in her case, she literally had to die to get there. Charlotte put this most painful realization aside for the moment as she continued to play "girlfriend."

"Yours it is!" Charlotte said as Damen pulled away from his "Reserved" spot.

Damen stretched and extended his right arm, the one she'd admired in the locker room, across the back of the passenger seat as he drove. Imagining that he was putting his arm around her, Charlotte straightened up slightly and leaned toward him. This was really happening. As she inched closer, his forearm and hand appeared to hang even lower, draping over her shoulder and onto her chest. She'd never been so close to him or so intimate with anyone ever before.

"Is he trying to cop a feel?" Charlotte giggled out loud hopefully.

Tossing her head back in the breeze, Charlotte was shocked right out of her romantic mood, her eyes widening in fear, by a whistle in the wind.

"Omigod, Pam!" she screamed, and turned toward the backseat.

There was Piccolo Pam staring at her like a parent who just flicked on the lights in the basement and interrupted a marathon make-out session.

"What? I've gotta figure out some way to communicate with him, don't I?" she said to Pam in her most persuasive voice. "Maybe this whole death thing can, you know, bring us closer."

"Oh, so now you think that being dead can actually *help* you

in the dating world?" Pam huffed. "Wait until the girls who got boob jobs hear about this one."

Realizing that Charlotte wasn't budging, Pam rolled her eyes and disappeared as fast as she'd come. Clearly, she wasn't about to waste her dead days as a third wheel.

Charlotte was so focused on seeing where Damen slept and going through his personal belongings that she didn't even consider the fact that he might not have been going straight home. As they pulled up to the curb in front of a sprawling manse, Charlotte noticed the driveway was empty. This was not his house. It was, however, a house that Charlotte had driven past all too many times, only to see his bright red sports car parked out front all afternoon and, sometimes, all night long.

No, this wasn't just any old house. This was Petula's house.

If she needed any more verification, Petula had already run the entire length of the long, landscaped bluestone walk to greet Damen, slamming into the passenger side door at nearly full speed.

"Hurry up, my parents will be home soon!" she said, prompting Damen to get out of the car at lightning speed and chase her back up the walk.

It probably wasn't the brightest idea, but Charlotte followed them. Up the sidewalk to the front of the house she went, full speed, ignoring a frenzied flock of blackbirds that had appeared above her. She approached the door just a split second too late — again — and watched Petula obliviously slam the door right in her face.

"Déjà vu," she said.

As she turned to walk away, she saw the birds fly off, leaving a drizzle of bird crap falling directly for her as they departed. She closed her eyes and braced for the impact. But it never came. The droppings just fell right through her and splattered on the front porch as an unexpected wave of optimism crashed over her instead.

"Of course," she reminded herself. "I'm dead!"

Charlotte thought back to orientation and the first few chapters of her *Deadiquette* textbook as she turned back toward Petula's front door. She'd only browsed them and hadn't had any time to practice, but desperation can sometimes breed confidence, and Charlotte was, after all, a can-do spirit.

"What was it?" she asked rhetorically. "Invisibility. No, stupid. Shape-shifting? Not technically . . ." She grew more frustrated with the fact that she couldn't remember. "Phasing? Riiiight. That's it. Moving through stuff!"

Charlotte got into position, bravely facing the door. Her basic knowledge of the properties of solids, if not her ghostly expertise, would surely get her through, she hoped.

"Okay," she began, "the denser the object, the more closely packed the molecules, and the more slowly they move. But what if I get stuck?" she said. "That would be bad. Very bad."

Whatever might come, Charlotte decided that this was not the right time to have a debate about finer points of molecular density.

She gathered herself and began to concentrate.

"I can do this . . . ," she said, remembering the words of the great philosopher Bruce Lee: "Empty your mind, be formless, shapeless — like water," he instructed. He certainly wasn't

part of the Dead Ed curriculum, or even a science teacher, but it was the best she could conjure up in a pinch. And he was dead too.

"Be the door, be the door, be the door . . . ," Charlotte chanted as she reached, open-handed, for the heavy wood and lead glass door.

To her amazement, the tips of her fingers, then her knuckles, palm, wrist, elbow — her whole friggin' arm — were passing right through the door! Then her leg. It was going well. Until she got to her shoulder. Where she got stuck. Half of her body on the inside of the house, and half on the outside. She was trapped, trapped in a door. Charlotte struggled to continue through, but it was futile.

"Crap" was the best she could come up with, standing in a pool of fresh bird shit.

Crap, indeed. Being half trapped in a door for eternity was not a very appealing outcome, and the downside of the whole phase-shifting thing was that you really had to get in and get out fast.

"I sure hope this gets easier!" Charlotte grunted as she slowly pulled the rest of her body through the door.

Charlotte climbed the stairs and searched for Damen and Petula. She heard voices behind a door down the hallway and headed for it. It occurred to her that this home invasion, like the locker room visit earlier, was more than a little creepy of her. Like reading someone else's e-mail. Still, she was not feeling guilty enough to change course. She poked her head through the door, this time with much less effort than before.

The room was Petula's very own shrine to herself. It was breathtaking in its shamelessness, filled with photos of herself and not-so-flattering photos of her friends. She outshined everyone, by design. It was HER room after all. Damen was lounging on the bed while Petula fussed in her walk-in closet, changing clothes.

"Hey, how about that girl dying in school . . . ," Damen yelled to Petula.

"He remembered," Charlotte said as her head poked through the door like a moose-head trophy on a hunter's wall.

Petula didn't respond. It was impossible to tell if she wasn't listening or just didn't care. Either way, Damen got up from the bed and walked closer to the closet, stopping in front of a dressmaker dummy on which Petula had been designing and fitting her dress for the Fall Ball. He fiddled with some loose threads and pressed the conversation.

"She is . . . I mean, was, my lab partner. Weird, right?" he asked Petula, a touch of sorrow in his voice.

Still nothing.

Meanwhile, Charlotte made her way through the door and over to the dummy, where Damen was standing. She came around behind it and stood staring face-to-face with the Man of Her Dreams, nothing between them but the dummy torso and the dress fitted on top of it. In a single step, Charlotte closed the distance between them, walking into the dummy, and the dress as well.

"Pretty dress," Damen mumbled, inspecting it more closely.

"Thank you," Charlotte replied softly, smiling.

Damen, feeling a bit strange, stood for a second longer, examining the bust intensely, and then walked toward the closet.

As he stepped away, Charlotte saw the reflection of the dress dummy in the full-length mirror he had been obscuring from her view. She felt beautiful for the first time, as she'd always imagined she would, wearing a gorgeous, expensive, custom-made frock — just like Petula. It made her so happy and, at the same time, so very sad, until she noticed that Damen was staring at the same mirror; his jaw dropping to the floor. Could he see her reflection?

She seized the opportunity, ran over to the mirror, and blew on it, writing "Can you see me?" on the foggy surface. Damen grinned seductively and walked toward her.

It was actually the reflection of Petula, there in the closet, in mid-change, that he was salivating over. As the fog receded from the mirror, Charlotte got a clear shot of Damen — who was now in the closet — and Petula, making out wildly. Stunned, Charlotte stood frozen as Petula practically dragged Damen right past her, out of the closet, to the bed.

Damen had a chunk of Petula's highlighted blond hair in his grasp, tugging on it as he forced her closer with every kiss, like he couldn't get enough of her.

The steamy scene took Charlotte's breath away. It was all so . . . physical. The only thing romantic about it at all was the fact that Damen kept his eyes closed, which was probably a good thing, because Petula didn't. She was studying every inch of her body in the mirror while they kissed. For her, it wasn't about making out so much as it was a sexy photo shoot.

Charlotte focused on Damen's shuttered lids, imagining all

the thoughts that must be going through his mind. He seemed strangely relaxed, even in the midst of it all. Maybe he was thinking about someone else. Petula was right there. He wouldn't need to fantasize about her, would he? Maybe he was thinking about her, "the girl who died at school."

But then again, maybe not. Maybe it was an involuntary response, kind of like the way people can't keep their eyes open when they sneeze. Maybe that was just the way he kissed.

The only way to really know was to be with him, in that moment, like Petula should have been. And that was impossible. Ironically, now that she was dead, she was able to go just about anywhere except the two places she most wanted to be: in his arms and in his mind.

Charlotte closed her own eyes, fantasizing it was her lips, not Petula's, sliding over his while his hands caressed her. The further her mind drifted, the more Petula's presence faded and the more intense their "virtual" kiss became.

She felt his hands. His warmth. She felt desire, passion, for the first time. She wouldn't ever have to imagine what he was like with a girl again. She would know firsthand. Well, secondhand. Talk about an out-of-body experience.

Charlotte continued to breathe him in, to feel his touch. She glided her tongue along her lips and tilted her head just as Petula tilted hers and then closed her eyes again. She opened her eyes only for a few seconds here and there, to catch a glimpse of what she was already feeling. If she looked for too long, her fantasy would be lost.

When she opened her eyes again for an update she saw that

Petula's legs were now straddled across Damen in some kind of a cheerleading split. Charlotte had always been conflicted about cheerleading, the basic idea being to validate male egos by doing stupid jumps and silly routines, all with pom-poms and a ton of makeup on. But she wanted to be ogled too. She wanted to be eye candy.

In that moment, Charlotte understood the benefits of being a cheerleader and why guys prized them so highly. Petula might not have been smartest girl in the room, but she was probably the most limber, Olympically so, and that skill was paying big dividends. The reality of what was going on began to hit her. This wasn't a movie or video game, this was happening in front of her face. As her own jealousy became unbearable, she headed out into the hall, ran to the adjacent bathroom, and slammed the door, sobbing uncontrollably.

"He doesn't even know I'm alive," she whimpered, hanging her head over the sink and forgetting that she wasn't alive.

After a few seconds of wallowing, she lifted her head to look in the mirror. Charlotte was so numb and distracted, she couldn't be sure if the condensation running down the glass was tears running down her face or not, and she hadn't yet noticed the hot steam from the shower filling the room.

"This must be how it happens," she said as her reflection slowly disappeared into the vapor. "I'm just going to vanish into nothing. Poof."

She reached for the shower curtain and clenched it like a toddler gripping her favorite blanket. She buried her face in the opaque vinyl and sucked in as hard as she could. She was

a dead girl having the worst panic attack she'd ever had. Not because she was afraid of dying, but because she knew that she would never live again.

The moist curtain clung to her face like a shrink-wrap body bag for a second, and then, almost automatically, her face passed through it into the shower stall. She stopped grieving for a moment to notice a bottle of shampoo with the instructions: "For dull, lifeless hair." "Dull . . . Lifeless . . . ," she said in utter defeat.

The next thing she saw through the hot mist was someone taking a shower. If she could have blushed, she would have. Wet, soapy, dyed-black, razor-cut hair dangling over her face, Scarlet rinsed out the last traces of shampoo and slowly opened her eyes, only to see Charlotte's head protruding through the curtain, into the shower.

Scarlet screamed at the top of her lungs as she tried to cover up with her arms and elbows, surprising Charlotte, who screamed right back.

Charlotte tried her best to escape from the curtain, but with each twist and twirl, she only got caught up even more.

Panicked, Scarlet noticed what appeared to be blood running down the side of the white porcelain tub and spooling down the drain. All she could think of was the shower scene in *Psycho*. She checked herself for wounds, cowered against the corner of the stall, and waited for the deathblow. It was only the traces of her red Urban Decay lipstick washing away, but Scarlet, who was an aficionado of grindhouse flicks, was prone to drama.

Meanwhile, Charlotte broke free and tumbled out of the shower just as Damen rushed into the bathroom to find out what all the commotion was about. He caught Scarlet coming out of the shower, naked, and was totally unaware of Charlotte perched up on the toilet, quivering in fear.

"What the hell are you doing in here?" Scarlet asked as she scurried to grab a black towel and cover herself.

"I heard screaming," he mumbled.

Damen tried not to "notice" Scarlet, but he found it hard to speak. This was the first time he'd ever seen her without any makeup, clothing, and/or accessories. She was naked in every sense of the word. Vulnerable.

"Not you . . . her," she snapped.

"What 'her'?" he asked.

She pointed to Charlotte, but Damen saw only the toilet.

"Her!" she said in her most frustrated voice.

"Me," Charlotte said with no hope in her voice.

Scarlet realized that Damen could not see Charlotte, and so she screamed again, this time in fear and frustration, and bolted. Damen was confused by her odd behavior, but he let it go and went back to Petula.

Scarlet ran to her room and slammed the door. She scrambled to put on a vintage magenta silk robe with black ravens delicately embroidered on it and proceeded to run right into her adjoining dressing room, slamming that door shut too for extra protection.

The room looked like a stall at CBGB's with graffiti of poems, drawings, and song lyrics on the wall. Her toilet bowl and vanity

were plastered with band bumper stickers. Scarlet rummaged wildly through her drawers to find something, anything, to defend her against the demon from the shower.

Within seconds, there was a gentle rapping at the door. She grabbed for her black plastic cross necklace, held it out defensively like Buffy, and shrugged.

"No. I need a real one!" she said as she threw the plastic one back like a small unwanted fish into the sea of crosses.

She picked up a sterling silver cross and ran to the door with it, striking the vampire hunter pose once more.

"What do you want?" she asked through the door.

"You can see me," Charlotte whispered.

"Wait a second, I know who you are," Scarlet responded nervously, cracking the door just a smidgeon.

"You do?" Charlotte asked, pleasantly surprised at some recognition.

"You're the girl that croaked at school," Scarlet said. "From Petula's Physics class."

"Yes! That's me!" Charlotte responded, over the moon. Death did seem to get her noticed.

"What? So like, you're here for revenge 'cause I was nasty to you?" Scarlet moaned.

"No, not at all," Charlotte reassured her.

"Or because I wrote a lame obituary?" Scarlet asked, sliding the newspaper under the door.

"I made the school paper!" Charlotte chirped.

She looked down at the copy and anxiously read it. Her whole life boiled down to two sentences alongside a general online "photo not available" icon.

CHARLOTTE USHER, HAWTHORNE HIGH STUDENT, DIED
TODAY IN A SENSELESS INCIDENT INVOLVING A GUMMY BEAR.
A MEMORIAL SERVICE WAS HELD.

"That's it?" Charlotte asked, dejectedly.

"I didn't have time to get details," Scarlet babbled, seeing
no need to bring up the poorly attended memorial just now or
the fact that the yearbook staff had no photos filed under her
name or that no one returned her calls for comment.

Scarlet opened the door with trepidation, holding out the
cross.

"It's real," Scarlet said in all seriousness, as if she were holding up a pistol to a bank robber.

"Wow, Jesus must have been tiny then," Charlotte said.

Scarlet couldn't help but laugh a little.

"I'm not a vampire," she said as she took the crucifix out of
Scarlet's hand.

Scarlet remained still as Charlotte entered the room. She
looked around and noticed all the vintage cult movie posters
like *Harold & Maude, Night of the Living Dead,* and *Delicatessen* hanging on her wall with creepy, quirky shadowboxes encasing grotesque figurines showcased in between. There was a
CD of William Burroughs reading The Tibetan Book of the
Dead and an Edward Gorey illustrated funeral planner lying
on her black ornately carved desk.

"Man, I think the wrong one of us passed," Charlotte said,
studying her stuff.

"Always a bridesmaid," Scarlet muttered under her breath.

The surrealism was growing, but Scarlet's fear had almost

totally passed. Almost. Neither girl could help herself as they blurted out questions simultaneously.

"What's it like to be dead?" Scarlet asked.

"What's it's like to be Petula's sister?" Charlotte asked.

Scarlet was dumbfounded at Charlotte's question. "You're kidding me, right?" Scarlet asked.

Charlotte proceeded with a question that was a little more appropriate. "Why can you see me? No other living person can. Well . . . except maybe for dogs and babies," she said.

"How should I know?" Scarlet responded sarcastically.

"There's gotta be some kind of logic to it," Charlotte said as she looked around her room. "What is it about you that lets you see me?" She examined the Celtic crucifix and some other Goth relics lying around the room. She then went over to Scarlet's dressing room, which was a huge open closet equipped with an antique chandelier that was dripping with jewel-colored teardrop crystals. There was a velvet upholstered chair peppered with what looked like tiny black polka dots, but at closer inspection, they were actually little skulls. And there was an old Venetian glass mirror on the door where a bunch of vintage jewelry hung.

The closet was filled with vintage clothing, handbags, jewelry, scarves, you name it. Mostly black, but bright pops of color here and there managed to peek out from the sea of sequin and lace gloom. It looked more like a cutting-edge couture shop or maybe the Dresden Dolls' Gothic-punk cabaret-style dressing room than a high school girl's closet.

"Everything in moderation," Scarlet said, noticing Charlotte admiring her collection.

Scarlet walked over and pulled out a worn-out Strawberry Switchblade band tee and paired it with a tartan kilt and black iridescent leggings.

"Where and how did you get all of this stuff?" Charlotte said almost in an accusatory tone.

"From my victims," Scarlet snapped. Charlotte looked slightly stunned.

"I work at Clothes Minded, the vintage store in town, during the summer," Scarlet said as she got dressed, sensing Charlotte's uneasiness.

"This is pretty," Charlotte said, running her hand over a midnight blue sequin dress.

"You think so?" Scarlet asked excitedly, but then stopped herself. "Yeah, I guess it's okay."

Charlotte rummaged through some black chiffon blouses, some bright vintage camisoles, and then explored a section of tees as Scarlet finished dressing.

"Maybe you can see me ... I don't know ... because you're ... well ... different ... or something?" Charlotte wondered.

"There you go, stereotyping," Scarlet accused.

"I didn't mean anything by it. Really. It's just that if I could figure it out, it would help me with ... well, with something I have to do," Charlotte said, trying to calm Scarlet down a little.

"Why are you here anyway? You could be anywhere," Scarlet asked suspiciously.

"I was just here for ... your sister," Charlotte responded.

"Don't let me hold you up ... down the hall to the right!" Scarlet said without missing a beat.

"I'm not the Grim Reaper, either," Charlotte said, putting a damper on Scarlet's hopes for a clean removal of her sister.

"Right . . . ," Scarlet said with extreme disappointment. "So why aren't you backstage at a concert or in Heaven or something? I don't know, somewhere cool?" she asked. "You're wasting your . . . Afterlife."

"What do you mean, I got to see Petula's dress for the dance!"

"You did???!!!" Scarlet said sarcastically as she jumped up and down with fake excitement. "I can barely contain my fluids."

"Who are *you* going with?" Charlotte asked, oblivious to Scarlet's wiseass behavior.

"Going where?" Scarlet asked.

"To the Fall Ball," Charlotte said anxiously.

"I'm not a part of the mindless herd that is the Hawthorne student body — in case you haven't noticed," Scarlet snapped.

Charlotte backed off.

"You know, you don't look . . . or act like you're dead," Scarlet said as she looked Charlotte up and down. "You're like a dead poseur."

Charlotte tilted her head down in disappointment. The old feelings of inadequacy came rushing back.

"Great, I can't even die right," Charlotte said as she plopped herself down on Scarlet's bloodred satin bedding.

"Wait, maybe I can help you, you know, look dead, at least?" Scarlet said.

Scarlet grabbed Charlotte's arm and headed for the bathroom.

"Have a seat," Scarlet said invitingly, plopping Charlotte down on the toilet seat next to the vanity. She opened the makeup drawer and immediately began her work.

"What are you doing?" Charlotte asked as Scarlet buzzed around her.

"You need a make-under. You know, live fast, die young, leave a good-looking corpse . . . ," Scarlet said, placing her instruments on a cloth beside Charlotte as if she were a surgeon prepping for a major lifesaving procedure.

"One for three," Charlotte mumbled as she sat back and let Scarlet work her magic.

Scarlet was focused and determined, a girl on a mission, as she reconfigured makeup colors, all the while applying some matte crimson lipstick on herself and combing her straight black bob and her perfectly short bangs. She applied some pale foundation and white powder to herself for good measure, realizing there was no need to waste it on Charlotte's already ashen complexion.

Scarlet looked Charlotte over cosmetic rep–style and planned her work. She laid out all the applicators, which were nestled in a makeup holster, and sprawled them out in front of her for easy access.

This is a pro, Charlotte thought, holding her hair back for Scarlet.

Before Charlotte could get any words out, any questions, Scarlet was heating up the tip of a kohl eyeliner pencil with a lighter, but every time the liner approached Charlotte's cold, dead skin, it froze. Trying again, she put the flame too close to Charlotte and freaked out.

"Don't worry, I'm no longer flammable," Charlotte said, reassuring her.

Scarlet ended up leaving the flame on the liner like a mini blowtorch while simultaneously applying it to Charlotte's eyes.

"Aren't you, you know, even a little freaked out or afraid of me?" Charlotte asked as Scarlet scanned her extensive eye shadow palette, careful to make the right color combinations. She applied the shadow over Charlotte's lid while Charlotte kept the other eye completely open.

"Aren't you a little freaked out or afraid of *me?*" Scarlet asked.

"Well, I guess I'm a little freaked out because you're not so freaked out," Charlotte said.

"Yeah, me too," Scarlet said with a little grin on her face as she prepared for the next procedure.

Scarlet scooped up some hot wax on a stick from a purple vat and proceeded to apply it carefully to Charlotte's eyebrow. After a few seconds, Scarlet applied a little piece of cloth over the wax, pressed it down, and then ripped it off, anticipating a reaction of major pain from Charlotte, but she didn't flinch at all.

"One definite advantage of being dead," Charlotte said as Scarlet laughed and nodded in agreement.

Scarlet did some more work on Charlotte, including her hair, and Charlotte enjoyed every bit of the attention. The best part about it for her was that Scarlet was genuinely happy to be with her. Charlotte wasn't used to that kind of attention, having been raised by a court-appointed guardian for most of her life.

After a short while, they were interrupted by Scarlet's an-

tique clock as a black raven popped out and trumpeted a hardy "F.U.," "F.U." instead of the standard "cuckoo."

Noticing the time, Charlotte got up to leave.

"Where are you going? I'm not finished yet!" Scarlet yelled after her, her portrait incompletely rendered.

"I'm late for a dorm meeting — see you in school tomorrow!" Charlotte yelled back.

She ran down the hall, stealing one more peak at Damen, who was sleeping comfortably on Petula's bed, exhausted, apparently, from their workout, while Petula continued to pin her dress. She left the house looking like a Mark Ryden portrait — her hair teased out, bleeding eyeliner, wearing crimson lipstick and dark nail polish — under the glow of the full moon.

Charlotte frantically continued down the sidewalk into the darkness, toward the moon, as the same black birds that had circled her head that afternoon converged on her again.

A dorm meeting? School tomorrow? Maybe death isn't that cool after all, Scarlet thought, watching Charlotte fade from view through her bedroom window and wondering what the hell had just happened.

"Wait!" she yelled again after Charlotte, but Charlotte didn't answer, she was well on her way, almost completely out of sight.

"Great. Not only do I see dead people, but now I'm needy on top of it," Scarlet said as she slammed yet another door shut.

8

Heart of Darkness

Last night I dreamt,
That somebody loved me
No hope no harm
Just another false alarm.
—The Smiths

Home is where the heart is.

It's a place to be yourself and a place to let your hair and your guard down. But as usual, Charlotte was having a hard time belonging. Hawthorne Manor was a place for her to stay but it wasn't a place for her to "live." And right now, she was more interested in finding a place for her heart than for her soul. Charlotte may not have had an actual beating heart, but she still had heart.

he Dead Dorm, which is what the Dead kids called Hawthorne Manor, might have sounded depressing to someone else, but to Charlotte, it sounded like a community. She would never get the opportunity to live in an actual college dorm, and this, to her, was the next best thing.

Would she have a roommate? Would they stay up and talk all night long? Would they study together and have secret codes in case one of them had a guy over? Would they share clothes and have raging fits of unbridled laughter? Would they order pizza late at night when they were studying and then complain the whole next day about their weight? No. Deep down she knew that and it was just another thing that she had to let go, but it was a "dorm" nonetheless, and that meant that she wouldn't be alone. That, to her, was enough.

All this and more raced through her mind as she sped to

the meeting. It was odd, but even though it was her first time going to Hawthorne Manor, she instinctively knew how to get there, as if some spirit-world GPS had kicked in. There was no Pied Piper or, more specifically, no Piccolo Pam actually guiding her, but she was being called just the same.

As she came around the corner of the long, lonely street, she knew right away which house to head for. It was a run-down Victorian manse, still beautiful in a decrepit sort of way, the kind of high-maintenance property that was once the pride of the neighborhood, until the surrounding McMansions and Father Time had eroded its glory.

From Charlotte's new "perspective," however, it had incredible character — a still-magnificent structure, covered in creeping ivy, with towering gables, oriels perched on intricate corbels and pristine, pointed stained glass windows. All the meticulously detailed masonry was straight out of Gothic fairy tale.

There were ornate lanterns hanging all along the wraparound porch, and each porch post was strung together in gingerbread fashion. Unlike the basement intake office, which was sterile, and Dead Ed, which was dull and antiquated, Hawthorne Manor was magical.

"Home, sweet home," she said somberly as she placed her hand on a rosette and pulled along the banister that led up to the heavy, dark double doors.

Charlotte walked up the steps and onto the porch, peered in through the leaded window, and noticed the enormous and very *Phantom of the Opera* chandelier that hung in the entryway. She entered and stood on the large black-and-white marble tiles.

She was amazed at all of the ornate cherry-wood carvings that adorned the arched doorways throughout the house. It was beautiful, unlike anything she'd ever seen, but best of all, warm. Even the grandiose foyer was welcoming. She was hoping that the bedrooms would be comfy too, because she was feeling tired. It had been a long, long day.

Before Charlotte knew it, Pam zipped down the huge, deep red–carpeted carved wood staircase.

"Where were you?" Pam asked, her tone more scolding than inquisitive. Pam already knew the answer to her question, and Charlotte, of course, knew that she knew.

"Oh, just *livin'* it up," Charlotte said, half-joking.

"Well, this is where you 'live' now and you're late for our meeting. Hurry!" she said as she grabbed Charlotte's hand and dragged her up the gigantic staircase. "Prue is *not* happy!"

Charlotte had never seen Pam so intense. In fact, Charlotte didn't feel her feet even hitting the ground as she was whisked up the steps like a helium balloon.

Pam and Charlotte headed for the meeting room at the end of the hall, which looked like an Ivy League literature classroom straight out of *Dead Poets Society.* Prue was calling the meeting to order just as Charlotte burst in.

Even though she felt Pam's hand in hers, pulling her along, she was startled to see Pam sitting there when she arrived as if she hadn't moved a muscle.

Before walking in, Charlotte quickly surveyed the space and noticed dozens of sorority-fraternity-type artifacts and relics peppered around the room. There was a banner with the insignia "theta," the Greek letter for death, strung across the

wall over sepia-toned "class pictures" framed by the Ouroboros. She loved that she was in such a dignified place, almost like she was part of a secret society, even if she did not feel like a full member just yet.

As Charlotte timidly entered, her dorm-mates snickered at her new look, well, all except for Prue, who was beyond pissed.

"Is this your idea of a joke?" Prue snapped.

Charlotte, having forgotten about her make-under in her rush to get to the meeting, tried desperately to flatten her hair by licking her hands and running them through her 'do. She tried to wipe off some makeup as well, but she was short on saliva, being nervous . . . and dead and all.

"It's not going to be so funny when this place is sold, is it?" Prue asked, commanding the room's attention and taking the focus off Charlotte while embarrassing her at the same time.

Charlotte made her way over to the one and only friendly face in the room, Piccolo Pam, and sat down.

"What's the big deal about saving this house anyway?" Charlotte whispered innocently into Pam's ear.

"What's the big deal?" Prue yelled before Pam could get a word out. "The BIG DEAL is that this is our home. It is where we exist."

"But aren't there a lot of other old houses in the world?" Charlotte asked sheepishly.

"Aren't there a lot of other Dead kids in the world?" Prue spat, throwing Charlotte's question back in her face. "It is not about other houses. It is about THIS house, which has been entrusted to *us* until the time comes."

"What 'time'?" Charlotte asked, making air quotes for emphasis. Pam, sensing a real problem brewing, jumped in.

"Everybody calm down," she interjected. "Charlotte is new."

This was a fact that carried very little weight with Prue.

"We *need* to be here, Charlotte, until the time comes when we can cross over together," Pam explained.

"To where?" Charlotte asked. "I just got *here.*"

"None of us really know for sure," Pam replied. "Resolving our personal issues is just one part of the process. Preventing this house from being sold is something we have to do as a team. It's our assignment to work together and forget about our own wants and desires."

"Unselfishness and obligation, Usher," Prue chided. "Two things you obviously know nothing about."

Charlotte bristled at Prue's cut because it was totally untrue, as far as she was concerned. After all, she tried to sign up for cheerleading didn't she? She had "team" written all over her.

"If we are going to save this house, everyone needs to pull their weight. If one person doesn't, it will ruin it for all of us," Prue said sternly as she repeatedly smacked a wooden pointer on her hand. "And I'm not going to let that happen," she concluded, staring threateningly at Charlotte.

Everyone instantly got serious, that is, everyone except Metal Mike and Deadhead Jerry, who tried to lighten the mood by making lewd gestures toward Abigail, the drowning victim who, oddly enough, still wore her swimsuit despite her varicose veins, sickly transparent pasty skin, and bulging eyeballs.

"I'd like to dive into that," Deadhead Jerry said to Mike,

referring to Abigail; a puff of smoke released from his mouth every time he opened it.

"Hard to believe she drowned with flotation devices like those." Mike snickered a little too loudly.

Charlotte tried desperately to keep her focus on Prue.

"So what can we do to save our house?" Prue asked.

There was dead silence as Prue began to make eye contact with each and every single Dead Ed student in the room.

"Anyone?" she barked like a mad dog.

In the audience, Charlotte desperately tried to avoid Prue's gaze.

"Please don't call on me ... please don't call on me ...," she pleaded to herself as she tried to stay as much out of sight as she could, ducking behind Simon and Simone, the fraternal twins who shared a desk in front of her. They were suspicious and secretive, dark and twisted, and they moved with a creepy elegance as one. Charlotte was just thankful that they were so inseparable and hoped they would provide a protective shield from Prue's accusatory gaze.

"Ah, if it isn't our prized Darwin Award recipient," Prue said, interrupting Charlotte's mantra. "Since this is all so friggin' funny to you, what's your plan?"

"Oh, I don't think it's funny," Charlotte said meekly.

"Could have fooled me," Prue said, once again referring to Charlotte's new look with her eyes.

"Oh no, this, this was just ...," Charlotte scrambled for an alibi.

"Well ...," Prue said as she continued to grill Charlotte, trying to prompt some kind of answer.

Just then, Abigail popped her eyes completely out of their sockets, straight at Jerry.

"Oh my God!" Charlotte screamed.

Charlotte startled the entire class with her outburst.

Hearing the scream, Abigail snapped her eyeballs back into place and her face returned to its normal shape.

"You're sick," Metal Mike said in disgust to Abigail.

Abigail smirked as she tried to cover her mouth with her pale, bluish hands.

"Oh God!" Prue mocked Charlotte, affecting a high-pitched squeal. "Not even God is going to be able to help you if you screw things up."

"No, wait! I think she just got an idea," Piccolo Pam chimed in, trying to save Charlotte's ass.

Charlotte nodded her head nervously in agreement.

"We can protect the house by scaring everybody away from it . . . ," Pam added as she nudged Charlotte. "Right, Charlotte?"

"Yeah, why can't we just, like she said . . . ," Simon said.

". . . scare the potential buyers away?" Simone finished.

"I've got it! We can decorate the whole house in 'Stuff by Duff!' That should do it," CoCo said as she shivered in fright.

Charlotte started to improvise, starting to get what everyone else in the room already knew.

"We are dead. Why not, you know, 'work' it?" she said to Prue, building confidence as she went along.

"Is this your plan?" Prue asked, trying to break Charlotte.

"I mean, it's obvious, but it's worth a try . . . ," Charlotte replied.

"Well, we can't actually haunt the house or it could backfire. It will either turn into a tourist attraction and a playground for drunk college kids or it will buy us a one-way ticket to becoming a parking-plex," Prue snapped.

"I think the best way to scare potential buyers away would be to make this place appear not up to code," suggested Buzz Saw Bud, a kid who'd died from a horrible shop class accident and now sported table saw wounds and a partially amputated arm.

"All right then, break up into scare squads!" Prue said, not really on board with Charlotte's plan but more than willing to give her enough rope to hang herself.

Charlotte immediately went to pair up with Pam, but just as she approached her, Prue grabbed Pam's arm like an abusive elementary school teacher taking a disruptive student to a hallway time-out.

"Pam, you're with Silent Violet," Prue ordered as she knocked Charlotte away and placed Pam with the eerie loner who had never, as far as any of the other kids in Dead Ed could remember, uttered a sound.

"Suzy Scissorhands!" Prue ordered, "You're with me."

Suzy tugged her sleeves over her hands and clenched them tightly as she walked over to Prue's side. Charlotte was left standing alone, just like in Physics class.

"Who am I supposed to be with?" Charlotte asked.

"Ask somebody who cares, *Butch*," Prue snapped, using a dig from class. "Maybe next time, you'll get here on time and take this seriously."

Charlotte tried to explain, but her words only echoed against the walls of the empty room.

She was alone again, but this time, not lonely. There was too much to take in. Charlotte trudged off to look for her bedroom, without the chitchat or the roommate that she had hoped for. No secret codes, no sneaking in after a night of un-bridled adventure, no giggle fits, no guy talk, no pizza. It was just as well. The confrontation with Prue was exhausting, emotionally and otherwise. She'd never felt so despised, even in Life.

She reached the next landing on the staircase, one flight up from the meeting room, and walked down to the first open door. It was wooden and heavy with carved moldings, like all the others at the Manor. She shoved it open, checking first so as not to intrude on anyone, and walked in.

The room was empty and she instantly felt at home. She knew instinctively that this was her room. The walls were cov-ered in delicate floral toile flock wallpaper, and Charlotte, who at first thought her eyes were playing tricks on her, noticed that some of the petals periodically fell off the flowers on the wallpaper, making for a surreal and dreamy effect. There was another chandelier, like a baby sister to the one in the foyer, that hung low from the beamed cathedral ceiling.

Mahogany bookshelves lined the walls, and a massive vanity like Scarlet's, which Charlotte loved, occupied the corner adja-cent to her four-poster bed. She was so spent she could barely take it all in or muster up enough emotion to be sufficiently impressed. She walked over to the bed and plopped down.

"Death is ruining my life," she said as she wrapped herself away in a crushed velvet blanket.

As her head hit the pillow for the first time, the drowsiness left her and her mind began to race. It was impossible for her to relax, and the thought of sleeping was suddenly frightening. As long as she remained awake, she reasoned, she was "alive," maybe not technically, but she was conscious at least. Present. Who knew what sleep would bring?

Then she remembered Deadhead Jerry falling asleep with his eyes open in Dead Ed, and the image of that freaked her out even more. Nightmare on Hawthorne Street. She frantically searched the room, looking for something that would keep her occupied and awake.

The closest book to her was her *Deadiquette* book, so she started flipping through it. Maybe there were answers in the book. Maybe there was hope tucked away in its antique pages.

As she flipped through, she noticed a chapter she hadn't seen earlier in class. It read "Possession" at the top.

Charlotte sat straight up in bed.

"Possession!" she exclaimed.

She thumbed through the '50s-style illustrations of a guy simply entering a girl and soaked up every word of the captions.

"Looks simple enough," she said with an insane amount of confidence.

Charlotte finished the chapter by the light of the moonbeams shining through her oversized windows, closed the

book, and finally gave in to the exhaustion that had been chasing her all evening. She was no longer sad or afraid.

"If he can't see me to ask me to the dance, I'll just possess the person he's planning to go with . . . ," she muttered as slumber fell upon her.

Charlotte took her hands and manually closed her eyes, just in case, while the light fall breeze blowing through the window flipped the pages of her book to the final page in the chapter — a page that she hadn't read yet. It warned: "Use Extreme Caution!"

9

Behind the Wheel

And I could purge my soul perhaps
For the imminent collapse
Oh yeah, I'll tell you what we could do
You be me for a while
I'll be you.
—Paul Westerberg

Attach here.

—◆◆◆◆—

An attachment to something or someone is holding on to the belief that a certain thing or person will fulfill you. Attachments keep us alive. They make us strive either to keep what we have or to pursue what we want. But sometimes they can also stick us in neutral, running in circles and getting nowhere. Charlotte was stuck, that much was sure.

etula and the Wendys sauntered into the bathroom as if they owned it. They made their usual tightly choreographed entrance, just in case someone was looking. It was their post–homeroom, pre–first period touch-up session, and the powders, brushes, and lip glosses were being pulled from every pocket and pouch of their ridiculously expensive handbags faster than the blink of a heavily coated RevitaLashed eye.

Their access to the mirror was momentarily blocked by a clueless group of sleazy freshmen not yet schooled in mirror protocol. Wendy Anderson took charge silently, parting the gaggle with an icy stare and pointing sternly to the exit. The freshmen learned fast, filing out quickly, quietly, and without objection.

"Wanna-MEs," Wendy Anderson grumbled as the three of them assumed their rightful place in front of the mirror.

Petula caught a glimpse of Wendy Thomas on the left side of her and got to thinking. She whipped out a stick of bronzer and drew a small line on the bridge of Wendy's nose, like a junior Dr. 90210 doing a pre-op markup.

"See, if you have this shaved down and then the tip lifted it will make a cute slope, just like mine," Petula said as she stepped back and admired her work.

"Ski?" Petula asked Wendy as she turned her to the mirror so that she could "see."

"Yeah, I ski," Wendy Thomas said with a chuckle, noticing the little but very conspicuous mark.

For Petula and the Wendys, this kind of brutal and shameless self-criticism was not so much a game as a hobby. And there was not an iota of embarrassment in them as they heard a rustling in the stall behind them.

If they had bothered to look at anything other than their own reflections, they might have noticed the clunky pair of black biker boots visible beneath the stall door. The toilet flushed and Scarlet emerged, tugging her mustard-colored camisole and shifting her black tank and vintage chiffon skirt into position.

Wendy Anderson, seeing in the reflection of the mirror that it was Scarlet, made a dismissive face, which only provoked Scarlet. Scarlet took the bronzer out of Wendy's manicured grasp.

"I'd go for the Marie Antoinette," Scarlet said as she drew a dotted line across Wendy's neck. "You need a total head removal."

"Shouldn't you be somewhere feeling ostracized?" Wendy Anderson said condescendingly.

"I'm sorry, I don't speak *whore*," Scarlet replied, heavy-tongued as she "signed" the sentence, ending with a thrust and extended middle finger much as Wendy had wagged her index finger at the lowly freshmen. Wendy got the message.

Petula brushed by her sister, not acknowledging her in the slightest, and walked out the door just as the bell rang.

Scarlet stayed behind, pondering how they could possibly be related. She instantly got an eerie feeling, looking around the empty room.

"Charlotte?"

No answer. Charlotte was outside the school, waiting for Petula and the Wendys to exit. She knew that the three of them had Driver's Ed first period with Mr. Gonzalez, and she didn't want to miss her opportunity.

Charlotte took one last look at the Possession page in her book as the triumvirate walked out of the school. She was nervous, this being her first time, and tried to convince herself just to do what came naturally. Still, this was the big time. She was about to enter Petula Kensington. To see the world through her eyes, to feel with her fingers, to possibly kiss with her lips. To look down and see a perfect body with curves in all the right places.

Maybe it was fashionable for beautiful news-show present-ers to go slumming in fat suits to experience "prejudice," but Charlotte was looking for the opposite — a chance to be

accepted. Admired. Popular. Petula's was a perfect suit, one with a perfect life and a perfect boyfriend, and it was all hers for the taking. For the first time ever, she was in a position to take control and make her dreams come true.

Meanwhile, Petula had positioned herself in the driver's seat of the car, adjusting her makeup in the side-view mirror as it idled. She left the door open so that anyone who wanted to see her could have a clear view before she left the school premises. She was really generous that way. Wendy Thomas and Wendy Anderson got in the back, leaving the passenger seat open for the teacher, who was chatting away with a colleague.

Petula, bored waiting for Gonzalez to finish his dialogue, decided to begin the Driver's Ed lesson without him. Only Petula could get away with taking a Driver's Ed car off school property without a teacher and without a license.

"In honor of Mr. Gonzalez, let's hit Taco Hell," Petula suggested to the Wendys, as if they had a choice.

"Sounds cool," they said in total agreement.

"Of course it does; I said it."

Petula hit the gas and pulled away from the curb with a screech and with the passenger door still open.

"Later, asswipe!" Wendy Thomas shouted out the window to the teacher.

"Wendy, he's also our Spanish teacher . . . *en Español, por favor!*" Wendy Anderson said with a smirk on her face.

"*Hasta la vista, Señor Assweep-a!*" Wendy Thomas screamed.

Mr. Gonzalez yelled to the wayward car, completely

humiliated in front of his colleague, but then again, Petula was a pro at humiliating people, especially teachers.

That instant, Charlotte put her head down and ran flat out toward the open passenger door, which Petula was reaching to close. She slammed directly into Petula, stopping half in and half out, like the shower curtain incident. Charlotte's intrusion unexpectedly sparked a reflex reaction in Petula, like a midday bout of restless leg syndrome, and forced her foot against the gas pedal and brake.

The car jerked spastically as Charlotte struggled to "carjack" Petula. It bucked so hard, in fact, that Charlotte was thrown from Petula and out of the driver's side window.

With Petula momentarily free of Charlotte, the car slowed and Petula felt for a second that she'd regained some control. From the backseat, the Wendys were loving the fact that Petula had just driven off without the teacher, but they were less enthused about all the stop-and-go action. Petula played it cool as she resumed the driver manual–recommended "ten and two" position on the steering wheel and picked up speed as she headed for the parking lot exit.

Charlotte regrouped also, reaching through the windshield to grab Petula's hands. Petula swerved wildly to the left and right. Charlotte's legs passed through the hood into the driver's compartment and into Petula's legs. She was stuck to Petula like a used piece of gum on the bottom of a shoe.

As the car careened further out of control, the momentum pulled Charlotte against the front windshield, face-to-face with Petula, both of their eyes wide with fear. Having never

been so close to her idol, Charlotte felt herself starstruck, even in these dangerous circumstances.

"I'm sorry, Petula," she said with utter sincerity.

Petula, oblivious, gritted her teeth, stared straight ahead, and tried not to hit anything. By now, the Wendys were starting to show signs of serious stress as they were tossed from side to side in the backseat.

"Motor vehicle accidents are the leading cause of teen fatalities," Wendy Thomas whimpered under her breath.

"It's because researchers have found that many teens have trouble regulating high-risk behavior because the area of the brain that controls impulsivity doesn't fully mature until age twenty-five . . . ," Wendy Anderson babbled nervously, uncharacteristically imparting a factoid she'd accidentally absorbed from one of her magazines.

Wendy Thomas and Petula sat in stunned silence at Wendy Anderson's outburst. Even Charlotte was momentarily impressed. The high-speed weaving of the car snapped them all back into reality.

"Petula, do you think you could slow . . ."

Before Wendy Thomas could get the words out, Petula snapped.

"Buckle up, bitches!" Petula screamed. "At least this is the most popular way to die."

Charlotte was hurt.

Petula was acting typically snotty and fearless, but she absolutely did not have a death wish. She just had no idea what was going on and needed to instill confidence in the troops until she could stop the car. That was leadership.

Petula was dressed to lead too. She always made sure to wear her cheerleading uniform to Driver's Ed. She'd caught the teacher eyeing her, er, pom-poms once and figured that with every drop of pedophilic sweat that bubbled up under his comb-over during lessons, she was that much closer to being the first in her class to get her driver's license.

Charlotte slammed into Petula again, awkwardly and aggressively, forcing her foot to slam abruptly on the brake.

The car came to a screeching halt and all the girls jerked forward and then back. Charlotte was once again thrown from Petula, this time headfirst, giving a whole new meaning to "going through the windshield."

"That better not leave a scar," Wendy Anderson said as she snapped off her seatbelt, lifted up her cheerleading sweater, and inspected her chest for anything that resembled a mark.

"Too late," Charlotte chimed in, noticing the implant scar showing from beneath Wendy's underwire bra. Charlotte pulled her head and shoulders back into the vehicle as Wendy pulled down her sweater.

Petula exhaled and tried to make light of the situation.

"I paid so much for these shoes, it's no wonder they have a mind of their own," she said, turning to the backseat passengers and referring to her self-designed Nike iDs.

The Wendys, who were as petrified as dead frogs in formaldehyde, burst out in sycophant-like laughter at Petula's joke as they approached the drive-through.

"There should be a warning: 'Do not operate heavy machinery while attempting possession,'" Charlotte said in frustration. Thinking that the third time is always a charm,

she hoisted herself high up against the passenger window as if she were Spider-Man and tried to get inside Petula once again, causing the car to lurch forward at the pickup window and onto the curb.

"What is up with you?" Wendy Anderson asked, unable to ignore Petula's odd behavior any longer.

"I . . . don't . . . know," Petula answered, honestly confused by her actions.

"*I* do," Wendy Thomas announced somewhat spitefully. "I overheard Coach Burres say that if Damen didn't get at least a C on his Physics test, he wasn't going to let him go to the Fall Ball."

Hearing this news, Charlotte flew into a tailspin. She paused for a second and then panicked.

"NO!!!" Charlotte cried as she tried to dig her way into Petula. The car sped off yet again, knocking the value meal order sign, and everything else in its way, to the ground.

A horrifying, white-knuckle ride of near hits and misses commenced as they barreled back through the school parking lot, completely out of control. Charlotte's final, desperate attempt at possession looked like some weird all-girl Ultimate Fighting match, with Charlotte and Petula's arms, elbows, knees and feet — both visible and invisible — flying in all directions.

As they headed back toward the school, the marching band was out front practicing their arrangement of Marilyn Manson's "The Beautiful People," that is until the car hurled through the cyclone fence and screeched across the practice field, scattering the band, crashing into the flag pole, and leaving the

world's biggest lawn job in their wake. A tuba that was knocked from the hands of its player collided with the car hood.

"What the hell is that?" Petula asked with utter disgust.

I think it's a . . . a . . . tuba," Wendy Anderson replied.

"There is spit in those things!" Petula, a world-class germophobe, screamed. "Band-people spit!!!"

Their priorities reestablished, they all rushed to exit the car as if it were on fire. They grabbed their gym clothes out of their bags and touched the car door handles using various articles of clothing as protection. As far as they were concerned, a group of men in hazmat suits should have showed up with truckloads of industrial-strength Purell to kill anything that might be growing on them.

Charlotte stayed behind, sitting in the dented, overheated car, wallowing in her disappointment. Not so much at what she did but at what she failed to do.

As the banged-up tuba seesawed on the car and the girls scrambled, an announcement came over the school PA system.

"Petula Kensington to the office," the announcer said.

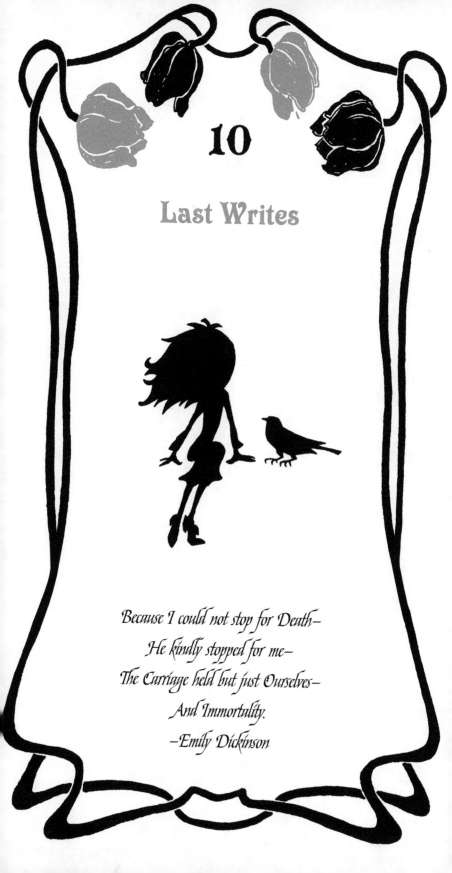

10

Last Writes

Because I could not stop for Death—
He kindly stopped for me—
The Carriage held but just Ourselves—
And Immortality.
—Emily Dickinson

Letting go, for anyone, at any time, can be the hardest thing to do.

———◆◆◆———

More than just depressing, for some people it is an admission of defeat, of failure. Charlotte was one of those people. Letting go meant that it was time to give up on everything she had hoped for and dreamed about. That everything she'd worked for was all for nothing. That life was more or less a crapshoot and she'd rolled a seven. This would never do. Her sole purpose became her soul purpose.

he time for "patience with the new girl" was passing, and Charlotte knew she had to get with the program. But what, exactly, was the program? She'd been so focused on her own goals, she hadn't a clue. Back in Dead Ed, Mr. Brain's lesson had begun and Charlotte was late — again. She had sneaked in while Brain's back was to her.

"She was so young," Mr. Brain said as he leaned over Silent Violet's desk, looking her right in the eye. "He had his whole life ahead of him . . ." Brain continued, turning to Mike.

"Huh?" Mike responded, unable to hear Brain's lecture.

"Life was just beginning for them," he concluded, frowning at Simon and Simone.

"Isn't that how the eulogy always begins?" Brain asked, returning to the blackboard as Violet and the other kids nodded their heads slowly in agreement.

"And whoever is doing the memorializing — priest, rabbi, minister, imam, parent, sibling, teacher, friend . . . whoever," he said, ". . . is right, of course. Dying as a teen is more than sad. It is tragic. But not for the reasons they think."

Piccolo Pam gave the evil eye to Charlotte, who was snaking along the perimeter of the classroom, trying to avoid being caught by Mr. Brain. She knew Charlotte, above all, needed to hear this particular lesson.

"Yeah. No one would believe you still have to go to school," Jerry said, cracking himself up. Prue looked over at him angrily, and he shut up instantly.

"Right, Jerry . . . ," Mr. Brain began as Jerry silently *nah-nahed* at Prue, who ignored him.

"The reason you have to go to school, even after you die, is not only to learn about your life after death, as the orientation film describes," Brain said to the confused students. "It is to learn the thing you never had a chance to learn in life."

"What 'thing'?" Charlotte asked, just as she had deftly slid into the open seat next to Pam. Prue glared at her.

"It is a different *thing* for each person, Ms. Usher," Brain said, oblivious to her tardiness. Score one for Charlotte. "That is for each of you to figure out.

"You see, infants and children are too young to have made serious mistakes, and older people live long enough to learn from and even correct theirs," Mr. Brain intoned, sounding more like a preacher than a professor. "But teens, like you all, live only in the moment, often behaving selfishly, impulsively, and with horrible consequences for yourself or others."

"No kidding," Pam said, the whistle sound from her throat becoming noticeably louder.

To make his point more forcefully, Brain polled the class on what should have been a very sensitive topic.

"Those of you who miss your family, please raise your hand," he asked.

Mike, Jerry, Kim, Pam, and the rest all looked around at each other and shook their heads no, arms dangling at their sides. Charlotte, come to think of it, had not given even a single thought to her family either.

"This," Brain said, "is a simply continuance of your natural state. You didn't pay much attention to them or to their wishes when you were alive. It is the thing that . . . 'undid' you, as it were, that remains with you here and needs to be confronted."

Charlotte didn't quite get it, but figured this familial blind spot could be as much a blessing as a curse. She really couldn't handle any more attachment to her life than she already had.

"So, we're being punished by being here?" Charlotte asked. "Is that what this is really all about?"

"Not at all," Brain interjected. "You have been given an opportunity. Dead Ed is your second and, listen well, *final* chance to understand what has happened to you and why, and to learn to accept it," Mr. Brain advised as he strolled back to the chalkboard. "To accept your death, but most of all, to accept yourself.

"When you do achieve acceptance, you will have found resolution, and with that comes rest, peace, and . . ."

"Graduation!" Mike screeched, thrusting both "rock hands" in the air.

"Exactly," Brain said.

Graduation? Charlotte wondered. She didn't even have a dress.

"The most important part of all this is that you will need each other to succeed. It is why you are here in this class together. The chain will only be as strong as the weakest link," Brain said.

At Brain's "weakest link" reference, Charlotte's eyes darted around the room to see if she could catch anyone silently accusing her. Only Prue's orbs were locked on hers.

Brain yanked on a loop above the chalkboard, which was connected to a dingy string, and forced a map of Mesopotamia to hurl up to the top, revealing a list of what appeared to be instructions written on the board.

"Now that you know *what* you need to do," Brain continued, changing his tone from preacher to motivational speaker, "this is *how*."

He began reading the list, underscoring each word, each line, on the board with his pointer as he did.

1. WE ADMITTED THAT WE WERE POWERLESS OVER OUR SELF-ABSORBED IMPULSES AND THAT, BECAUSE OF THIS, WE DIED.

2. WE CAME TO BELIEVE THAT A POWER GREATER THAN OURSELVES COULD RESTORE US.

3. WE MADE A DECISION TO TURN OUR WILL AND OUR LIVES OVER.

4. WE MADE A SEARCHING AND FEARLESS MORAL INVENTORY OF OURSELVES.

5. WE ADMITTED TO OURSELVES AND TO EVERYONE ELSE THE EXACT NATURE OF OUR WRONGDOINGS.

6. WE WERE ENTIRELY READY TO HAVE ALL THESE DEFECTS OF CHARACTER REMOVED.

7. WE HUMBLY ASKED TO REMOVE OUR SHORTCOMINGS.

8. WE MADE A LIST OF ALL PERSONS WE HAD HARMED, AND BECAME WILLING TO MAKE AMENDS.

9. WE MADE DIRECT AMENDS TO SUCH PEOPLE WHEREVER POSSIBLE, EXCEPT WHEN TO DO SO WOULD INJURE THEM OR OTHERS.

10. WE CONTINUED TO TAKE PERSONAL INVENTORY AND WHEN WE WERE WRONG PROMPTLY ADMITTED IT.

11. WE SOUGHT TO IMPROVE OUR CONSCIOUS CONTACT WITH ONE ANOTHER AND TO UNDERSTAND OUR SPECIAL ABILITIES.

12. WE TRIED TO CARRY THIS MESSAGE AND TO PRACTICE THESE PRINCIPLES IN ALL OUR AFFAIRS, INCLUDING WORKING TOGETHER TO SAVE OUR HOUSE AND OURSELVES.

Everyone looked at the twelve steps as if they were written in hieroglyphics. It reminded Charlotte of that sinking feeling you get when a pop quiz in Trig is passed back to you and the only words you recognize on it are "Name" and "Date."

"Oh, it's not so bad, people! The main thing here is to admit the reason you died, eventually accept that it was your responsibility, and figure out what you could do to change yourself and to banish your personality flaws, or, as they say in the program, your addiction. If you could first admit your flaw to your classmates, and more importantly to yourself, then you could earn a one-way ticket to a Better Place! This class is essentially a rehab to resolution," Brain said, trying to rally his team.

None of this was striking a chord with Charlotte.

"Why don't you get out your personal 'DIEaries' and we can get started on our journey to a little place I like to call Success," Brain enthused.

It was hard enough having to get up and admit your faults to the whole class, but reading your deepest, darkest thoughts from your own DIEary was particularly humiliating, even for a Dead kid.

"Mike, why don't you go first?" Brain suggested loudly, or more like insisted.

Metal Mike took his DIEary out of his pocket and dragged himself up to the podium.

"Hi, I'm Mike, Metal Mike, and I love music," he said unenthusiastically, obviously just placating Brain.

"Hi, Mike," the class droned with equal excitement.

"I would like to share with you with these inspirational words of wisdom that I carry with me wherever I go." Mike cleared his throat, perused his DIEary briefly, looked up, and quoted the lyrics to "Back in Black" by AC/DC.

"Mike. That's a song," DJ said. "Not a personal observation."

"Music is . . . was, my life," he confided. "It is personal. It speaks to me."

"That's the problem, Mike, you lived for it. We're not alive anymore," Simone said.

"What's the problem with wanting to hold on to something that you love? Something that you lived for?" Mike asked defensively.

"And that you died for, Mike. Music killed you. Have you forgotten that?" Simon said.

"Music is a murderer," Deadhead Jerry said halfheartedly.

"No, his love of music is the murderer," Call Me Kim chimed in.

"So? Why would I give up something I love so much that I died for it?" Mike asked.

"Maybe it's not about giving it up?" Charlotte asked rhetorically.

"You're damn right it's not. I don't give a crap about crossing over and getting any kind of resolution if it means giving up my music," Mike said stubbornly.

With the class in an open discussion, Pam took the opportunity to nudge Charlotte.

"Where were you?" Pam whispered to Charlotte as Mike continued his rant.

"Oh, my ride was late," Charlotte said with a smirk.

"Not again," Pam moaned.

"Care to share your conversation with the rest of us?" Mr. Brain, perturbed by Charlotte and Pam's sideline conversation, asked the age-old question.

"Why can't I do any of this stuff?" Charlotte blurted out to everyone's surprise, including her own. The Fall Ball was a few weeks away and the clock was ticking. She was feeling pressure.

Mr. Brain turned around, a bit startled that Charlotte spoke up rather than shut up, which was what he'd intended.

"What stuff?" he asked of Charlotte.

"All the Deadiquette stuff. I'm totally failing," she replied.

"Breaking news," Prue chortled sarcastically.

"Quiet, Prudence," Brain ordered with a seriousness of tone unexpected in such a touchy-feely session.

"You've all had your period of adjustment, haven't you? She hasn't been afforded that yet," Mr. Brain said, seriously ruminating over Charlotte's point. "And speaking of 'periods,' perhaps that is the best way to explain," he continued cryptically.

Giggles erupted from Jerry, Mike, and DJ at the word "period."

"Mind and body mature at different rates. This is especially true of adolescents, isn't that right, gentlemen?" Mr. Brain asked as Mike, Jerry, DJ, and the rest instantly choked back

their laughter into embarrassed coughs. Having made his point, Brain continued.

"Just because your body is hormonally programmed to begin your peri . . . ah, menses, that is, because you are physically capable of reproducing at a certain age, does not mean you are emotionally or psychologically prepared. In other words, yours is a woman's body, still ruled by the mind of a girl."

Everyone was getting a little uncomfortable now at the depth and detail of Brain's lesson.

Pam unexpectedly piped up.

"His point is," Pam clarified, "that just because you've died doesn't mean you're ready to let go of your Life. You aren't disconnected, mentally."

"And until you are," Brain advised, "you will not be able to exercise each of your powers fully or correctly, which is essential to moving on. In fact, trying to do so may even be dangerous to yourself — and others."

"So I have to be 'mentally dead' to get something like possession to work?" Charlotte asked naively.

The whole class gasped when Charlotte said the "p" word.

"You think you're too good to be dead, don't you?" Prue railed, squinting her eyes like a bully about to start a fistfight.

"This isn't film class, Charlotte," Mr. Brain said, more than annoyed.

Charlotte looked confused as Mr. Brain started writing on the board like a wild man.

"Possession is not something I teach, because to take

custody of a living person's body defeats the whole purpose of acceptance, what we're all trying to achieve together." Brain continued pointing once again to the twelve steps on the board. "It is the ultimate act of selfishness."

She had clearly touched a nerve with Brain and even her classmates.

"Besides, possession is impossible except under the most extraordinary circumstances," Brain said, hoping to defuse Charlotte's fascination with the topic much like an unprepared parent does when the subject of sex is raised.

"Impossible?" Charlotte asked, the last flicker of hope leaving her eyes.

"You need a willing participant, and none of us can be seen by anyone, so it's not really an option. It has to be consensual," he replied, trying to lay the topic to rest.

"Consensual. Makes sense," Charlotte mumbled, recalling her struggle with Petula in Driver's Ed. "So, you have to be seen by someone in order for them to agree to be possessed?" Charlotte summed up.

The bell rang not a minute too soon for Mr. Brain or her classmates, and everyone collected their belongings and started to leave.

"Just a reminder, the house is going to be shown tonight. TONIGHT, PEOPLE. Just like a soul needs a body, you need that house," Mr. Brain yelled as the class dispersed.

Charlotte trailed behind, deep in thought, trying to figure everything out. As she passed by Brain's desk, he stopped her.

"Charlotte, are you visible to someone?" he asked.

"You said we couldn't be seen," she replied.

Charlotte, not really trusting that she should come clean just yet, tucked her DIEary under her arm, turned, and headed out of the room, the word "willing" still bouncing around in her mind.

11

So Alive

My motto—sans limites.
—Isadora Duncan

Life support.

———◆◆◆———

Respirators, heart monitors, IV drips and resuscitators, though crucial to the sick and dying, are useless to the dead. The support Charlotte required was not the technological kind. She needed someone with enough faith in her to give herself over completely. Not just someone to stand behind her, but someone who would let Charlotte stand inside her, inhabit her, become her. A soul mate.

ou wanna do what??!!" Scarlet, flabbergasted, spit a mouthful of split pea soup all over the cafeteria table. She could not believe what she'd just heard.

Charlotte flinched, closing her eyes as if she might be hit by Scarlet's spew, and smiled for a second at the *Exorcist* moment.

Piccolo Pam watched the tête-à-tête from the Dead table, feeling slightly left out.

"So what do you think?" Charlotte asked once more, looking for a few wayward soup flecks to wipe from her dress and hoping for a more favorable answer this time.

"I think you were a no-show this morning in the bathroom when I needed you and now you want to use me," Scarlet said.

"I'm sorry for not showing up. I was into something else," Charlotte replied.

"Or into *someone* else?" Scarlet quipped.

"I do have a life . . . I mean, well, you know what I mean," Charlotte responded defensively.

"What do I get out of all this?" Scarlet asked.

"Well, haven't you ever wanted to be invisible?" Charlotte said.

"Every day," Scarlet replied.

"Well, then, here's your chance," Charlotte said.

Scarlet got a smirk on her face from ear to ear as Charlotte grabbed her hand and led her out of the cafeteria.

"Wait, where are we going? I'm still hungry," Scarlet said as Charlotte pulled her along.

"Yeah, but wouldn't you rather eat in the teacher's lounge?" Charlotte said, hinting at the possibilities to an already curious Scarlet.

As they made their way to an abandoned room, they continued their conversation. It appeared to the students they passed in the hallway that Scarlet was talking to herself. Scarlet could give a shit. Charlotte loved this about Scarlet. This lack of shamelessness in public was worn as a badge of honor, definitely something Scarlet shared with her sister, although in a very different way. Petula was a leader, Scarlet an outcast. One got off on being idolized, the other on being iso-

lated. Charlotte was too little of both: neither cool enough to be loved nor cool enough to be loathed.

The girls came upon an abandoned room at the end of the hallway. Charlotte went in first to see if there were any students hiding in the corners and then signaled to Scarlet that the coast was clear. She came in and shut the door. The lights were off and the only light shining was from fluorescent chemicals bubbling blue, red, and violet in beakers on Bunsen burners. It was cool if you were lying on the floor, zoning, with your iPod cranking, but under these circumstances, it was unsettling.

They both knew that what they were about to attempt was something that no one else had done. This was beyond the unknown — beyond life and death. Neither of them knew exactly what would happen or how they would end up, but they were both willing to try because, well, they could.

"How long does a possession session last?" Scarlet asked.

"As long as you want it to," Charlotte reassured her.

"Here's to good chemistry then," Scarlet joked nervously as Charlotte crammed the possession incantation in her book.

"My book says we only have to do this ritual at the beginning of each session." Charlotte instructed. "After that, we'll be able to switch at will."

Scarlet was willing, but anxious.

"Don't worry," Charlotte said. "I set it all up. I signed

you, well me, up to be Damen's 'Physics Friend.' He's going to meet me on the football field for his tutoring session," Charlotte continued with all the precision of a covert FBI operative.

"I hope this works because . . ." Scarlet let the preposition hang in the air, not wanting to add any of the predicates describing what might be. ". . . I don't know a thing about Physics."

"Once I'm inside you, you will," Charlotte said reassuringly. "Trust me."

But the floodgates of Scarlet's imagination opened anyway. She didn't want to even entertain the thought that she might get stuck on another plane and be lost forever. Maybe she would end up in a narcoleptic state where she knew what was happening but couldn't communicate. A kind of hell where no one could hear her and she couldn't quite die or couldn't quite live. Maybe she'd get trapped for eternity. That could be a very long time.

"I still don't get why you care if he passes or not," Scarlet asked, as much to delay the moment as satisfy her curiosity.

"It's my unresolved issue to help Damen. That's what was about to happen when I died," Charlotte said sincerely, knowing that Scarlet had a built-in bullshit detector and taking every precaution not to sound any alarms.

"Tutoring a guy in Physics is your big unfinished business?" Scarlet asked, sensing something was up.

"Look, you're Petula's sister . . . so you being able to see me

makes sense," Charlotte said as she set up her Deadiquette book on the lab table so that she could read and face Scarlet at the same time. "You are my only path to resolution."

"I'm glad you think so . . . my body is headed to the football field to tutor a popular guy," Scarlet said sarcastically.

"No one will even see you," Charlotte said. She took Scarlet's shoulders and began to position them in line with her own. "Our hearts have to be in perfect alignment," she said, reading out of her book and manipulating Scarlet as delicately as she could.

"I don't want to hear any details," Scarlet said, wincing at the thought of her blood-filled beating heart being messed with.

"Hey, your first time is always the most memorable, right?" Charlotte said, trying to divert attention from what was happening.

"Yeah, 'cause it's always the most awkward and horrible," Scarlet replied.

"We don't have to do anything you don't want to do, and we can stop at any time," Charlotte said, trying to put Scarlet at ease so she didn't feel trapped and out of control.

"That's what they all say," Scarlet joked nervously, signaling for Charlotte to begin the ritual.

"Hey, you can't get any more punk than possession," Charlotte said, trying to ease her fears. "Ready?"

"Go for it," Scarlet said.

Charlotte began reading the incantation aloud from her *Deadiquette* book, silhouetted against the colored beakers.

"'You and me, our soul makes three. . . .'"

Scarlet took in a deep breath and looked into Charlotte's eyes as they clasped hands tightly, drawing strength and courage from each other.

"'Me and you, our soul makes two . . . ,'" Charlotte said as her delicate pale hands started to meld into Scarlet's as if they were hot candle wax. They were both startled at what was physically transpiring in front of them. Their bodies continued to merge in a kind of otherworldly osmosis, from their feet to their torsos.

"'We are me . . . ,'" Charlotte said, pushing her heart into Scarlet's as she faded into her body.

Glimpses of Charlotte inside Scarlet's body could be seen periodically through Scarlet's eyes like a series of misfired synapses.

"'. . . inside of YOU,'" Charlotte said as her mousy brown eyes rolled back and sank deep down into Scarlet.

Scarlet's eyes were now absent. Two dark voids replaced the pretty hazel hue in each of her sockets.

With a final blink, Scarlet's translucent soul departed from her own body, leaving it entirely to Charlotte. Scarlet's eyes reappeared, but with a much different gleam in them. Her body language now reflected Charlotte's personality, not her own.

Realizing the possession was a success, Charlotte took a deep breath and felt her new body. Scarlet floated up to the ceiling, where she paused momentarily and looked down to see Charlotte running her hands all over her body.

"Hey, quit feeling me up!" Scarlet yelled as her spectral form began to pass easily through the white ceiling tiles.

"Sorry . . . ," Charlotte said distractedly, just as Scarlet passed completely through the ceiling and out of earshot.

"I just feel so . . . alive."

12

Busy Bodies

Nothing in the world is single,
All things by a law divine
In one spirit meet and mingle—
Why not I with thine?
—Percy Bysshe Shelley

Inside out.

— ◦•◦•◦ —

Being inside of someone else's body could be equated to getting your stomach stapled to treat obesity. You lose a whole bunch of weight, but there's still that insecure little fat girl inside. The same nut, just inside a different shell. Charlotte was still a geek. Still unsure of herself. Still wanted to get noticed, but in Scarlet's body, that didn't quite compute.

harlotte opened the Chem Lab door and gingerly stepped out into the hallway, She was thrilled to be "alive" again, and it showed. Scarlet's typical glower was softened now into a hopeful grin closer to Charlotte's, with students doing a double-take as she helloed her way down the hall, greeting total strangers with unexpected warmth. It was not just her personality that had morphed, but Scarlet's body also began to look and move differently in Charlotte's control. Her posture became more upright, her gait became less plodding, and her demeanor — heaven forbid — even became more feminine.

Charlotte was pleasantly surprised that she was having a much easier time inhabiting Scarlet than she had Petula. She recalled Brain's lecture and the importance of willingness in this whole possession process, and silently thanked him.

"He knows everything," she thought, running Scarlet's fingers along the painted cinder-block walls.

She felt each crevice and chip in the wall like a blind woman reading Braille, drinking in the sensation she had been deprived of for what felt like forever.

Despite the new lease on "life" Scarlet had so generously provided, Charlotte was not entirely confident in her plan yet. Possessing Scarlet was, after all, Plan B. Hers was not the body, the hair, the clothes, the look Charlotte had hoped for and certainly not one that many guys, let alone the most popular guy in school, found, to put it kindly, welcoming. Besides, this takeover was a temporary thing and — moral issues aside — it was surely going to take a lot of time and effort to get a guy to leave his super-hot girlfriend for her Goth younger sister.

Still, Damen had come to Scarlet's rescue in the shower, she recalled. At least that was something to build on. Charlotte's attitude came full circle and she started feeling some gratitude. Who was *she*, after all, to be critical of Scarlet's appeal in any way? Oh yeah, she was the stupid geeky girl who choked to death on a candy, according to Petula.

Charlotte continued down the hall, being quite the social butterfly, leaving blank, confused faces in her wake as she headed out the back doors and toward the football field.

❧

Scarlet, meanwhile, was enjoying herself too. Having floated up through the ceiling and into the crawl space above with

surprising ease, she drifted along aimlessly for a minute until she heard the booming, uptight voice of her arrogant literature teacher in the classroom just below. Mr. Nemchik seemed more interested in humiliating students than teaching them, and self-importantly wrote out each topic on the board as if he were delivering the Ten Commandments. She could not resist the opportunity to screw with him, just a little.

"Today," Mr. Nemchik began, "we will be comparing C-h-a-r-l-e-s D-i-c-k-e-n-s and H-o-m-e-r." He was careful not to speak more quickly than he wrote, which was incredibly irritating.

When he turned from the board to begin discussion with the class, Scarlet changed a few letters in their names so that they now read "Charles Dickhead" and "Homo." The class burst into laughter, and Nemchik stood there totally humiliated and quite baffled.

Next, Scarlet passed through a wall into Health class next door, where two knucklehead football players, Bruce and Justin, were mocking Minnie, a shy, defenseless girl sitting next to them. Scarlet feverishly scribbled on a piece of paper and stuck it into Bruce's hand, in plain view of the teacher.

The teacher snatched it out of Bruce's sausage fingers and proceeded to read it to the whole class.

"Justin, I love sticking my . . ." Ms. Bilitski paused, not wanting to carry on.

"This classroom's policy has always been, 'if you pass a note and get caught, it gets read aloud to the whole class,'" Minnie

confidently reminded her, knowing that the note was incriminating.

Unable to argue Minnie's point, Ms. Bilitski continued. ". . . I love sticking my hands between your thick, hot, sweaty legs when you hike the football to me. I will savor your smell on my hands until we are able to be together again. See you after practice tonight. Love, your ball-boy, Justin."

"No way!" Bruce cried in disgust as Justin leaned as far away from his buddy as anatomically possible.

"Maybe you boys might want to explore 'Repressed Homosexual Urges in High School Athletes' as your essay topic?" the teacher asked as their stunned classmates spun around and stared accusingly at the red-faced jocks, who slowly shrank beneath their desks.

"Come out, come out, wherever you are," Minnie's quiet voice echoed in the uncomfortable silence, highlighting the boys' much-deserved humiliation. Scarlet laughed with satisfaction, reached for an unreciprocated high five with Minnie, and moved along.

She then headed to the bathroom, the next stop on her vengeful path. There on the counter she noticed a latte, which obviously belonged to the girl who occupied one of the stalls. Scarlet looked underneath the stall and noticed that the girl was actually a snob who always picked her last in gym class.

Scarlet calmly made her way over to the open stall next to her and picked up a pubic hair off of the toilet seat. She walked back over to the girl's coffee and dropped it in.

It was a perfect fall day for football practice — cool and brisk. The late afternoon sun prepared to set as the coach's whistles rode the crisp breeze that blew past the players' ears and scattered crimson leaves across the field. There were groups of kids at all ends of the complex, running drills, stretching, a few hard cases even running laps around the track instead of taking detention.

Charlotte walked along the edge of the track and found a quiet spot under a secluded bleacher, where she spread out the tartan plaid blanket she'd tucked into "Scarlet's" backpack and waited for Damen to show. She obsessed over the best way to position it, like a sun worshiper looking for the best angle to catch optimal rays, which was ironic, because Scarlet's porcelain skin looked like it hadn't seen the sun in years.

In the end she decided just to let the blanket fall where it might, which turned out to be the right decision. It alighted on a sea of bright wildflowers that grew unattended in the shade, creating a perfect little island of wool and blooms, patiently waiting for a couple to strand themselves. Charlotte sat down slowly on her knees just as Damen stepped down the bleachers above her.

She reached up through the gap and grabbed his leg.

"What the . . . ?" Damen yelled, jerking his leg away in surprise.

He looked down, saw that it was Scarlet's hand gripping his ankle, and relaxed.

ghostgirl

"You scared me half to death," Damen said as he jumped down onto the ground and crouched under the bleachers.

"Hey, I hadn't thought of that," Charlotte said, almost to herself.

"What?" Damen replied, obliviously.

"Oh, I mean, then you, ah, wouldn't have to take the Physics test," Charlotte said, thinking fast. "Just a little 'inside' joke," she finished, desperate to change the subject. "Anyway, sorry about the leg thing. I wasn't sure if you'd see me," she added, trying to start over.

"I see you," Damen said, unsure how anyone could miss Scarlet; she stood out so blatantly.

"So let's begin," Charlotte instructed, getting all professional. "I'll be your 'Physics Friend.'"

"Um, this is another joke, right?" Damen said. "I mean, we know each other. Kind of, anyway."

"Oh right, of course," Charlotte responded. "Petula, the shower, etcetera."

"Yeah . . . ," Damen said, thinking that she was indeed admitting that this was all a joke.

"Yeah, I mean, no, I needed the extra credit, and you were the first name on the list. I signed up before I even read your name, and then I noticed I signed in ink, so . . . ," Charlotte said, realizing she was babbling.

"Why don't we start over and try this a little more informally, okay?" Damen asked politely. He grabbed her upper arms and applied the tiniest amount of pressure to them, guiding her down to the blanket. It was a gentle but firm motion

that had Charlotte totally gobsmacked. Damen slumped down after her.

"Nice blanket. I thought you'd bring a black towel," Damen said, attempting a joke of his own.

Charlotte, confused about what he was referring to at first, finally caught on. "Oh ... the black towel from the bathroom ... ," she said, laughing just a bit too loudly.

Damen laughed at his towel joke for a second, made himself comfortable, and opened his book. He looked over to see that Charlotte's book was covered with a brown bag and a GRAVITY IS A DOWNER bumper sticker.

"Let's begin," she said, pointing to the sticker.

"I don't get it," he said, looking at it really hard.

The whooshing sound that followed might have been the wind, but Charlotte would have sworn it was the sound of irony flying right over Damen's head.

"You must think I'm the most uncool moron," he said, showing surprising self-awareness that, although he might have been worshipped by most at Hawthorne, there was a small percentage of kids, very small he liked to think, like Scarlet, who would mock him mercilessly behind his back. The fact that this tutoring session took place under such covert circumstances proved that Damen felt he had at least a little something to hide.

"Not at all," Charlotte said sympathetically.

"It's kind of weird being tutored by my girlfriend's little sister," he said sneaking peeks through the bleachers at Petula in her cheerleading outfit, who was stretching in preparation for tryouts on the field.

"So would it be cool if we just kept this, you know, between us?"

"Anything we do will be kept strictly confidential . . . ," she said, leaving a door open for, well, for her wildest dreams to come true. "Anything," she repeated.

The niceties complete, Charlotte and Damen got down to business. Charlotte might have been in awe of Damen, but she was no-nonsense as she began the tutoring session. The Fall Ball was on the line, and she was determined to keep her eyes on the prize, refusing to be sidetracked even by her own passions.

Damen was struggling, and within a short period, his eyes began to glaze over and wander. Sensing that he needed a break, Charlotte looked up to see what was distracting him. Of course, it was the cheerleading tryouts happening downfield.

"You know, I was thinking of trying out," Charlotte blurted, trying to reclaim Damen's attention.

"Yeah right. You wouldn't be caught dead trying out for cheerleader," he replied, totally dismissing her comment.

Without warning, Charlotte slammed her book shut and headed to the football field. Damen was dumbfounded at first, but then started to laugh, thinking that Scarlet was just playing or that she was going to pull off some kind of prank.

The Wendys were running cheerleading tryouts like prison guards, checking names on the list against school IDs and looking candidates over for any bleached hair out of place. They were primping and prepping everyone in line so

that they'd be perfectly presentable for when Petula analyzed them.

Watching from the bleachers, Damen eyed the line of new-bies, placing bets with himself on which girls he thought would make the cut, when he saw Charlotte-as-Scarlet take a place at the end of the line. She did not look like a good bet. Positioned next to the future Miss Teen USAs, she looked more Goth and out of place than ever.

Charlotte ripped material from Scarlet's skirt to make pom-poms, shredding it with a single-edge razor that Scarlet always kept in her pocket. It was definitely innovative but hardly guaranteed to win friends or influence the Wendys. The rest of the girls in line were indistinguishable, wearing the school-mandated candidate apparel of plain white tops and skirts — a parade of perfectly coiffed heads and perfectly fit bodies.

The Wendys saw Charlotte as they approached the end of the line. They cringed at her custom-made outfit and pom-poms, but rather than reject her immediately, they decided to have a little fun with her first, seeing a perfect opportunity to humiliate her once and for all.

"Look at that," Wendy Thomas giggled. "Satan has spirit."

Both girls broke their clinch and turned to the potential candidates.

"Anyone here ridin' the cotton pony?" Wendy Anderson asked, seeing if it was anyone's "time of the month."

"No!" the girls yelled back in unison as they giggled.

"No? Aw, sorry Gothlet, no blood here," Wendy Thomas said with fake disappointment.

"I'm here to try out," Charlotte said firmly.

The Wendys turned their backs on Charlotte to discuss what their next move or "cut" would be.

"I don't know what she's trying to pull, but let's give her enough rope to hang herself," Wendy Anderson whispered curiously.

"Fingers crossed," Wendy Thomas said nastily. "Petula is going to freak!"

The girls turned to face Charlotte and gave her their verdict.

"We've got room for one more, don't we, Wendy?" Wendy Thomas jibed, much to the surprise and dismay of the rest of the candidates.

"Yes, we do, Wendy," Wendy Anderson concurred.

"I don't know why you're here, but I do know that you're going to wish you weren't," Wendy Thomas said.

"I'm here to cheer," Charlotte affirmed, twisting Scarlet's trademark sourpuss into an ultra-bright smile.

"It's your . . . funeral," Wendy Anderson scoffed, looking over Charlotte's outfit, scribbling a number, and tossing it to her.

Charlotte proudly pinned on the number: 666

Damen looked on skeptically, wondering what the Wendys had up their identical sleeves as Petula walked onto the field.

"What the hell is her jaded, friendless virgin ass doing contaminating MY football field?" Petula griped as she approached.

Scarlet was having the time of her life as she made her way to the teachers' lounge, completely oblivious to what Charlotte was up to in her body.

"So this is their habitat," she said, watching the teachers eat and socialize.

She noticed two teachers playing footsie under the table — one wearing high heels and the other wearing chunky black boots. Both were women, doing a dirty little toe dance under the table.

"I knew it!" Scarlet screamed as she sat down on the windowsill, thrilled to be in possession of such secret knowledge.

One of the teachers, feeling a cold chill, walked over to the window, looking right through Scarlet to the field outside. Scarlet was nervous, not knowing what was actually going on.

"Oh my God!" the teacher shouted, leaning even farther into the window, eyeball to eyeball with Scarlet.

Scarlet thought the jig was up as she scrambled off the windowsill into the corner.

The teacher opened the window and waved the other faculty over to get a look for themselves. The teachers came running to see, and finally, so did Scarlet.

"What the hell!" Scarlet yelled, standing side-by-side with the teachers, totally in shock at what she saw.

"That's not very Goth, is it?" Miss Pearl, one of the freshly outted teachers, said with a smirk on her face as Charlotte, making her audition, jumped, spun, and tumbled her heart out effortlessly, with skill and passion far beyond anything the coaches or Petula had ever seen. Damen, meanwhile, watched

from the bleachers in awe and seemed to enjoy every moment of Charlotte's routine . . . and Petula's agony.

"GOOD LUCK!
"HEY, HEY . . .

"L*U*C*K!" Charlotte cheered, spelling out the word and punctuating each letter with a kick or jump.

"What are you doing?" Scarlet yelled out to Charlotte.

Scarlet raced toward Charlotte, hoping that she could end the public humiliation that she — well, her body, at least — was being subjected to.

Charlotte was in the zone and continued her cheer, totally unaware that Scarlet was watching.

"I SAID, GOOD LUCK!
"HEY, HEY . . ."

Terrified of what would come next, Scarlet took action. She slammed right into Charlotte, knocking her out of her body and into the air. As she tumbled back to earth, Scarlet regained control of her body and finished the cheer, her way.

"F*U*C*K!" she spat out, landing sure-footed, a most impressive feat for a would-be cheerleader.

The buzz was buzzing around the football field and a small crowd had gathered to watch Scarlet's otherworldly gymnastics. It was that shocking. The other cheerleaders, feeling

threatened, immediately organized a huddle to plot a response.

The cheerleaders broke their huddle with a handclap and,
with game faces on, lined up in cheer formation, facing Scarlet.
Three stepped forward — Petula and the Wendys — to com-
mence the cheer-off. Scarlet was outnumbered, but she
was ready. Wendy Thomas stepped forward and fired the first
shot.

"OH, NO, YOU DIDN'T.
AT LEAST WE LOOK ALIVE!
YEAH, THAT'S RIGHT,
WE'RE NOT SUN-DEPRIVED!"

She clapped her hands sharply. Scarlet watched and listened unfazed, then responded with a dis of her own.

"OH MY, 'DEPRIVED.'
WHAT A BIG-ASS WORD.
YOU JUST WON A FREE VISIT
TO PLANNED PARENTHOOD!"

Scarlet crooked her index finger and scored "one" on an
imaginary scoreboard. Wendy Anderson was next. She did a
back-bend walkover and began:

"YEAH, YOU WISH,
YOU CAN'T EVEN GET A DATE —"

Before Wendy could get the rest of her spiteful screed out, Scarlet interrupted.

"AT LEAST I DON'T STRESS
ABOUT MY PERIOD BEING LATE!"

The jocks broke down with hysterical laughter in total disbelief at what Scarlet just said. Scarlet held her finger to her mouth, blowing on it like the barrel of a warm gun. The applause was deafening.

"Oh no." Charlotte sulked, her dreams of impressing Damen and being accepted by Petula fading as fast as the Wendys' egos.

The crowd grew larger and faces were plastered against every window now. The Main Event was coming right up, and the tensi on was palpable. It was Petula's turn, and she decided to get creative and show some real cheerleadership. Rather than bust a rhyme, Petula grabbed the Wendys and they broke out in song. A nasty, hurtful campfire singalong that touched a nerve in Scarlet the way only a sister could.

"IF YOU'RE A REJECT AND YOU KNOW IT,
SLASH YOUR WRISTS.
IF YOU'RE DEPRESSED AND YOU KNOW IT,
SLASH YOUR WRISTS.
IF YOU'RE DESPERATE FOR ATTENTION
OR JUST BORED IN DETENTION.

I̶F̶ ̶Y̶O̶U̶'̶R̶E̶ ̶A̶ ̶R̶E̶J̶E̶C̶T̶ ̶A̶N̶D̶ ̶Y̶O̶U̶ ̶K̶N̶O̶W̶ ̶I̶T̶,̶
IF YOU'RE A REJECT AND YOU KNOW IT,
SLASH YOUR WRISTS!"

Petula and The Wendys turned to everyone and took a bow, rubbing the humiliation further into Scarlet's face.

Scarlet took center field, walked dismissively past the Wendys, and let loose on the Queen Bitch, her sister, Petula.

"AFTER GRADUATION,
YOU'LL BE ALL CELLULITE AND FATTY,
SITTIN' NEXT TO MAURY
SEARCHIN' FOR YO' BABY'S DADDY!"

"Ohhhh," the crowd cringed in unified embarrassment for Petula.

Scarlet was just getting started when Charlotte once again tried to inject herself into Scarlet's body. Maybe she wanted to help her friend or maybe she was jealous that Scarlet was getting the attention she'd earned, but either way she was determined to make a scene.

"What are you doing?" Charlotte asked desperately. "You are going to ruin everything."

"Me?" Scarlet cracked. "I'm not the one trying out for the Special Olympics!"

The struggle between the two spirits forced Scarlet's body into the air like a rag doll, flipping forward and back in a gravity-defying *Crouching Tiger* dance. As the girls bounced, twisted, and turned faster and faster, all that could be seen was a whirling dervish of arms and legs burning up the field.

The crowd went wild over the supernatural finale.

The cheer ended dramatically with Scarlet back in control of her body and Charlotte tossed out onto the ground, disappointed.

The kids in the upper bleachers and the ones peering speechless from the windows of the classrooms noticed that Scarlet had burnt an *H* for *Hawthorne High* in the grass.

"Those skills cannot be denied," one candidate said in the emergency huddle.

"Well, she is *my* sister," Petula said, trying to take credit for Scarlet's performance.

The cheerleaders reluctantly reached an agreement and walked over to Scarlet.

"We talked it over and . . . well . . . you are now a Hawthorne Hawk," Petula said begrudgingly.

"And there's a slumber party tonight at Petula's . . . well, your house, F.C.O.," Wendy Anderson said.

"F.C.O.?" Scarlet asked, skeptical of the warm reception she was receiving from these lifelong enemies.

"For Cheerleaders Only," Wendy Thomas said.

"You are one of us now," the Wendys said in their best Stepford-wife monotone, sandwiching Scarlet between them, symbolically absorbing her in their clique.

Scarlet made her "walk of shame" off the field in a stupor.

"I'm a cheerleader," Charlotte said, her spectral form hovering just inches over the grass turf but totally over the moon at this unexpected piece of good fortune. She stayed for the rest of the tryouts, thinking that she was now finally "in," and watched Scarlet walk off the field and almost past Damen.

"How did you do all that?" Damen, still hidden under the bleachers, whispered, fascinated by what he'd just witnessed.

"Years of pent-up pep," Scarlet replied, deadpan, noticing the blanket and the whole setup, and just wishing it was all a nightmare.

13

The Fall of the House of Usher

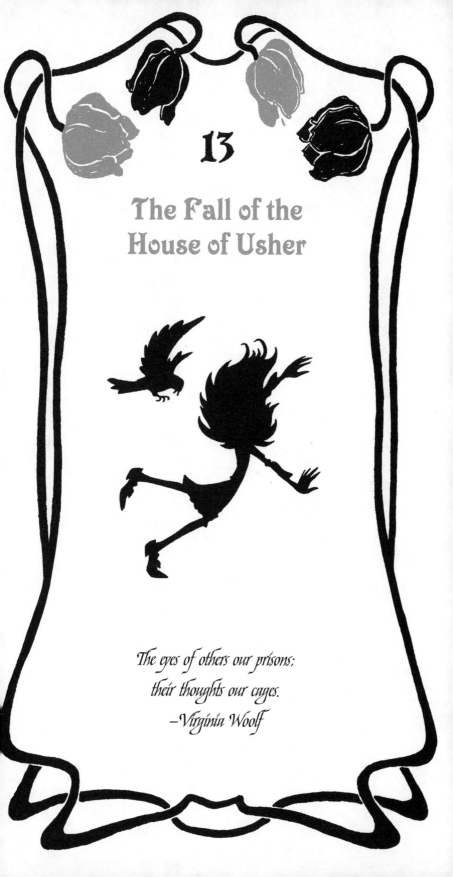

The eyes of others our prisons;
their thoughts our cages.
—Virginia Woolf

Being someone who you're not is exhausting.

—⋄⋈⋄—

But better to be phony than lonely. That was the way Charlotte saw it. She convinced herself that what she was doing wasn't any different than those girls on the football field. She even rationalized that she was doing a good thing for Scarlet — a service — by bringing her into the inner circle at Hawthorne, because if she was on the outside, she was a sitting duck. And in her experience, sitting ducks were dead ducks. But with her whole duck scenario, the question was: was it better to waddle alone in agonizing fear that you would be caught and dragged away at any given moment, or was it better to know that you were surrounded by other "ducks" that looked and acted exactly like you, possibly sparing your life by sacrificing theirs? Our will to survive is inherent, Charlotte thought, and our will to be popular is survival.

harlotte arrived early for the big slumber party F.C.O., buzzing with the thought of being included in such a clique for the first time. She began to ring the bell at Petula's house, but then thought better of it and proceeded to just walk through the door. It was getting easier.

There in the living room was Scarlet's semi-lifeless body, sprawled out on the couch wearing dark sunglasses and looking spent and depressed.

"Well if it isn't the school spirit," she said, barely lifting her head.

"Nice shades," Charlotte said, breaking the ice.

"Looks like I'm the only one enjoying a possession hangover," Scarlet snapped back, peering over her glasses. "The cheerleading squad???"

"Damen wasn't paying any attention to me, so I thought

he'd pay attention if I tried out for cheerleader," Charlotte argued in her own defense.

Scarlet, however, did not budge.

"Look, I didn't know we would make it! But it will be easier, now that you are a cheerleader. I so appreciate what you're doing for me, and this is going to help me get resolution. You'll see," Charlotte said.

"No, I won't see. Find someone else who's user-friendly. I've seen enough," Scarlet said.

"What do you mean?" Charlotte asked nervously.

"I mean, I'm done. No more 'Scarlet on Demand,'" Scarlet said, confirming Charlotte's worst fear.

"You're the one who said you're always a bridesmaid," Charlotte pleaded. "Come on, wasn't it cool being invisible, doing whatever you wanted?"

Scarlet stayed silent, knowing she'd had a good time but not wanting to admit it.

"Come on, admit it, it was cool . . . no boundaries, no limitations, no authority," Charlotte said, prodding her. "Fight the power!"

"You did not just bust out with 'fight the power,'" Scarlet said as she rolled her eyes. "Look, I didn't say it wasn't cool. . . ."

"Hey, maybe we can raise the stakes a little, you know, make it a little more exciting for you?" Charlotte said, getting things back on track.

"Oh yeah, like how?"

"I don't know, maybe have a slumber party of your own at *my* house while I'm at yours?" Charlotte teased.

"The Dead Dorm?" Scarlet asked, her voice dripping with excitement for a change.

☙☙

At Hawthorne Manor, Prue addressed the Dead assembly at their "scare" meeting.

"Okay, so, exactly how are we going to make the potential buyers believe that this place is not up to code?" Prue barked, starting to spin her head around and make specific assignments. "Jerry. You're in charge of plumbing."

"Yeah, make this place smell like Britney Spears's bare feet walking out of a public restroom," CoCo added.

Deadhead Jerry gave the peace sign, signaling that he was onboard.

"Bud. Destabilize the structure of the house," Prue snapped as Bud held up his stump and agreed.

"We're talking Paula Abdul–unstable!" CoCo yelled, amusing everyone, but mostly herself, with her clever, but somewhat dated, pop culture references.

"Where's our little German exchange student?" Prue asked, preparing to give her final assignment.

A small decaying girl slowly raised her hand as minute maggots welled restlessly in the pores of her face.

"Rotting Rita. You're on Infestation Patrol," Prue announced.

"Yeah, we wanna see bugs swarming like the paparazzi around Brangelina!" CoCo broadcasted at a fever pitch.

Prue telekinetically opened the doors and everyone scurried out of the room. She noticed that Charlotte was absent.

"Where's Usher?" Prue asked.

Piccolo Pam started to tremble, producing a high-pitched whistling sound from her throat as she tried to speed past Prue.

"Pam, why is your piccolo so pitchy?" Prue asked smugly. "Do you know where Usher is?"

"She asked me to, ah, take notes for her . . . ," Piccolo Pam said, thinking on her feet.

"Note this. She better get here!" Prue threatened as she got into Pam's face, totally intimidating her. "I am *dead* serious."

☙

Back at Petula's, the Wendys arrived for the slumber party, toting enough luggage for a month — Vuitton wheelies, carry-ons, and crates. After they rang the doorbell, they hung back and recited Scarlet's cheer from that afternoon.

"Sittin' next to Maury . . . ," Wendy Anderson chanted.

"Searchin' for yo' baby's daddy . . . ," Wendy Thomas chanted back.

Upstairs, Charlotte's persistence paid off and Scarlet agreed to be possessed once more.

"Oh, just one thing before you go. Don't be afraid of anything you might see," Charlotte warned casually. "It's just something that we have to do for an assignment tonight, okay?"

Scarlet shook her head in agreement.

"There's this girl, her name is Prue . . . ," Charlotte began.

"Prue," Scarlet repeated.

"Yes, just make sure you stay out of her way, okay?" Charlotte emphasized.

"Okay," Scarlet agreed.

"Promise," Charlotte said, holding onto Scarlet's shoulders and looking her square in the eyes.

"Yeah, I'll stay out of her way. You're freaking me out," Scarlet said, shaking free.

Anyway, I'm sure everyone will be so busy, they won't even notice you're there," Charlotte explained.

"Yeah, and you don't be afraid by anything you might see tonight either," Scarlet said as she disappeared out the window and into the clear autumn night. They were excited about what the night had in store for each of them, and neither wanted to miss a single second.

Charlotte heard the doorbell and rushed downstairs, since Petula didn't seem to be in any rush to get it. She was all fake smiles, just like the Wendys, as she opened the door and let them in.

"Let's get this party started," pseudo Scarlet screamed a bit too enthusiastically, hitting the play button on the CD remote. With the music blaring and new friends arriving, Petula trudged unhappily down the staircase, more than a little peeved at the glory her sister was so uncharacteristically basking in.

❧

On the other side of town, a doorbell was also ringing. Miss Wacksel, a strange, uptight, eccentric real estate agent who was assigned to sell Hawthorne Manor, was standing on the porch about to show the house to the Martins, an anxious young couple looking for a deal and hoping to buy the relic as an affordable fixer-upper. It was windy and very cold, and the

longer they stood on the porch, the more unpleasant it was. Wacksel long suspected that the house might not be entirely unoccupied, but tried to put on a brave face for the twosome.

Behind them was a huge old "For Sale" sign that creaked loudly as it was blown to and fro in the wind. Piccolo Pam was perched in the branches of a dead, twisted tree, desperately looking out for any signs of Charlotte. The melancholy notes from Pam's throat mixed with the howling wind, producing a mournful soundtrack for Miss Wacksel to begin her tour.

"Ah, why are you ringing the doorbell if there's no one living here?" the husband asked, wanting to get inside as soon as possible.

"You are exactly right, Mr. Martin," Miss Wacksel said nervously. "No need to ring, I have a key."

Steadying her grip, she pushed the antiquated skeleton key into the lock, but each time, it was forced back into her hand.

"There is no one living here," she repeated over and over, continuing to struggle with the lock and key. If Miss Wacksel could only see Silent Violet plugging the keyhole with her finger on the other side of the door, she might have just called it an evening. But Wacksel was determined, and the thought of her commission on the old dump was a big motivator.

"This house has so much . . . personality," she babbled to the increasingly impatient newlyweds, finally thrusting the key in the lock and turning it open before Violet could get her finger all the way in. Silent Violet, Dead Ed's first line of defense, had been breached. She instantaneously disappeared and reappeared at the top of the steps before the couple could enter.

Immediately, she started purging black tarlike sludge from the pit of her stomach out of her throat, causing it to creep down the steps and seep into every crack of wood in its path.

"'Come into my parlor . . . ,'" Miss Wacksel said as she pushed the heavy chestnut door open and ushered the couple inside. A cold wave of air instantly engulfed them, nearly taking their breath away.

"That's odd, it's colder in here than it is outside," Mrs. Martin observed.

"We don't keep the burner running until later in the season," Wacksel advised, looking around for a cracked window or perhaps some other explainable source of the chill. "These old houses are drafty anyway. It's part of their charm, dear. Nothing an extra blanket or cuddle can't cure," she said through a tight smile.

The trio made their way through the foyer at the bottom of the steps on their way to the living room, and as they did, they slipped and slid around uncontrollably.

"Wow, they don't make wax like they used to," Wacksel said, nervously trying to stabilize herself and the others.

Once they were all under control and steady, they continued on to the living room and admired the high ceilings, brick fireplace, plaster walls, and original woodwork, which was still fairly well intact. The detail, color, and craftsmanship of the moldings, banister, and flooring were impressive.

"They don't make them like this anymore," Mr. Martin said, secretly calculating how much profit he could make flipping the house in the current market.

"They sure don't." Wacksel nodded in agreement, kicking away small, unnoticed piles of Suzy Scratcher's sawdust building up in each corner.

Just then, Mr. Martin thought he saw a piece of furniture move. It was so gradual that he wasn't sure if his eyes were playing tricks on him or if the drab black needlepoint chair with pink rose pattern had actually moved. Before long, they all began to notice the room getting . . . smaller.

Bud, who was positioned beneath the floorboards, had shifted one of the support beams, causing the house to tilt ever so slightly. As the furniture crept closer to them, they couldn't deny there was something supernatural going on in the house, but Miss Wacksel laughed it off.

"What do the Orientals call that?" she asked, showing just how politically incorrect she was. "Phuk Me . . . Feng Shui . . . or something?!" she said as she hurried the suspicious couple into the upstairs bathroom.

The only thing any of them could see in the bathroom was the shower curtain, which was fully drawn over the claw-foot porcelain tub. By now, their imaginations carried them almost totally away as they fixated on what might lurk behind the curtain. Prue was starting to get a little worried, because they should have been scared off by now, and the kids really had no alternate plan. She hadn't counted on the depth of Wacksel's, or the couple's, greed. She signaled Mike, Jerry, and Bud, who were on bathroom detail, to do their thing.

Wacksel walked over to the curtain slowly, deliberately, as if on eggshells, holding her breath, and grabbed the curtain, flinging it open. There was nothing there. The couple slowly

leaned in for a look with trepidation. Suddenly, a disgusting brown sludge blasted up out of the tub drain, drenching the couple in smelly goo from head to toe.

Mike, Jerry, and Bud had rigged their "pipes" to the plumbing and began blowing sewage back up the drainpipes into the bathroom, creating a deathly stench.

Miss Wacksel whisked the Martins into the kitchen to get cleaned up, fearing that this would definitely be the deal breaker.

"You said you wanted a fixer-upper," Mr. Martin said, trying to remain optimistic and make his wife feel better about having crap all over her face, hair, and clothes.

Wacksel took a long, deep breath, grateful for the husband's lifesaving comment. As they wiped off, the couple couldn't help but admire the artisan cabinetry. The husband opened a cabinet door, and a blinding swarm of testy bugs flew out into the room. Rotting Rita was spewing them from every orifice, including her milky, film-covered eyes.

Miss Wacksel quickly reached into her pleather purse and grabbed a travel-size can of bug spray.

"Those appear to be termites," Mrs. Martin said, grossed out as she swiped at the little creatures flitting around them.

"Appearances can be deceiving," Wacksel said, spraying the bugs dead.

☜☞

It was all about appearances back at Petula's house, where Charlotte-as-Scarlet was enjoying the mani-pedi session with everyone sitting around gossiping. This little popularity

summit was now an endless sea of pink baby-doll nighties, everyone wearing one just like Petula's, except for Charlotte, who was wearing Scarlet's deep teal vintage silk slip with black lace accents. The big topic for the evening was "Dates for the Fall Ball." Who had one, who didn't, and what they were planning to do about it.

"... He's cute, but he went out with that slut from Gorey High," Wendy Thomas said, shooting down a suggestion for a potential date for the dance as she vigorously removed the black polish from Charlotte's toenails and painted them pink.

"You'll find somebody. You're so pretty," Charlotte replied.

"I *know*!" Wendy Thomas concurred.

Petula, who was sandwiched by the Wendys, turned to Wendy Anderson on her right.

"I can't believe she is acting like this," Petula whispered about Scarlet.

"Poor thing. That Chem Lab explosion must have been worse than we thought," Wendy Anderson said. "You know, everyone's talking about how strong, brave, and selfless you are to deal with a sister who has been brain-damaged."

"Well, it's hard, but I'm a very spiritual person," Petula answered. "I mean, Jesus, don't I have enough to worry about right now with Principal Styx on my back about the Driver's Ed thing?"

"Don't stress, Pet. You'll find a way ... ," Wendy Anderson said, pointing to Petula's breasts, "... or TWO, out of it."

"Yeah, you can't miss the Midnight Kiss," Sue, another cheerleader, chimed in.

"It's school tradition. If you miss the Kiss, it will change the course of your future," Sue said to Charlotte, sensing that she had no idea about the Kiss legend.

"Yeah, like Marcy Hanover missed the Kiss last year because her car broke down, and now she's a model," one of the girls said, ". . . for Lane Bryant!"

The girls reacted in shock and horror.

"That Kiss decides your Destiny," Sue said. The girls nodded in agreement.

The distraught look on Charlotte's face was beyond the capacity of even the most expensive makeup to conceal as she obsessed about her Destiny and the fabled Midnight Kiss. She didn't need these girls to tell her how much was riding on getting to the Fall Ball. She knew. But the Midnight Kiss?

ॐ

As worry crept into Charlotte's almost perfect night, Scarlet was flying high . . . above the cookie-cutter rooftops until she came upon a massive gloomy structure that hovered like a dark cloud over the otherwise indistinguishable row houses. She floated from window to window, peeking through, until she saw an unpacked bookbag, day-planner, and laptop all spread out on a chenille bedspread.

"This has got to be hers," Scarlet said.

She entered Charlotte's room through a long, narrow floor-to-ceiling stained glass window in the uppermost gable. She'd seen the house from the outside many times, and the best that could be said about it was that it was old. But now, looking at

it in her current state, it was transformed, gleaming in deep, rich colors, ornate furniture, and elaborate candle sconces and chandeliers dripping with jewel-toned crystals.

"I think I've died and gone to heaven," she said, taking in the décor. Scarlet threw herself on the large four-poster bed, landing next to Charlotte's mountain of stuff.

"I guess you *can* take it with you," Scarlet said, rummaging through Charlotte's personal belongings.

She noticed Charlotte's laptop, which was displaying a cut-out design of a couture gown with Charlotte's head pasted on top. Scarlet hit the spacebar and saw a guy appear in her arms and start to dance around the screen.

"Sick!" Scarlet yelled.

Before she could inspect it more closely, Scarlet's attention to the laptop was interrupted by a loud noise coming from downstairs. She decided to go check it out instead of waiting around for it to find her.

෨෬

Meanwhile, downstairs at the Manor, Miss Wacksel entered the great room with the Martins.

"Don't you just love the sense of space in this room?" she asked.

The room was indeed large, but the couple was more fix-ated on the ceiling and the chandelier hanging from it. Mrs. Martin was the first to notice it and nudged her husband.

"Isn't that a lovely old thing?" she said.

Just then, thanks to Simon and Simone, the huge fixture began swinging like a pendulum, slowly at first, and then

picking up speed. Prue had anchored herself on the staircase and was tugging on the twins, who in turn were grabbing hold of the chandelier.

"Yes, these old chandeliers do take on a life of their own," Miss Wacksel commented, not realizing how right she was.

The Martins were nearly frozen in place, hypnotized by the motion as their shadows appeared larger and more ominous on the wall with each pass of the chandelier.

"Once you put the new windows in, this won't be a problem," Miss Wacksel reassured them.

Prue pulled Simone even harder, causing the chandelier to sway faster. Just as she leaned back, Scarlet came out of Charlotte's room, startling Prue.

"Who the hell are *you*?" Prue snapped, losing hold of Simon and Simone. Out of Prue's grip, Simon and Simone were unable to stop the swinging chandelier, and it went careening across the divide. The twins, tangled up in the fixture, crashed into the wall, creating a gaping hole in it.

"Oh. My. God!" Mrs. Martin screamed as her husband tried to shelter her from the raining shards of crystal. Had it been in slow motion, it would have been a beautiful sight, with all the crystal remnants catching the sunlight from the nearby window and falling peacefully to the ground like diamond spears. Mr. Martin yanked his wife out of the way just as a last large shard came straight down to the ground, piercing the floor where the woman had been standing.

"That could have killed her!" Mr. Martin said, trying to examine his wife for shrapnel.

Miss Wacksel was speechless.

"No termites, huh?" he asked sarcastically.

Miss Wacksel gathered herself one last time.

"Well, er, I'm sure this, ah, newly discovered wear and tear will be accounted for in the price," she said, desperately trying to keep them on track, but hoping just as much she would escape with her life as well as a sale.

Smelling a deeper discount, Mr. Martin's avarice kicked in once again. He went over to inspect the hole.

Scarlet, who was totally petrified by the entire scene, had been hiding out behind the broken plasterboard to avoid Wacksel and the Martins as well as Prue and the other Dead kids, whose plan she had just ruined.

"What is this?" Mr. Martin asked, approaching Scarlet and a pile of plasterboard that had crashed down from the ceiling.

Scarlet bolted out of the hole, but Prue quickly grabbed hold of her ankles before she could make a clean escape.

"We are not buying this house!" the man announced with conviction.

The Dead kids could not believe what they just heard come out of his mouth.

"No one is," the man added.

Everyone who was Dead screamed and cheered and danced around the house in celebration, including the twins still trapped in the twisted remnants of the chandelier.

"What are you talking about?" Miss Wacksel asked, thoroughly depressed.

"Look at this!" he demanded, crumbling a piece of the ceiling board into a powdery gray dust. "Looks like asbestos," Mr.

Martin said sternly. "This house will have to be . . ." Prue clamped down even deeper into Scarlet's spectral ankles as she waited to hear what the verdict was.

". . . condemned," Miss Wacksel acknowledged softly.

Having the house sold was bad enough, but the prospect of it being demolished was devastating.

"Condemned?!!" Prue growled, twisting Scarlet's ankles.

"Shit," Scarlet muttered, unable to break free.

As the shock subsided, Prue realized things were now as bad as they could get. She loosened up her grip on Scarlet, who wriggled free and headed for her own house like a bat out of hell.

"If the house is condemned, then so are we all," Prue said angrily.

14

Kiss Off

*Ever get the feeling
You've been cheated?*
—Johnny Rotten

The end doesn't always justify the means.

———◆◆◆———

Everybody gets used at some point or another in his or her life. In fact, we often welcome it. It is a deal we make to get what we want or what we need — a ride to school, a ticket to the game, a hot date, a party invite. A mutually agreed-upon fair trade...usually. But feeling used is an entirely different matter. In that case, you are nothing more than a conduit for someone else's ambition. A member of their audience and a bystander in their fantasy.

amen and his friends, already nestled in the bushes outside and secretly peering through the windows of Petula's house, were spying on the girls sitting around in their nighties.

"Excuse the P.D.E.," Max said as they all fought for space in the window.

The guys stopped, looked at Max, and gave him a quizzical look.

"Public Display of Erection," he chortled, to winces from the other guys.

Petula noticed the guys outside and proceeded to put on a show for them.

"It's so cold out here tonight. We wouldn't want you boys to get stiff," Petula said teasingly, leaning over.

"Too late," Max said.

"Are you coming?" Petula asked as she threw open the sash.

"Not yet!" Max said, making his way through the window first.

As the rest of the guys climbed through the window, one of them accidentally knocked over a diet soda bottle. It spun around and stopped, pointing at Wendy Anderson.

"Spin the bottle," Max said lasciviously.

"That is so junior high," Wendy Anderson quipped. "Me first!"

Wendy Anderson spun and ended up sucking face with Max.

"Your turn," a desperate guy said to Charlotte-as-Scarlet, prompting her to spin.

Charlotte was reluctant but stole a glance at Damen and got her courage up. The bottle turned and landed on the mooky guy.

Horrified, Charlotte concentrated all of her energy on tele-kinetically moving the bottle so that it would land on Damen. To her amazement, it worked.

Damen hesitated, not knowing quite what to do. He didn't want to kiss Petula's sister right in front of her. It was an awkward situation to say the least, but then again, it was a game.

"Come on, man, play the game!" Max said.

Petula was mortified, but she tried her best to play it cool. "Go ahead. It's just a game," she said, giving Damen the okay in front of the group.

Damen, however, knew that she was pissed, and so he could either kiss Scarlet and get everyone off his back, or he could not kiss her and spare himself from Petula's vengeful ranting later. He decided to just follow through with the kiss and not be a spoilsport.

Charlotte closed her eyes and leaned in at the same time Damen did. Everyone watched with bated breath as the two moved closer and closer together in the middle of the circle. Just as their lips were about to touch, Scarlet flew in the window; she was a total mess and obviously terrified.

"Charlotte!!!" she screamed as she took off toward Charlotte. "This is not consensual!"

She slammed into her body, knocking Charlotte out, but the force of the intrusion also caused her to fall into Damen, forcing an awkward "kiss" on his shoulder. Damen was intrigued by Scarlet's peculiar gesture and chuckled. Petula was relieved, and the game continued.

"Man, that girl is a freak," Max whispered to Damen. Still dazed, Charlotte looked up and saw Prue fly through the window in hot pursuit of Scarlet.

"Prue?" Charlotte said worriedly, now able to see her.

"So you wanna interact with the living? I'll show you what interacting with the living is all about," Prue threatened as she set her eyes on Wendy Anderson. "My turn!" she hissed, insinuating herself into the game. "You wanna get high?" she asked Wendy Anderson shortly before levitating her ever so slightly above the ground and spinning her around like the bottle in their kissing game. Everyone freaked out.

"Hey, this is some good shit," Max said, referring to his cup of punch.

Wendy Anderson, still trying to protect her manicure, reached out for anything she could grab to stop spinning. She was looking bad and feeling worse.

Prue stopped spinning Wendy abruptly, leaving her pointing directly at Charlotte.

"Kiss this," Prue raged at Charlotte as Wendy puked explosively from vertigo and dropped to the floor.

Everybody scattered to avoid the vile Wendy chunks, except for Max, who kept swigging his drink.

"Liar! I thought you said you didn't eat today," Petula scolded, watching the vomit drip down the walls like a spin-art painting.

"Didn't we tell you to stay with your own kind?" Prue warned Charlotte, who was too scared to respond.

Prue dematerialized and returned to Hawthorne Manor, unsure of what to do about Charlotte, Scarlet, and the house, which really needed saving now. Meanwhile, Scarlet ran upstairs to her room.

Wendy Anderson just lay on the floor, humiliated.

"She'll do anything for attention," Wendy Thomas whispered cattily to Petula as they both stared at their bruise-and-bile-covered friend. Wendy Anderson gathered up all her strength and slowly managed to bring her hand up to her face, wipe some vomit from her fingertips, and inspect her manicure for chips. On that note, the party was over. Nobody needed to be asked to leave.

Charlotte sat there, busted and all alone.

"I was sooo close," she cried, feeling sorry for herself. "It's over, and I'm dead," she concluded, imagining what awaited her back at the Dead Dorm and Eternity.

☙☙

In her bedroom, Scarlet put on a silk Chinese dragon robe, looked over her shoulder for any sign of Charlotte, and booted up her PC. She clicked on her Web browser and began searching for local obituaries.

"She's got to be here somewhere," Scarlet said, determined to find out as much about this so-called Prue as possible.

After trolling through pages of irrelevant links, she found one that looked promising and clicked on it. It was an archive of local crime stories from a newspaper that had folded ages ago, so long ago that Scarlet had seen only a page or two of it when she unwrapped her grandparents' old Christmas ornaments one year. The *Hawthorne Advance.* The archive had a searchable database, and Scarlet entered the only info she had.

"P-R-U-E," she said as she typed, and hit return.

Three articles were retrieved, none of them obits.

"Great," Scarlet fumed, already frustrated.

She read through a couple of them but found nothing pertinent, just pieces about "Prue" the old maid who canned "the best damn vegetables in the county," and even a turkey nicknamed Prue that had won a Thanksgiving reprieve from the mayor. Two strikes.

Just then, Charlotte slid in through the door. Scarlet switched off her computer.

"Who the hell was that crazy bitch Prue?" Scarlet asked.

"*That* was one of my Dead classmates. . . . She's angry because I was spending time here and not at the house, where I was supposed to be. I'm so sorry," Charlotte said, sincerely trying to assess if Scarlet really was okay or not.

"Sorry for what? A) For making the cheerleading squad? B) For trying to kiss my sister's boyfriend? Or C) For almost having me killed by some evil demon seed?" Scarlet replied.

Charlotte shrank down in Scarlet's pink-and-black skull chair.

"I happened to see your little screen saver when I was at the Dorm," Scarlet said, suspicious of who the "guy" was on it, but not letting on to Charlotte that she wasn't 100 percent sure.

Charlotte was cringing silently, imagining exactly what Scarlet had seen on her computer. There were folders and folders of Damen-head jpegs she had taken over the past two school years. Smiles, frowns, profiles, portraits — every mood and angle. But most damning of all was the crude screen-saver animation she had Photoshopped from scans of vintage magazine cutouts and pictures of their heads. When Scarlet hit the spacebar, did she see the composite of a couple — Charlotte's head pasted atop a beautiful dove gray Chanel dress and Damen's pasted atop a gray Givenchy suit with a white silk pocket square — dancing close? If so, she was busted for real, and there was no point in trying to spin it. She decided it was best to come clean. About everything.

"Okay! Okay. I'm not really tutoring Damen so that he can pass Physics," Charlotte said, realizing that she couldn't lie to Scarlet any longer.

"I got that," Scarlet snapped, realizing that the guy was, no doubt, Damen.

"I'm tutoring him so that he can go to the dance," Charlotte admitted.

"Why would you care if he goes to the dance with my sister?" Scarlet asked.

"I don't. I'm tutoring him so he can go to the dance with . . . me," Charlotte said. "I don't just want to go — I have to go."

"That's a good one," Scarlet said sarcastically.

"Really. See, when we die unexpectedly, we carry unresolved issues with us. Issues that need to be resolved before we can . . . move on," Charlotte explained.

"So let me get this right. You have to go to a stupid dance with a moron to reach a higher spiritual plane?" Scarlet said, not believing Charlotte's audacity.

"It's true. Look, you don't know what it's like. I am now and have always been invisible to everyone," Charlotte replied.

"I will not let you use my body to go to a dance with my dumb sister's boyfriend . . . or to do anything else for that matter," Scarlet announced as she shooed Charlotte out of her room and slammed the door.

"But what about Damen? What about his test?" Charlotte yelled from the hallway, which prompted Scarlet to open the door, shoot her a look, and slam it again.

15

Do or Die

Kiss me and you will
see how important I am.
—Sylvia Plath

Perception vs. reality.

In high school, they are pretty much the same thing. We put on makeup and football helmets, buy nose jobs and fast cars, all to reinforce perception and keep reality at bay. There might, in fact, be much more to someone than meets the eye, but in order to make such a discovery, you have to be willing to dig beneath the surface. Most people aren't, because it would upset the social order; but a few, very few, are.

harlotte peered through the glass of the Physics room door, the same door that she'd peered out of when she took her last breath, only this time she was literally on the other side. She saw that Damen was struggling with his Physics quiz under the watchful "eye" of Mr. Widget. Everyone in the room was on edge but not nearly as tense as Charlotte.

Damen was already stuck on the first "easy" question, unable to make up his mind between two answer options. Was it a trick question or was it really easy? He was so nervous that he began to overthink everything and second-guess what he knew.

Charlotte was beside herself as he agonized and finally decided to go in and help him. She walked through the door and back toward Damen's desk. As she did, the mini solar system on the ceiling started to whirl around as she made her way toward Venus, the planet Damen was sitting under.

Charlotte stood behind Damen and tried to move his hand telepathically to the correct answer, but as usual, found it

difficult to use her powers around him. Leaning over his shoulder in such an intimate position, staring at his paper nearly cheek to cheek, was thrilling for her but not so lucky for him. Charlotte unwittingly knocked the pencil from his hand, attracting totally unwanted attention from Mr. Widget, who was deep into the new issue of *Physics Today*. Widget caught Damen fishing around for it under Bertha the Brain's desk.

"Eyes on your own paper, people," he reminded the class without singling out Damen. He'd seen enough clever cheating techniques in his tenure to write a book, from plain old sneaking a peek to the more hi-tech tactics of the digital age — taking cell phone pictures of tests, texting answers, Googling from cell phone Web browsers. . . . Basically, he'd seen it all, and so he kept an eye — his good one, that is — trained suspiciously on Damen.

"Cramp," Damen mouthed, pointing to his hand, as Widget shook his head and resumed reading his magazine.

Charlotte immediately tried again. She wrapped herself around Damen and got so excited that the hot pink electrical current that periodically sparked in a glass ball next to Damen brewed into an all-out electrical storm. She stepped away, not wanting to call any more attention to Damen, but this only caused the eraser on his pencil to jerk all the way up his nose. Damen was getting a little freaked and Widget, who continued to eye Damen, was on high alert.

Concerned that she might cost Damen not only just a ticket to the Fall Ball but also his place on the football team if this kept up, Charlotte made her best effort to focus on the task at hand. She ignored his broad shoulders, his strong arms, his beautiful head

of thick hair, his gorgeous eyes, his sweet lips, and his perfect nose, and without any further distractions took his hand in hers and gently guided it to the right answers just as time ran out.

"Pencils down, people!" Mr. Widget said with the gumption of a cop trying to disarm a dangerous assassin. "Time's up!"

The stragglers blindly filled in the last answers without even reading the questions as they passed up their papers.

Mr. Widget personally snapped Damen's paper out of his hands with the last question still blank. Charlotte desperately grabbed Damen's hand, which caused him to dive out of his seat like a receiver catching a Hail Mary pass, and fill in the last answer.

໑৩

Hoping for a more normal day (or as normal a day as was possible for someone like her), Scarlet was in the hall getting stuff out of her locker when there was a knock on the other side of the steel door.

"Go away," Scarlet said, not even looking to see who it was. A few more knocks followed, irritating Scarlet enough to get her to pay attention. She closed her locker and saw Damen's quiz, marked with a big red "A," covering his face.

"Can you believe it?" Damen asked, shoving the paper into her face now.

"I can believe just about anything at this point," Scarlet replied.

People started to stare at them, so Scarlet ducked down and tried to keep a low profile, but Damen didn't seem to care who saw them. He was way too excited.

"It didn't even feel like we really studied," Damen said excitedly.

"Tell me about it," Scarlet replied.

"I hope we do half as good on the big exam," Damen added, walking backward away from her. "See you after school."

"We?" Scarlet asked. "Wait, I'm busy. . . ."

He was already out of earshot, leaving Scarlet no time to object but plenty of time to resent Charlotte.

☙

Damen arrived at Scarlet's, well, Petula's house, parked in front, and entered as he usually did, without ringing the bell. He knew Petula was at cheerleading practice and wouldn't be home for a little while. He walked down the hall of the second floor but made a left turn to Scarlet's room rather than the right turn he usually made to Petula's. It felt a little weird to him.

He approached Scarlet's room, ignored the authentic KEEP OUT sign posted on the partially closed door, and walked in. The lights were dimmed and there were what seemed to be hundreds of ornate candles flickering around the room. It was beautiful. Damen looked around for Scarlet but couldn't find her until he noticed her silhouette on the ceiling, projected by the candlelight. On his way over to her, he noticed a pom-pom pinned to the wall with a steak knife. He walked toward Scarlet, on the floor next to her bed, her iPod cranked as she rocked out mindlessly.

"I guess this means you won't be attending any more pep rallies?" Damen said as he pulled the knife out of the wall, freeing the pom-pom above her.

Scarlet was lost in the music and didn't hear him. He tapped her on the shoulder while holding the steak knife in his other hand, which was the first thing she saw. She yanked her ear buds out and jumped up on her bed to get away as the morbid strains of the new Arcade Fire spilled out into the room.

"Oh, sorry," Damen said, realizing that he looked like an attacker.

As he put the knife down on her nightstand, he noticed the tag line on a poster for the cult indie film *Delicatessen,* which read, "A modern tale about love, greed, and cannibalism."

"Hey, isn't that the one where the guy has a deli in the apartment building and grinds up tenants and sells them for meat?" he asked.

Scarlet was blown over by the fact that he knew the movie, but she didn't want him to know that, so she just brushed it off as best she could. "I'm thinking about doing my own version at Hawthorne where a disgruntled student gets a job as a waitress at the local country club and grinds up popular kids into pâté and then feeds them to their unsuspecting parents," she said, trying her best to intimidate him.

"I just got here a little early, but I thought, if you were free now, we could study for a few minutes?" he asked.

"Yeah, I've been meaning to talk to you about this whole tutoring thing . . . ," she replied.

Damen noticed her guitar — a pale purple Gretsch hollow body — sitting on a stand and picked it up, interrupting her.

"I didn't know you played," he said as he placed the black leather guitar strap over his head.

"Why would you?" she asked, somewhat sarcastically.

Damen plopped down on Scarlet's bed and started fiddling around.

"Oh, sorry, do you mind?" he asked.

"No, no, not at all . . . ," she replied, using it to stall him, ". . . go right ahead."

Damen looked at the guitar, closed his eyes, and felt his way through "I Will Follow You into the Dark," by Death Cab for Cutie.

"I didn't know . . . ," Scarlet uttered, unable to believe not only that he could play, but that he knew one of her favorite songs, ". . . that you played."

"Yes, you did. Remember? I told you," he said.

"Right. I guess I forgot," she replied, figuring that it must have been when Charlotte possessed her.

Damen was intrigued, since in all his experience with girls, they hung on his every word, remembering every little thing he said.

"I never thought I'd be playing this song for a 'cheerleader,'" he said, laughing as he strummed.

"Ex-cheerleader," she snapped, cracking a little smile. Scarlet smiled throughout, impressed by his song choice.

"You know, I have tickets to see Death Cab Saturday night . . . ," he said as he played the last few notes of the song.

"Oh yeah?" she said in her deadpan tone, not wanting to let him know that she would kill a small cuddly animal or even a close family member for a ticket.

"Petula's really not into them and she's making other plans," he said tentatively. "Would you . . . I don't know, be willing to cramp your style and maybe go with me . . . ?" he asked.

The question hung in the fragrant air as the most awkward silence ever followed.

Lost in their moment, neither of them heard a car pull up to the house or the front door open or Petula cursing about practice being unexpectedly canceled and what a waste of her precious time that was.

"I mean, you know, as a thank-you for all your help and all?" he added.

"Umm . . . yeah . . . I guess, sure," she agreed, trying to keep her cool, but on the inside she was ecstatic. Her reaction surprised her.

"Damen?" Petula yelled, calling through the house for her boyfriend.

Scarlet and Damen both blushed, as if they were just caught making out in the fiery grips of passion.

"I better go," Damen said, setting her guitar down and straightening his shirt and pants.

"Yep . . . ," she replied, trying to act like she couldn't care less.

"So, okay then, Saturday, we'll just meet outside the theater," he said as he left the room. "Hey, you were going to say something about tutoring?"

"Oh right, it was nothing . . . ," she said.

Damen ducked into the bathroom that adjoined the sisters' bedrooms and flushed the toilet, creating a little audio alibi for himself as he opened the door and walked hurriedly down the stairs.

"Coming!" he yelled down to Petula. "Just draining the dragon."

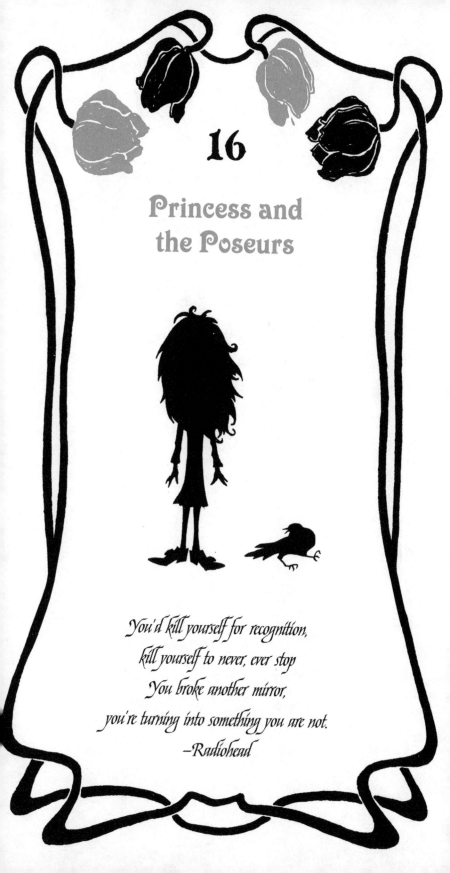

16

Princess and the Poseurs

You'd kill yourself for recognition,
kill yourself to never, ever stop
You broke another mirror,
you're turning into something you are not.
—Radiohead

We all want to be stars.

---◆·❖·◆---

The idea of being revered and envied must be encoded somewhere deep in our DNA. So must the desire to revere and envy others we imagine to be better, more accepted, and more popular than we are. The only problem is that the most necessary qualities required to be a celebrity—self-absorption, egomania, shamelessness—are the least attractive in a friend.

aybe it was another possession side-effect?" Scarlet ruminated as she walked down the hall to her locker. Could she actually be starting to like Damen Dylan as, dare she say . . . a person? A guy? In a desperate attempt to drown out the unpleasant thoughts plaguing her, she sought the solace of the iPod volume control yet again, spinning the toggle wheel to ear-bleeding levels, so loud that the people halfway down the hall could ID her playlist.

As she headed to her locker, wearing a washed-out vintage Suicide tee, she looked around for Charlotte, who had been noticeably absent of late, but saw only Damen standing in the hallway, leaned up against an adjacent locker.

"Hey," he said as she came into view.

Damen reached into his backpack and pulled out a bootleg Green Day CD from under his coat.

"I burned this for you last night. Thought you might dig it," he said as he handed it to her.

"Thanks," she muttered, not really trying to hide her ambivalence.

Scarlet's tepid response suggested to Damen that he was off the mark.

She reached into her locker, scoured the customized CD rack that she kept at the bottom, and picked one for him.

"Dead Kennedys?" Damen asked.

"Truer now than ever," Scarlet replied.

"'*Fresh Fruit for Rotting Vegetables*,'" Damen read the title out loud. "How thoughtful."

While they were caught up in their music discussion, a few football players noticed their exchange, and then some girls noticed the football players noticing Scarlet.

"People are looking at me funny," Scarlet said to Damen as the girls stared her up and down.

"Is that a new thing?" he asked, impressing her with a surprisingly quick-witted comment.

"Hey, just because I'm paranoid . . . ," she began.

". . . doesn't mean they aren't out to get me," Damen said, completing her thought with a nod.

They weren't exactly soul mates, but there was no denying they were becoming increasingly comfortable around one another. Scarlet decided to surf this wave a little further, or at least until it crashed. She shrugged off her anxiety for the time being and agreed to meet Damen later for a tutoring session. Her only problem: she didn't know a thing about Physics.

☜☞

Charlotte sat at her desk in Dead Ed, thumbing robotically through the pages of her *Deadiquette* text. She had been feeling inexplicably uneasy ever since Damen's test and thought she might lose herself in her studies. It had always worked for her before, but unfortunately, not this time.

"They sure are spending a lot of time together," she thought, the sudden twinge of insecurity taking her by surprise.

Pam, who was studying on the other side of the room, couldn't help but throw an " I told you so" look Charlotte's way.

"Eavesdropper," Charlotte said sarcastically, closing her book and staring vacantly ahead.

☜☞

Later that day, Damen and Scarlet were in the middle of a "tutoring" session in the Hawthorne music room, only their books were shut on the floor as they traded licks on the guitar. They looked up long enough to notice that the same girls who noticed the football players noticing Scarlet were all now wearing the exact same Suicide tee that she was wearing, thanks to the indie T-shirt store around the corner.

"Call the exterminator. This place is infested with poseurs," she said as she strummed on the guitar.

"You are an icon. Now everyone knows how cool you really are," Damen said with a smirk on his face.

Scarlet appeared annoyed but was actually flattered. She let the comment go without acknowledgment, deciding to play it

cool. To let on would be to give in to everything she detested, including, until just recently, the guy in front of her.

Damen reached into his guitar case, pulled out another CD, and handed it to Scarlet. She was more impressed with his selection this time.

"My Chemical Romance bootleg? Getting warmer," she said, barely able to contain her excitement. He was getting more than warm with that pick. She encouragingly handed him a copy of My Bloody Valentine's *Loveless* album in response, and they both laughed.

"Almost forgot this," Damen said as the bell rang. He snapped up his Physics book from the ground and put it in his backpack.

"Yeah, wouldn't want to forget that," Scarlet said with a slight detection of guilt, and relief, in her voice.

Scarlet left the room for Gym class, wondering if she was getting herself in a little too deep. She decided to clear her head and enjoy this little unrealistic break where one drops everything and plays a mandatory team sport for forty-five minutes. The thing that sucked most about her class was that it was split in half, half sophomores and half seniors, as if it wasn't demeaning enough to have to change in front of your own. The school actually managed to introduce a whole new level of humiliation. They thought it would close the gap between the student body, but all it really did was reinforce the feelings of terminal inadequacy when it came to every student's body.

She entered the locker room and came across a platoon of her easily influenced poseurs, who had obviously studied and memorized her MySpace profile and were now decked out for

the next Trash and Vaudeville convention, wearing her shade of lipstick and sporting sharp bobs, brothel-creepers, vintage rhinestone cuffs, and a smorgasbord of underground tees: The Birthday Party, PiL, Bauhaus, New York Dolls, Sonic Youth, The Damned, Sick of It All, The Creatures, BowWowWow, The Germs, and Killing Joke, to name a few. As each of the girls undressed, their shirts came off and dropped to the locker room floor, creating maybe the coolest pile of locker room clothes ever.

Ordinarily Scarlet would have been offended and lashed out at their sartorial brownnosing, but she found herself thinking about Charlotte instead. All she could think was how happy Charlotte would be to see that popular people were starting to emulate her, and how it was all because of Charlotte. Not that she welcomed that, but she knew how much it would mean to Charlotte, even if they weren't on speaking terms.

Scarlet unzipped her gym bag, and as she rummaged through to find gym clothes — a ripped-up, gray GOTH IS DEAD tee to slip over her magenta camisole, black faded shorts, and canvas Converse All Stars — she noticed the CD *Disintegration* by The Cure at the bottom of her bag.

"You're burning up," she said in triumph as she put the CD in her music player and blasted "Plainsong" on her way up the steps to the gym.

❧

Petula wasn't taking any of Scarlet's newfound fame at Hawthorne very well, but she spitefully clung to the hope that it

would just be flavor-of-the-month syndrome and everyone would return to their senses in short order. She had been the standard of All-American beauty for the past four years, and she wasn't going relinquish her crown to anyone, especially her sister. Primping as usual in her locker mirror before the next class, Petula noticed the reflection of a jock in a new Goth-style football jacket, all black with circling red hawks as the logo. Next she caught the Wendys approaching. They were feeling Scarlet's influence too.

"Spread the dread!" Wendy Anderson said dismissively as they passed Petula.

The most irksome thing, however, was not the newly acquired shiteous fashion sense of her friends and classmates; it was the reports she'd been getting back about Damen and Scarlet and their little jam sessions. Petula had been biding her time at her locker, waiting for an opportunity to confront Damen. An opportunity that was about to arrive as she saw him stop at his locker.

"I heard you've been slumming it," Petula said, sidling over to him.

"What?" Damen asked.

"Do you know how this looks?" Petula asked.

"How what looks?" Damen replied, not really wanting to have this discussion in public.

Petula spied Scarlet's CD in his locker and snatched it out with her hot pink talons.

"Oh my God, she *has* infected you!" Petula said, confirming her worst fear.

"Look, she's been tutoring me in Physics, okay?" Damen

said, wanting to come clean so that Petula wouldn't spontaneously combust in the hall.

"Is that what they're calling it in freak circles?" Petula asked.

"It's just so I can pass my test and go to the dance," Damen explained.

"Well, then, get another tutor," Petula said, slamming her pump into the newly waxed floor.

"You're paranoid," he laughed unconvincingly.

"And you're getting another tutor," she said as she held up the CD.

"It's either this," she said, presenting herself like a second-rate *Price Is Right* spokesmodel in front of a new living room set, "or . . . ," Petula held the CD away from her body in a pinched grasp, ". . . this."

Just then, Scarlet emerged out of the gymnasium and saw them arguing. She snuck around the corner so she could watch undetected. Petula continued with her ultimatum, ripping off Damen's old varsity jacket, and threw it at him. Damen, for the first time ever, found Petula's little tantrum more funny than threatening. Scarlet, who knew better, did not.

"You'll be sorry," Petula said vindictively as she walked away.

"I already am," he quipped.

17

While You Were Out

*My one regret in life
is that I am not someone else.*
—Woody Allen

Regret.
The saddest word in the English language.

———◆·•·◆———

There are consequences to every action; it is just not always so obvious at the time. You never really know how things are going to work out or how you're going to feel until afterward. Thus, regret. You may not be able to change anything, but at least you can feel bad about it. Never mind that it might haunt you for the rest of your life or, in Charlotte's case, beyond.

ord was getting around Hawthorne Manor that Charlotte was becoming increasingly unreliable. It was now obvious that her single-mindedness and total inability to let go of her "life" had placed the Dead kids' mission in jeopardy. The house was on the chopping block, and as far as Prue was concerned, so were their heads.

Charlotte watched from the parlor doorway as the Dead kids killed time to ease the tension they were all feeling.

DJ was spinning platters in the air, aiming the old vinyl LPs like buzz saws at Simon's and Simone's heads. Silent Violet sat at a desk ramming a finger down her throat like a determined bulimic, searching for her voice. Call Me Kim was picking the scabs from her head wound mindlessly as she chatted away. Suzy Scratcher absentmindedly carved "wash me" into Rotting Rita's back as Rita grabbed at maggots crawling from

her nostrils, rolled them in her fingers, and flicked them at Mike and Jerry, who held their thumbs and pinkies up like goalposts.

"Score!" Mike hollered each time Rita split the uprights.

CoCo, meanwhile, was digging through shards of broken mirror glass, tearing her fingers to shreds while trying to piece enough together to see her own reflection.

Everyone stopped what they were doing when Charlotte walked in the room. Dead Ed was always kind of chilly, but the cold shoulders Charlotte was getting from the other kids in the parlor left her absolutely frosted.

"Hey, Kim," Charlotte said. "Who ya talking to?"

"I'm busy," Kim mouthed dismissively as she continued her phone "conversation" and walked away.

Charlotte turned to music mavens Mike, Jerry, and DJ next.

"Hey, what are you guys jammin' to?" Charlotte eagerly asked. "Mind if I listen in?"

The boys were tempted to answer her, seeing as they would take any opportunity to talk about music — especially Mike, who literally had to bite his tongue — but their disappointment in Charlotte was too much to overcome. Mike removed one of his ear buds and declined.

"We'll pass," he said, answering for Jerry and DJ too.

"Too late, you already have!" Charlotte quipped, trying to joke her way back into their good graces. Jerry just shook his head.

"We're Outtie," DJ said in his best retro hip-hop lingo, motioning the guys away from Charlotte as if she had the plague.

Feeling rejected, Charlotte turned to Silent Violet and just began talking aloud to herself, using Violet as a sounding board. Violet just stared impassively.

"What did I do that was so wrong?" Charlotte whined. "I wasn't even at the house. I didn't mean for any of this to happen."

Pam, who was on the other side of the room, couldn't bear any more of her rationalizing.

"Take some responsibility, Charlotte!" Pam scolded, the whistle in her throat sounding loudly. "You knew enough not to get involved with the Living and not to bring your little living protégé into our world. What were you thinking?"

"I wasn't, I guess," Charlotte answered humbly.

"From the first second we met you've been obsessed with being important to people who couldn't give a flying crap about you," Pam said, throwing up her hands.

"If I could take it back, I would," Charlotte confessed.

"I'm not so sure," Pam said skeptically. "You sound like a broken record."

DJ was right on it, providing a perfect sound effect for Pam by scratching his vinyl with a long, sharp fingernail.

By now, all the other kids had fallen in behind Pam, listening to the conversation with crossed arms and raised eyebrows.

"What do you want me to say, Pam?" Charlotte asked, her emotions, and her gag reflex, intensifying. "That I'm happy to be here while life goes on without me?"

"That was your Fate, Charlotte," Simon said.

"Stop fighting it," Simone added.

"No, I don't believe that!" Charlotte responded.

"Then what?" Pam asked.

"I failed," Charlotte said quietly. "I'm a failure. We all are."

"Speak for yourself," CoCo warned.

"*We* failed to live, and I, personally, am having a little trouble dealing with it," Charlotte went on. "*She* failed to pay attention. *He* failed to obey the speed limit. *She* failed to listen. *He* failed to eat right!" she said, going around the room.

The hurt in her classmates' eyes was evident, but Charlotte was determined to make her case, no matter how harsh, as much for herself as for the others.

"Living isn't winning and dying isn't failing," Pam retorted.

"It is the ultimate rejection," Charlotte said. "And I've had enough of that to last forever."

"So you'll jeopardize all our futures for your own selfish desires?" Kim asked. "What about resolution? Self-acceptance?"

"I accept . . . that I'd rather be alive," Charlotte affirmed.

"Do you know why Prue is so powerful?" Pam asked, seeming to change the subject.

"Because she's been here the longest?" Charlotte guessed, thinking that Prue might even have had decades of Dead Ed under her belt for all she knew.

"No. It's because she understands her purpose," Pam informed her. "She doesn't ask why."

The truth rang loudly in Charlotte's ears. Prue was really good at being dead and was in full control of her abilities. She had none of the internal conflicts that held Charlotte back. In fact, from the first moment she met her, Charlotte believed that Prue actually liked being dead, if that was really possible.

"Prue may be a bully at times, but at least we know whose side she's on," CoCo said sharply.

With that painful cut, Pam and the rest turned and left Charlotte alone in the room to think it over.

The nighttime street was peppered with puddles after an early evening shower had left its mark outside the Buzzard's Bay Theater. The shiny black pavement was as close to patent leather as pavement could get, and the muddied reflection of headliners "Death Cab" on the turn-of-the-century marquee could even be read in it. Scarlet waited beneath the canopy, wearing a vintage mauve minidress with a black sequined sweater hanging loosely over it and her biker boots. Her raccoon eyes were lined heavily, as black as her hair. Her lips were painted pale.

She was twitchy and anxious, waiting impatiently for Damen to arrive. He was running late. Scarlet, her palms sweaty and her foot tapping rapidly, wasn't sure if she was more nervous that he would show, or that he wouldn't.

"Need tickets? Tickets. I got tickets," a shady scalper said as he surreptitiously brushed up beside her.

"No thanks, I got one," she said as he faced the other direction.

"What location? I got some good seats here," the huckster persisted.

"Oh, I don't know, my friend has the tickets," Scarlet responded, trying to shoo him away.

"Well, where's she at?" the scalper asked.

"*He's* on his way," Scarlet responded as she moved to the other side of the entrance.

"Well, when your date gets here, maybe you'll want to pay a little extra for some better seats," he called after her.

"It's not a date!" Scarlet yelled, not wanting him, a complete stranger, to walk away with the notion that she was on a date, because if it appeared to be a date to a scalper, then maybe it was a date, and she wasn't going to stand by and let a scalper of all people determine if she was on a date or not.

"*Not a date!*" she yelled again as he slipped away into the shadows and Damen appeared in his place.

"Not a date?" Damen asked.

"Oh yeah, ah, the scalper was trying to sell me a ticket on a night that wasn't today's date," she said, playing it cool.

"Gotta be completely gullible to buy a ticket for a date that wasn't even real," Damen added.

"Yeah, gullible," Scarlet said.

"This sure beats studying," Damen said as he dropped his backpack on the outside table to be searched.

"Yeah, about that . . . I was thinking, maybe we should stop . . . ," Scarlet said with hesitation. ". . . You know, the tutoring."

"Why?" Damen asked.

"Well, I was just thinking that it might be better . . . for you . . . if you studied with someone more . . . on your level?" Scarlet replied.

"On my level? If I did that, I definitely wouldn't pass," Damen said with a laugh as he snatched up his backpack from the table and slung it around his shoulder.

"No, I don't mean on your Physics level, I mean, you know, on your level . . . ," Scarlet said as she dropped her purse on the table to be searched.

"Oh, I get it. . . . If you don't want to tutor me anymore, just say it," Damen said, feeling the impending blow of rejection.

"No, that's not it. I just don't know if this is working out . . . for you," Scarlet said, trying to give him a way out.

"Thanks, but . . . for me . . . it's working just fine, and I'm completely cool with the level we're on," he said.

Guilt was starting to get the best of her, but she wasn't about to go crawling back to Charlotte. She took her purse up off the table and, at the same time, noticed that the band inside was playing "I Will Follow You into the Dark," the same song Damen played on the guitar. "Hey, listen, they're playing our . . . I mean, your song."

"Yeah . . . maybe we should head inside," Damen said as he dug in his pocket for the tickets.

"So how much do I owe you?" Scarlet asked.

"Oh, nothing, it's my pleasure . . . ," he said as he fished out the tattered tickets. "I told you it was a thank-you for the tutoring," Damen said firmly, stepping to the side and holding the door open for her to enter the orchestra section. He took her hand and ushered her in, the other hand gently placed against the small of her back.

"Oh, right . . . of course," Scarlet said, pleasantly surprised by Damen's thoughtful gesture.

The concert passed much more quickly than the two hours the band was onstage — at least that's how it felt to Scarlet. Song after song took on greater meaning for her than

ever before as she experienced them with him. There were thousands of people in the arena, but for her, there were only two.

They didn't hold hands, but as they swayed to the music, their eyes would meet accidentally, or their shoulders, elbows, or knees would touch lightly, flustering Scarlet and Damen too.

The crowd exited to the mournful strains of "Title and Registration." Scarlet and Damen sat quietly waiting for the room to empty, satisfied with the hit-packed show and in no rush to leave.

They didn't talk much on the way home. Damen drove slowly to Scarlet's house and walked her to her door. They spent an uncomfortable few seconds saying goodnight, not sure if they should kiss on the cheek, hug, or shake hands, turning what should have been a tender moment into an awkward rock-paper-scissors parting.

"Um, thanks," Scarlet said. "I had . . ." She searched her brain for the perfect word, but could only come up with a limp, ". . . fun."

"Me too." Damen nodded shyly. "See you . . . soon?" Neither of them saw Petula watching bitterly from her bedroom window. They didn't even think to look, seeing that it was Saturday night, and for Petula Kensington to be home on a Saturday night was, well, Amish.

Damen walked down the stone path as he had so many times before, but noticed this time it felt very different. He got in his car, pushed the CD function on his Bang & Olufsen stereo, and as *Transatlanticism* played, he replayed every detail of the night.

The next morning, Scarlet went to tape a more formal thank-you note on Damen's locker, but noticed it was open and decided to place her note inside instead. His recent Physics assignment was leaning against the door and fell out onto the floor. She picked it up and immediately noticed the big fat "F" written in red on the top.

Scarlet knew that Damen hadn't failed — she had. Without giving it a second thought, she ran down the hall and straight to the abandoned wing of the school, sucking air and swallowing her pride along the way.

There was no life in that wing of the school. It had been "under construction" for longer than anyone could remember, but no work ever seemed to be done or even planned for it. It was a place lost in time, a place forgotten. At least it looked that way to Scarlet.

Scarlet pulled away a few of the loose boards that walled off the wing from the rest of the school and entered. It smelled like old people and wet cardboard. She walked around, looking in different classrooms, but didn't see anyone, "anyone" being Charlotte. She started to fear that maybe something had happened to her or maybe Scarlet couldn't see her anymore because of their falling out at the F.C.O. party. Maybe Charlotte was gone for good.

Scarlet gazed out through the dirty glass windows into the courtyard nestled in the middle of the square wing. Overgrown with weeds and creeping ivy, cracked pavement, stone benches and statues caked with moss, the courtyard resembled

an old cemetery more than the English-style garden it was supposed to be.

Charlotte — who was in the corner, out of Scarlet's view — approached Pam, who was studying. She held up a really cool dream catcher that she had made herself.

"Peace offering," Charlotte said as handed it to Pam.

"Dream catcher? You just don't get it," Pam huffed.

"You can hang it in your room," Charlotte said hopefully.

"How ironic, seeing as I'm not going to have a room much longer thanks to you," Pam said as she turned away, showing Charlotte her back.

"Look, I'm sorry." Charlotte said, mustering the courage to apologize even though she knew how trivial it would sound after the way she'd disregarded Pam and the others.

"It will never happen again," Charlotte assured her. "I'll make this up to you and to everybody."

Pam, who always had a soft spot for Charlotte and her antics, smiled and decided to let Charlotte grovel a little and apologize profusely and then to let bygones be bygones.

"I'm done with all the fantasies, Pam. I want to come back," Charlotte said.

Pam turned to face Charlotte and accept her apology but saw someone she didn't expect instead. There was Scarlet, standing in the entranceway. Pam felt hurt and played for a fool.

"What are you trying to do, set me up as an alibi?" Pam bristled, showing an angry side Charlotte had never seen.

Charlotte flashed a confused look. She tried to speak in her own defense but broke out in a hacking cough instead.

"I've tried to help you, Charlotte, but I'm not going down with you," Pam continued, sounding wounded and feeling betrayed.

Watching Charlotte cough her head off, Pam was tempted to smack her on the back as she'd done before, but walked away instead.

Now that Charlotte was alone, Scarlet walked out from the shadows and tapped her on the shoulder from behind.

"Hey," Scarlet said.

"You scared me," Charlotte said, startled.

"How's that for role reversal?" Scarlet said, trying to make light of the situation.

"What are you doing? You can't be seen out here," Charlotte whispered as she led Scarlet deep into a corner behind thick brush.

Scarlet reached into her bag and pulled out Damen's F paper.

"An F?" Charlotte said, stunned.

"This isn't just about us anymore. He trusted me, well, us, and now he's got no girlfriend, he's failing Physics, and will probably be kicked off the football team," Scarlet said.

"So, does this mean that you're back in?" Charlotte asked, unable to control herself and live up to the promise she made to Pam just minutes before.

"It's more like *you* are back in," Scarlet replied.

Pam watched from a distance as Scarlet and Charlotte reconciled and realized that Charlotte had once again picked Scarlet over her and the Living over the Dead.

18

Play Me

Get me away from here I'm dying
Play me a song to set me free
Nobody writes them like they used to
So it may as well be me.
—Belle and Sebastian

Life is a series of choices.

Fun-house magicians and psychics ask us questions and offer us choices as a way to ascertain the things we most want to hear. In other words, they manipulate us. Charlotte and Scarlet wanted Damen to make his choice on his own. But he had no idea there was even a choice to be made.

I t was a gloomy, stormy afternoon and the band room was set up for the big Fall recital. The risers stretched the entire length and width of the room, and there was very little space to walk. The periodic lightning bolts caused the snare drums to vibrate on cue, and the woodwinds, hanging like marionettes on their cold, sterile stands, were rattling along with rolling thunder in the distance.

Charlotte, in possession of Scarlet once again, entered and looked around for Damen in the half-lit room. As she scanned the chairs, a piece of paper hit her in the head.

"Up here," Damen said in a loud whisper.

She lifted her delicate chin and saw him at the top of the band riser, waving her up.

"Are you okay?" he asked as she took her seat.

"Oh yeah, I just have something else on my mind," she

replied as she opened up the Physics book and laid it out for both of them to see.

Yeah, me too," he said as he closed her book. "Let me get unzipped so we can get started."

Charlotte was dumbfounded. She opened her book back up and tried to keep it together, but at the sound of a zipper opening, she lost it.

"Wait! What are you doing?" she said as she sank her nose down deeper in her book and tried to forget the locker room incident.

"Pulling it out," he responded.

"No, no, no . . . ," she pleaded as she closed her eyes. Relief swept over her as she peeked and saw him take out his guitar out of its case.

"Play that song you played yesterday," Damen said.

"Oh, no, no, I can't. I mean, I couldn't," Charlotte replied nervously.

Damen placed the guitar in her arms and she awkwardly tried to cradle it like someone holding a newborn for the first time.

Charlotte tried to act naturally, but it was obvious that she didn't even know how to hold a guitar, let alone play one.

"Hey, what about the cello? I can play that," she suggested.

Damen laughed, thinking she was joking. "What cello?" he asked.

He leaned in closer and prompted her to begin. Uncertain what to do, she grabbed a bow from a nearby violin and rubbed it over the six-string like a virtuoso classic rock guitar God.

"Scarlet unplugged," Damen said in utter surprise.

"That's me," Charlotte replied.

She smiled nervously and, after fumbling around on it a little, started playing a beautifully airy tune. Damen was charmed.

"Definitely not the song you were playing yesterday," he said.

"Do you like it?" she asked.

"Yeah, I like it. It's . . . different," he replied.

"Well, you know how much I love playing guitar, but maybe we should actually study?" Charlotte said.

"Study?" Damen replied. "What's with you today?"

Charlotte couldn't keep up the guitar charade much longer so she turned the conversation back around to her strength. Her thing was Physics, and she wanted Damen to like her thing just as much as he liked Scarlet's.

"Check this out." Charlotte opened her Physics book to a diagram.

"Yeah?" Damen replied.

"It's a sound wave," she proudly announced as she plucked the guitar string.

"I don't get that stuff," Damen said.

"Sound is the disturbance of mechanical energy that flows through matter as a wave," Charlotte explained. "It's invisible, but it is still there."

Charlotte noted the vacant look on Damen's face.

"How can I explain this?" she thought out loud. Charlotte held up the neck of the guitar.

"A guitar string makes no sound," she instructed, pointing to the silent E string, "until it makes contact with your body."

She took Damen's hand in hers and plucked the guitar string with his finger.

"When the connection is made, the vibration of the string

creates a wave, which you hear when it reaches your eardrum," she finished.

Damen was amazed that he was learning his assignment without even realizing it.

"So, without a body . . . the strings couldn't do much at all," Charlotte said, making a larger point. "They need each other."

"*A Bell Is a Cup Until It Is Struck*," said Damen proudly, hoping his summation of Charlotte's lesson via an obscure reference to Wire's classic album title would score him some points. It didn't. "That's cool," Damen said, feeling like an idiot.

"That's sound," Charlotte gushed. "You'll definitely be a better guitar player if you know how one works, so just think of acoustics as guitar practice."

As Damen flipped back through the Physics lesson of his own accord, it was clear that she had made an impression.

"I almost forgot . . . I made you something," she said as she ran down to the bottom of the riser and fetched her bag.

She ran back to Damen and handed him a small container. Just as she did, Scarlet's shadow moved across the floor as she peeked in through the doorway.

"What's this?" Damen asked as he opened the bag and pulled out a black-and-white cookie.

"You made me a cookie? I didn't figure you for the Betty Crocker type," he said.

"Oh, it's nothing . . . ," she said. "Lame, right?"

Damen took a bite right down the middle, where the black and white icing met.

"The best of both worlds," he joked, devouring the cookie.

Desperate to interfere in the warm and fuzzy scene, Scarlet forced open the window, allowing the cold rain to dampen their little moment. Damen immediately took off his varsity jacket and put it around Charlotte's shoulders, much to Scarlet's dismay.

"I like this side of you . . . ," he said.

Suddenly an emotion that had been completely alien to Scarlet washed over her as her shadow receded back through the doorway. She was jealous.

ॐ

The next day, before class, Charlotte snuck a smiley-face cupcake into Damen's locker. When he finally got to it and opened the door, he was stunned to find the cupcake, only it had been "Scarletized" with a facial piercing, horns, and evil grin.

Damen turned to find Charlotte-as-Scarlet coming down the hall, fresh from that day's possession ritual.

"Hey, Betty Rocker!" Damen called out to her.

Charlotte looked confused.

"I can't believe you did this. I never know what you are going to come up with," he said as he sunk his finger into the icing and licked it.

Charlotte looked at the cake and saw what Scarlet had done.

"Neither do I," she said.

"It's almost like you're two different people," he said.

"Which one do you like better?" Charlotte responded, seeing it as her opportunity to settle things once and for all.

"Thankfully, I don't have to choose," he said as he took a bite out of the cake.

19

Dirty Little Secret

Never seek to tell thy love
Love that never told can be;
For the gentle wind does move
Silently, invisibly.
—William Blake

You can't have it both ways.

———◆———

Love is too powerful to hide for very long. Deny it and suffer the consequences. Acknowledge it and suffer the consequences. Revealing it can either be shameful or it can be liberating. It is for others to decide which it will be.

harlotte and Scarlet were hanging out in Scarlet's room together, but each felt as if they were living in different worlds for the first time. Scarlet was sprawled out on her bed, surrounded by deep crushed-velvet cushions, sketching innocent, big-eyed porcelain dolls with freaky out-of-proportion body parts while Charlotte paced the floor like a caged tiger.

The tension was thick and Charlotte was dying to confront Scarlet over what happened with Damen and her cupcake, but she didn't want to rock the boat, fearing that Scarlet would ban her from her body again.

Desperate for approval, Charlotte walked over to Scarlet's guitar and pressed her fingers on the sharp bronze thatch of twisted strings on the gearhead.

"He's only with you because of me," she blurted out antagonistically.

Scarlet continued sketching and didn't even look up.

"I mean, you know that, right?" Charlotte said as she plopped down on the bed and got in Scarlet's face.

"This whole thing was your idea and you're mad?" Scarlet asked, still refusing to look Charlotte's way. "Maybe you should go stick your head in the freezer; it's going bad."

Charlotte got up and walked over to Scarlet's Death Cab for Cutie tour poster on the wall. Trying to unnerve Scarlet, she ran her fingers down the side as if she was giving herself the worst paper cut ever. For anyone else it would be hard to watch, but Scarlet did not want to give her any satisfaction.

"I just want you to realize that he only responds to you when I'm in you, that's all," Charlotte added.

They both turned their attention to the antique-framed plasma TV on Scarlet's wall: a promo for a dating show was on.

"Find out who he'll choose . . . next," the announcer said ominously.

Scarlet and Charlotte exchanged a look.

"Really? Well, why don't we let him decide?" Scarlet replied smugly.

⊗☾

The following morning, Scarlet and Charlotte decided to play out their own little game in the school's pool well before gym classes started.

The only lights on were the ones under the water, which made for a very spooky setting as the dim beams of light were refracted all around the concrete cocoon. The smell of chlorine and mildew reddened Scarlet's eyes just a little.

"Okay, so, just like the TV show, we're going to take turns being with him. I'll go first, then we switch, and we'll see which one of us he 'responds' to," Scarlet said.

"This isn't fair. This place is so dark . . . so creepy . . . so . . . you," Charlotte said as she looked around the room. "I never took you for the swimming type."

"We're not here for the water," she said as she turned up her iPod and slid it into the LifePod stereo system that doubled as a messenger bag. The music bounced off of the cement walls and tiled floor as if they were in a nightclub. "We're here for the acoustics."

"How is this going to work for me?" Charlotte asked.

"Sorry, I can't hear you!" Scarlet yelled, cranking the music up even louder.

Both girls' attention turned to the door as it creaked open. Damen walked through the darkened doorway, heard the music blaring, and walked toward it.

Charlotte quickly disappeared and then reappeared at the top of the diving board, watching the scene below.

"Why are we meeting at the pool? We usually at least *pretend* to study," Damen said as he moved closer.

Damen took a seat on the bench next to her. The pool light gave off an eerie glow that surrounded them like lava at the mouth of a volcano. Shadows from the rippling water danced across Scarlet's face, mesmerizing Damen as he tried to get a few words out of his head and over his tongue.

"I-I've been wanting to tell you something . . . ," he stammered.

Charlotte was beside herself. Fearing what he might say to

Scarlet, she swooped down from her perch on the diving board and possessed her prematurely.

Scarlet was expelled abruptly from her own body, landing on the side of the pool, confused at first and then just angry.

"I hope that it's not that you're afraid of the water ... ," Charlotte said, finishing his thought and continuing the conversation barely missing a beat. Without waiting for his reply, Charlotte seductively stripped down to Scarlet's vintage camisole and matching boy short–style underwear and jumped in the pool.

"No way," he mouthed, not believing his eyes or his luck.

Damen pulled off his shirt, kicked off his shoes, and dived in after her.

Scarlet was paralyzed with disgust and rage. She couldn't believe the depth that Charlotte had sunk to.

"I thought a little dip before studying would clear our heads," Charlotte said.

"Yeah, I'm thinking clearer already," Damen said with a slight shiver, staring at her makeshift bathing suit, which was becoming sheerer and tighter the wetter it got.

"Hey, race you to the end?" he said, trying to burn off some of the hormones raging inside him.

Both of them took off for the far side of the pool, arms and legs flailing. He could have won easily, but that wasn't really the point. Charlotte was swimming so hard, he eased up in admiration of her competitive spirit and determination, and they hit the wall at the same time.

"That was great," he said as he wiped the water from his eyes, blinded for just a second. In that heartbeat, Scarlet re-

gained control of her body in what was becoming a ridiculous otherworldly tug-of-war.

"Okay. Pool time's over," Scarlet announced like an impatient mom.

"Why? We were just getting used to the water. I'm kind of confused here," he said as he swam to the other side of the pool.

Scarlet dipped back under, pushed off the wall, and swam over to him. As she came up, she brushed her body ever so slightly against his.

"Well how about I un-confuse you, then?" Scarlet said as the crystal clear water dripped from her black hair, raced down her body and gently fell back into the water. "Close your eyes and tell me which kiss you like better."

Damen closed his eyes. Scarlet playfully pinned him in the corner and powerfully planted one on his wet lips.

"Okay. Compare that one to . . . ," Scarlet said as she motioned for Charlotte to enter her body.

". . . to this one," Charlotte said, finishing the sentence.

Charlotte leaned in to kiss him but hesitated, caught off guard by his beautiful face. She started softly kissing her way up his neck, teasing him and herself. She opened her eyes to look at his lips before she kissed them, but nearly swallowed her tongue when she saw Prue hovering beside the pool.

"Whorepool!" Prue yelled, ordering the rest of the Dead kids to start swimming in a circle. Charlotte was forced away from Damen by the supernatural vortex just as she was about to kiss him. By this point, she'd had enough of these kinds of déjà vus.

Scarlet, realizing that she'd rather be humiliated in front of

the entire school than face the wrath of Prue's anger toward Charlotte, panicked and took back her body.

The whirlpool built up pressure until a wave rose up above the coping, spilling out of the pool and rolling into a wall divider that separated the pool area from the gym. The rushing water rattled the divider and seeped under it and into the gym. The Living kids in Gym class saw the beginning of the flood heading toward them and ran for the exits.

"Tsunami!!!" they screamed a bit dramatically, warning their classmates, but it was too late for most of them. Gym bags, ball bags, book bags, tracksuits, sweatpants, hoodies, and all kinds of athletic gear were left behind and drenched. Old wooden floorboards came loose, electrical outlets sparked, lights blinked, and circuit breakers popped all over school. It wasn't quite Biblical, but the damage was significant.

Most damaging of all, however, was the moment the divider finally fell like a domino. Scarlet and Damen were revealed, huddled together, holding onto each other for dear life, like two *Titanic* castaways spit ashore by an angry sea.

Everyone in the gym was more shocked at seeing them together in such a compromising position than they were by the actual path of destruction that was left in the flood's wake. As the water began to drain out through the doorways, Prue whisked herself and the others back to Hawthorne Manor. Her work here was done.

☜☞

The chaos in the gym had yet to come to Principal Styx's attention, but for the time being, he had an equally catastrophic

problem to deal with — meting out Petula's punishment for the Driver's Ed incident.

"Honestly, Principal Styx . . . I don't know anything about a car accident. What makes you think it was me?" Petula asked in an inappropriately flirtatious tone.

"Is this yours?" Styx asked while holding up a tube of lipstick.

"Where'd you get that?" Petula asked.

"In the car," Styx replied.

Petula ripped the lipstick from his hand and her facial expression transformed from vixen to plotting über-bitch.

"I'm afraid this incident with the car cannot be overlooked," he warned. "The damage to the vehicle, the town, the tuba, and the school is considerable. It needs to be accounted for. People could have been hurt or worse," Styx lectured.

"But they weren't," Petula tossed off dismissively. "Were they, Mr. Shits, I mean, ah, Styx?"

"I'm afraid that I'm going to have to ban you from the Fall Ball," Styx said, issuing his verdict.

"You can't ban me from the dance! I *AM* THE DANCE!" Petula screamed. Still looking for a reprieve of any sort, she scanned the disciplinary report and mustered a defense.

"Wait, your report just says 'Kensington.' I have a younger sister!" she argued. "I have evidence. This is her lipstick! Look, it's crimson. Do I look like I wear crimson?"

"My decision is final," he explained, ignorant of Petula's penchant for pink frosted lip liner and clear glosses.

Just before Petula could get out another nasty word on her own behalf, Styx's secretary burst into the office.

"The gym is flooded!" she yelled excitedly, enjoying all the drama that had just insinuated itself into her humdrum life.

Principal Styx, still examining the lipstick, and with Petula in tow, ran toward the gym.

As he arrived to assess the damage and any injury report, Petula spied Damen and Scarlet, still clinging to one another, half naked, but at least out of the water.

"That's her!" she ranted. "She did it to steal my boy-friend! MOTIVE!" Petula yelled, but the principal was too busy assessing the damage to pay any attention to her accusations.

Petula approached them as if they were radioactive and scoffed at the vulnerable and compromised position she as well as the entire student body had discovered them in.

"Hey, I hear they're having a sale on scarlet letters at Hot Topic," Petula said as she looked down her nose at Scarlet.

"Back off!" Damen demanded as the janitor handed them towels.

"You'd like that, wouldn't you?" Petula snapped, looking ready for a Jerry Springer–style smackdown as she turned back to Scarlet.

"That's okay. You can expect these type of outbursts from the calorie-challenged," Scarlet quipped.

"No one is ever going to take you seriously. Look at you! You're a joke," Petula said, trying her best to humiliate Scarlet in front of Damen.

"Petula, stop!" Damen yelled.

Scarlet looked embarrassed and hurt, but she did her best to play if off. Charlotte looked on sadly.

"He'll never take you out in public on a real date. What did

he say to you, 'oh, let's just keep this between me and you'?" Petula probed. "Did he say that?"

Scarlet fell silent and Damen looked a little guilty.

"You've got it all wrong," Damen said.

"You're a dirty little secret," Petula said, continuing to slash away at Scarlet.

"Yeah, well, this dirty little secret is going to the Fall Ball with me!" Damen announced.

Petula and Scarlet were speechless. Even Damen was surprised that he blurted the proposal.

Scarlet, numb from the verbal and physical beating she had just taken, wandered off without a word. As she dried off, Charlotte appeared to her.

"I can't believe it! We're going to the dance!" Charlotte exclaimed, barely able to contain herself.

"I can't believe you!" Scarlet said in utter disgust. "What, if you can't have him, no one can . . . is that it?"

"I didn't do anything," Charlotte replied. "You know I didn't!"

Scarlet cut her off before she could explain.

"You almost got me killed too! Every time I agree to let you possess me something horrible happens," Scarlet berated her. "I can't let you do this anymore."

"Scarlet, please . . . ," Charlotte pleaded. "Please don't do this!"

Scarlet turned away, unable even to face Charlotte, and continued to wring out her clothes. As she did, droplets fell on to Charlotte's face, making it appear as if she were crying, which is what she wanted to do more than anything.

20

To Wish
Impossible Things

*In all relationships, there are
always aching holes and that's
where the impossible wishes come into it.*
—Robert Smith

Life is random and love can be just as random.

---◆·◆·◆---

If you sit back and really think about it, you will be left with one thought — a profound one — why bother? The only reason to live is to love and the only reason to love is to live. Charlotte had neither...at least she didn't yet. She still loved him. She always would. He was her "why bother."

he unmerciful rain fell through Charlotte and to the ground as she walked somberly down the darkened street, lamenting her misfortune. She wished she could feel the cold drizzle against her skin again, but she couldn't. It was just a reminder that she was as hollow as Damen's Ovation guitar, and there was not much she was going to be able to do about it now or ever. Nothing could touch her, not even the downpour, she thought as she traversed the accumulating puddles. The truth was, Charlotte had nowhere to go, and there was nowhere to be. No curfew, no one waiting up for her, and no need even to sleep.

She wandered down the quiet streets until the sky cleared, revealing the final fleeting moments of sunset silhouetted against Hawthorne's skyline. Even mired in her disappointment, she noticed a cold front blowing through, clearing the

dampness but not her conscience. She'd brought embarrassment and pain to her friends and quite possibly condemned herself and her Dead Ed classmates.

She wasn't just sad, she was jealous too. She felt cut out. Her plan to win Damen's love and Petula's respect had totally backfired, and it was mostly her own doing. Mostly, that is, because some of the blame belonged to Scarlet, right? And to Prue. Charlotte didn't intend for any of this to happen, she rationalized. It was just collateral damage.

"Talk about unresolved issues," she babbled to herself.

Sunset gave way to evening and evening to night as she continued aimlessly in the bitter cold under the watchful eye of the gables that hovered majestically over all. Being alone in the middle of night, trudging through dark alleys and side streets, would have had anyone else constantly looking over her shoulder, but the only thing Charlotte had to fear was the reality that her dreams would never come true.

"This is what ghosts do, isn't it?" she thought out loud, resigning herself to oblivion. "Wander. Repent."

As she passed under a stone trestle and through a thicket of dead trees strangled by braided vines, she was unable to stop obsessing over Damen and Scarlet — they were under the same full moon as she was — and wondering what they were doing.

It was eating her up inside when she inexplicably found herself outside of Damen's house. It was a place she'd bicycled by many times over the summer. She needed to see that he was sleeping, that he was alone, and that, for the time being,

there was nothing happening between him and Scarlet. She needed at least that much peace of mind.

Charlotte crept up under his window and saw him there, bathed in moonlight, asleep on his twin bed. Maybe, just like her, he needed to drown out all that was wrong, all that was being thrown at him, and to check out for a while. He had one leg sticking out of his blanket, a naked leg, and she could see part of his white boxers peeking out from his green army blanket. She knew that he had volunteered with the Red Cross last summer because she had the newspaper clipping on her mirror, and she thought it was so cool that he was issued an official blanket. His window was cracked a bit to let the dry heat from the radiator escape into the cool fall night. She considered this opening a silent invitation and slipped in.

She had never been in a guy's room before, let alone a guy like Damen, and to her surprise it was everything she thought it would be. He was sleeping under a rack of CDs, trophies, and his stereo, which was cranked up so loud she wondered how he could sleep at all.

After declaring their situation a state of emergency, she slid underneath the Red Cross blanket with him, cuddled close to his warm body, resting her head gently on his chiseled chest. She had nothing to lose and she needed him to herself, for just a little while.

"Damen?" she whispered desperately into his ear, reaching out to any part of him she might still be able to touch.

He didn't respond at first, but then he slowly turned around and opened his eyes, looked deep into her eyes as if they were

familiar to him, and then . . . then . . . he screamed bloody murder.

Charlotte flew back against the wall and watched helplessly as he sat up in bed, his body dripping with sweat, in a stressful post-traumatic state. She had penetrated his dream, but not in the way he penetrated hers.

"I'm his nightmare," she admitted as she fled his room.

There was no escape for her. No relief. She had exhausted all possibilities and all her hope was gone, washed away with the heavy rain and Damen's night sweats.

Charlotte's tireless walk of shame lasted the entire night. In the still light of dawn, she changed her direction and headed toward Hawthorne High, where she curled up in a ball on the concrete steps and waited for signs of life. She closed her weary eyes and drifted off to sleep.

With the morning sun came the buses and staff and students and classes, and with the noise from the last few stragglers, Charlotte awoke and realized she was late for her class. She felt like unpopular roadkill. Like she had been trampled by hundreds of Living kids, which she had. She immediately headed for Dead Ed, but when she arrived, the classroom was empty, with everyone already out in the courtyard for break, except for Prue, who was kept back by Mr. Brain.

"The swimming pool?" Brain said, fuming. "You, of all people, should know better."

"Me?" Prue asked. "Why don't you talk to the 'grim weeper' about that?"

Prue was tempted to snitch about Scarlet, Damen, all of it, but bit her lip and kept quiet. It was an unspoken code of soli-

darity among the Dead kids that even Prue's anger would not allow her to breach.

"I know you have a problem with Charlotte," Brain said, "but you are just making things worse."

"Things couldn't be any worse," Prue cracked.

"Yes, unfortunately, they could be," Brain said firmly. "The last seat is filled, Prue, and our time is coming."

". . . Or not," Prue said. "She could ruin it for all of us."

"Then find a different way to bring her around," Brain said, stating the obvious. "We are not going anywhere without her."

"You don't know that for sure," Prue said. "The other kids are coming along and —"

"I do." Brain cut her off. "And so do you."

Prue just stared at him vacantly.

"I know it's hard for you to step back and let Charlotte take the lead," Brain said sympathetically. "You've always been head of the class."

"The lead?" Prue balked. "She's a follower! She doesn't care if we are stuck here for Eternity."

"Then make her care," Brain said. "That's *your* challenge."

"But she never listens," Prue whined.

"Sound familiar?" Brain asked knowingly.

The creaking of a classroom door being opened interrupted their conversation as both Prue and Brain turned to the doorway.

"Speak of the devil," Prue said.

"Hello, Charlotte," Brain said in a welcoming tone.

"I guess my time is up," Prue sniped, her jealousy poking

through the words just as Charlotte poked her head into the classroom to see if Brain was free.

Prue turned and left in a huff, just barely crossing paths with Charlotte, and then telekinetically slamming the door behind her, speaking volumes to both of them about her opinion of Charlotte.

Not content to leave bad enough alone, Prue turned back to the door, pressed her face against the glass, and slid downward, leaving a gooey trail as she mocked Charlotte's death.

"Why does she hate me so much?" Charlotte asked Mr. Brain.

"She doesn't hate you, Charlotte," Brain explained. "But we all need to rely on each other here to achieve a common goal, and so far, you've proven yourself to be . . . undependable."

"I'm trying," she said.

"Are you?" Brain asked somewhat rhetorically.

Charlotte thought about it and paused, her demeanor becoming increasingly desperate.

"I don't know what I'm doing," she admitted. "I'm failing at everything that matters to me."

"Maybe that's the lesson, Charlotte," Brain offered. "You need to stop living and start dying."

"I am trying to let go, but every choice I make is the wrong one," she said dejectedly. "No dance, no Damen, no friends, no house, no *life*."

"You are in complete denial," Brain said.

"I worked so hard to get that Midnight Kiss . . . ah, I mean resolution," she said, giving herself away.

"Midnight Kiss?" Mr. Brain asked, beginning to put some

pieces together. "Charlotte, I'm asking you again, can you be seen by someone?"

Charlotte's silence told Brain everything he needed to know.

"Did you ever consider that being seen was about more than just getting what you want?" he asked, moving in closer to her.

"What do you mean?" Charlotte asked.

"Your choices impact all of us, Charlotte, not just you," Brain said sternly. "Interacting with the living, almost without exception, is strictly prohibited. The risk is too high for them . . . and for us."

"Since when have my choices ever mattered?" Charlotte whined. "I don't want this responsibility. I can barely solve my own problems, let alone everyone else's."

"I'm afraid it is out of your control whether to accept it or not, Charlotte," Brain replied. "You're problems are becoming everyone else's."

"Great, I walked in here for a little advice . . . ," Charlotte said as Brain stared straight ahead, lost in thought.

"But there is another possibility," Brain conjectured.

"And that is?" Charlotte attempted to drag it out of him.

"Perhaps the fact that you can be seen," Brain hypothesized, "and the rest of us cannot be, is actually a key to solving your problem . . . and ours."

"Are you saying that I am meant to go to the dance?" Charlotte asked, some hope returning to her voice. "Could it be that the Midnight Kiss is *my* key to resolution?"

"Let's not get ahead of ourselves," Brain cautioned. "I didn't say that."

"But there's a chance, right?" Charlotte asked, pressing him.

"We won't know that until afterward," Brain offered cryptically. "There are so many variables. . . ."

Charlotte interrupted Mr. Brain's explanation, weighing her options out loud and quite dramatically. "To kiss or not to kiss," she said, pacing the floor frenetically like the lead in a third-rate middle school production of *Hamlet*.

"The stakes are high, Charlotte," he warned. "We may be trusting you with . . . our future."

The possibilities ran through Charlotte's mind and she made a calculation. Her answer was never really in doubt.

"It's a risk I'm willing to take, Mr. Brain," Charlotte said, suddenly very willing to shoulder this heavy burden.

"Remember, just because you *can* do something, doesn't mean you *should*," Brain stressed.

She was barely listening any longer. Brain had told her exactly what she wanted to hear. The dance, Damen, the Midnight Kiss, it was all hers for the taking.

"Thank you," Charlotte said sincerely. "You are a lifesaver."

"A lifesaver?" Brain said, a look of concern flashing across his face. "That's not exactly what I had in mind."

"To *kiss*." Charlotte sighed, nearly swooning as she left the room.

Prue, who was hiding behind the open door, was now more determined than ever to stop her.

"Or *not* to kiss," Prue muttered cryptically to herself.

Charlotte, meanwhile, had a smaller but no less important issue to resolve. Scarlet. They were still not on speaking terms, and without her cooperation, nothing would be possible.

Just then, an announcement from Principal Styx echoed through the vacant halls of the school.

> *"Attention Hawthorne students. Due to the flooding of the gym, we are unable to hold the annual Fall Ball in that location this year. Unless we find another suitable venue, we will be forced to cancel. I should inform you now that there are no good prospects at this time."*

Everyone seemed to have a different reaction to the breaking news. Petula, who was in front of her Speech class reading an article on "How to Please a Man" from her latest issue of *Cosmo,* was bubbling with vindictive delight over the news. Damen, almost suited up for football practice, was visibly bummed, and Scarlet, who was sitting in her History class, was secretly crestfallen.

Outside in the courtyard, Charlotte strolled past Prue with renewed confidence.

"I've got it!" she squealed with excitement.

21

Dead Can Dance

They shifted the statues for harboring ghosts
Reddened their necks, collared their clothes
Then we danced the dance till the menace got out
She gathered the corners and called it her gown.

–R.E.M.

Pretty persuasion.

In order to be influenced by someone, especially to do or believe something that is totally out of character for you, that person must have some credibility. An element of trust between two parties. That trust, once broken, is hard to mend. Charlotte had become more persuasive, but until now, it wasn't so pretty.

he brass, woodwind, and timpani arrangement of Joy Division's "Love Will Tear Us Apart" assaulted the first period classes as the Hawthorne High marching band circled the building. Charlotte was above it all, perched on a stone ledge over the entranceway. Before long, she saw Scarlet coming toward the building. She appeared in front of her and scared her half to death.

"Look, I know we're not friends anymore," Charlotte said, getting right down to business, "but what about being 'frenemies'?"

Scarlet pulled out her ear buds, paused her iPod, and crossed her arms tightly, appearing, as far as Charlotte could tell, to be a tiny bit open to the conversation.

"Go on . . . ," Scarlet challenged, giving her a second to make her case.

"Right now you can't go to the dance and get back at your sister . . . unless they find a new place," Charlotte explained.

"Well, that seems unlikely," Scarlet snapped, "so I wouldn't get your shriveled little organs in an uproar."

Charlotte naïvely thought taking revenge on Petula was motivation enough for Scarlet, but what Scarlet could not admit to Charlotte or even herself completely was how excited she was at the prospect of going to the dance with Damen.

"What about having it at Hawthorne Manor?" Charlotte blurted before Scarlet could put her ear buds back in and take off for class.

"There are two major problems with your suggestion. One being 'rigor mortis on the rag,'" Scarlet said.

"Let me worry about Prue. If you agree to let me possess you at the dance, I'll find a way to get all of them out of the house," Charlotte replied.

". . . and two: How the hell are you going to get the Dance Committee to agree to that when the house is about to be condemned?" Scarlet asked.

"I'm not," Charlotte responded. "You are."

☙

That night at the Dance Committee meeting, Scarlet sauntered in uninvited and addressed them.

"I know where we can have the dance," Scarlet said, not wasting a single breath.

The room got quiet and everyone put down their refreshments, curious as to what Scarlet had to say.

"We already checked the graveyard and it's booked . . . there are tons of people dying to get in," a snarky guy yelled out from the back of the room. As a popular girl nudged him in the arm to shut up, Scarlet continued, surprised by the respect she seemed to have earned.

"Where?" the girl asked.

❧

Meanwhile, Charlotte was in a meeting of her own at the Dead Dorm.

"Have the dance here? How is that gonna save the house?" Metal Mike asked.

"If we vacate the house and let the Living kids have their dance here, the authorities will see that it is safe and won't bulldoze it," Charlotte responded confidently. "It will also show that there can be other purposes for the building." She nervously awaited their reaction, fearing the worst, hoping for the best.

❧

Scarlet continued her argument simultaneously on the other side of town.

"It's big enough. It's vacant . . . ," Scarlet said, ". . . kind of."

Lucinda, Hawthorne High's resident faculty cheerleading sponsor, immediately stood up in support of Scarlet's plan. She looked like Dolly Parton, sans the talent, with huge white hair, a heavily painted face, and long talons polished whore red.

"Well, someone does owe me a favor downtown . . . I'm

sure we can get an okay from them to use the space for one night," she said, winking at Scarlet.

Scarlet was relieved that someone was on her side.

"We can even have a haunted house fund-raiser to repair the water damage in the gym," Scarlet said, thinking on her steel-toed, fishnetted feet.

"It's kind of cool, having the dance in a creepy, abandoned manor," the popular girl added, sealing the deal in a bizarre twist.

❧

"So, it's agreed. We let the Living have their dance here," Piccolo Pam said as she winked at Charlotte. "Besides, what do we have to lose?"

Charlotte couldn't believe that, after all she'd done, Pam still had her back.

"Will there be a red carpet?" CoCo asked, completely glazed over.

Everyone was bursting with enthusiasm, except Prue, who was beyond livid that Charlotte had sealed the deal.

Charlotte was being congratulated by everyone as they filed out of the room. It was her moment to shine, and did she ever. She was glowing until Prue popped up at the end of the line.

"I know you think you're *meant* to go to the dance," Prue said antagonistically. "That fits right in with your selfish little agenda."

"What are you talking about?" Charlotte asked sheepishly.

"You may have fooled everyone else, but you don't fool me," Prue declared. "Saving the house for our sake means nothing to you."

"Weren't you just in the meeting?" Charlotte retorted, finding some backbone. "I've got it all worked out. You're just jealous because I am The One and you're not," Charlotte said naïvely.

Prue paused for effect before replying. "You're a choker, remember?"

∞

Scarlet and Charlotte wasted no time, for fear that either side would have a change of heart, and feverishly wrangled everyone to prepare for the dance.

The Clean Teams assigned by the Hawthorne Dance Committee worked their little hearts out making the old house presentable. All the broken ceiling tiles and Sheetrock were scrapped and carted away. Floors were scrubbed, dust vacuumed, furniture and lighting repaired, and woodwork polished.

Before long, the makeshift haunted house was coming to life. Totally unaware of the ghostly presences surrounding them, the Living kids sprayed fake spider webs in all the corners and over all the doorways, dripped red-tinged Karo syrup and red dye down the walls, put down a flimsy track for the haunted house "ride" and loaded in dry ice for the smoke machines. The Dead kids' decorations were a little bit more . . . authentic.

Rotting Rita spit real spiders out of her mouth to populate

the webs. Kim pressed her head wound on an opposite wall and rolled it, leaving a purplish bloody stain ringed with scabrous flesh. She stepped back and admired her work as one would a priceless Renaissance painting. Everyone was getting into the spirit.

Scarlet was setting up the DJ booth and sound checking, alternating between her trusty iPod and the two CD mixers. She had her headphones on and was deep in thought, weighing every selection with the utmost importance.

"I need to talk to you," Charlotte said, broadcasting her voice through Scarlet's iPod.

Scarlet, freaked out, threw off her headphones, and saw Charlotte standing eerily behind her.

"Can't you just tap me on the shoulder like a normal person?" Scarlet asked. "I know what you're gonna say. Don't worry; you'll get your turn."

"Well the thing is, I have to be the one who dances with him at midnight because of the kiss," Charlotte said.

"What are you, CinderHELLa?" Scarlet asked. "That's just a myth. A joke."

"It's not a joke. Mr. Brain explained it to me," Charlotte replied, Prue's words taunting her in her head. "Scarlet, I'm The One."

"You're The One?" Scarlet asked, still cynical about Charlotte's motives.

"Yes, for once, I really am." Charlotte explained breathlessly. "This kiss, you being able to see me, everything, it all proves that Damen is my unfinished business. That this kiss will bring resolution not only to me but to all of us Dead

284

kids," Charlotte said. "He's my destiny, and you are my only hope."

Scarlet just wore a blank expression as Charlotte continued to explain that she was the chosen one.

"Scarlet, you may not believe me, but you believe *in* me, right?" Charlotte asked, seeking to rekindle just a little bit of the trust they had between them.

"Sure, yeah, it's only one kiss, right?" Scarlet agreed, reminding herself that it was only one night for her but an eternity for Charlotte.

☙

While everyone was working hard to prepare for the dance at Hawthorne Manor, Petula and the Wendys were working just as hard to ruin it. There was no catty gossip to be heard coming from Petula's bedroom. They were all business, and Petula was clearly becoming a little unhinged.

"So, what do you guys think?" Petula asked as she turned around, smearing on Scarlet's crimson lipstick, the one that she took from Principal Styx, and smacked her lips.

"You look just like Marilyn," Wendy Anderson said in amazement. "Marilyn Manson, that is!"

The Wendys burst into uncontrollable laughter at the sight.

"You are so funny, Petula." Wendy Thomas giggled.

"Oh really? Am I funny to you?" Petula said with a deadpan expression. "Funny, how?"

"You know, funny, like funny ha-ha," Wendy said nervously.

"So you mean funny like a joke?" Petula asked, wide-eyed. "Like I'm here to amuse you?"

The mood in the room got deadly serious.

"Kidding," Petula said, her psychosis passing for the time being.

The Wendys looked at each other, exhaled, and returned eagerly to plotting Petula's revenge.

"Come on, guys, *think,*" Wendy Thomas said.

"I want the punishment to fit the crime," Petula said through her gritted unnaturally bleached pearly whites.

"Well, it's all about the dance, then," Wendy Anderson reasoned. "But she will be hard to get to there."

Petula thought for a minute and interrupted.

"What is the absolute worst thing you can do to a Goth girl in front of the whole school?" Petula asked.

"We can drop a bucket of blood on her," Wendy Anderson suggested.

"It's been done, Wendy. Besides, she'd probably love that," Petula said. "But you might be on to something there. . . ."

⌘

Scarlet decided to take another crack at researching Prue. She figured that knowledge was power, and she wanted to be prepared. She typed "Prue" again, only this time armed with her newspaper advisor Mr. Filosa's password — "fit2print" — which she "got" from his desk drawer.

With it, she would have greater access to the school database and online archives. She waited and waited for the

advance search to complete. Finally, a link to just one article popped up on screen.

"Hawthorne Hit-and-Run Ruled an Accident," the headline read. Scarlet scrolled down farther, her hand shaking, knowing that she finally had found what she was looking for.

A DISTRICT COURT JUDGE RULED TODAY THAT THE HIT-AND-RUN KILLING OF SEVENTEEN-YEAR-OLD HAWTHORNE REGIONAL HIGH SCHOOL STUDENT PRUDENCE SHELLEY WAS AN ACCIDENT. SHELLEY WAS RIDING WITH HAWTHORNE TRACK STAR RANDOLPH HEARST TO THE ANNUAL HARVEST BALL WHEN, BY HIS ACCOUNT, SHE REQUESTED TO BE LET OUT ALONG THE WAY. IT WAS THE LAST TIME SHE WAS SEEN ALIVE. AFTER A TWO-DAY SEARCH HER BODY WAS FOUND IN A DITCH BY A MILK DELIVERYMAN.

"Pru*dence*," Scarlet said, smacking her forehead.

LAW ENFORCEMENT HAD LONG BELIEVED THERE WAS MORE TO THE DEATH THAN HEARST ADMITTED AND CHARGED HIM WITH MANSLAUGHTER AND VEHICULAR HOMICIDE, BUT WAS UNABLE TO PROVE EITHER COUNT AT TRIAL. THERE WERE NO OTHER SUSPECTS.

"GIVEN THE NATURE OF THE WOUNDS TO HER BODY, I WILL NEVER BELIEVE THIS WAS A SIMPLE HIT-AND-RUN," THE PROSECUTOR TOLD US EXCLUSIVELY.

HER AGGRIEVED PARENTS SAID, "WE TOLD HER NOT TO MIX WITH THOSE RICH KIDS. THAT IT WOULD ONLY BRING TROUBLE. BUT SHE WOULDN'T LISTEN. SHE NEVER LISTENED TO ANYTHING WE SAID."

"Ouch," Scarlet said. "Her own parents threw her under the bus, so to speak."

HEARST IS RETURNING TO HIS STUDIES AT A UNIVERSITY WHERE HE IS MAJORING IN FINANCE. HE HAD NO COMMENT ON THE DECISION, BUT HIS ATTORNEY, RUFUS BENCH, SAID HEARST WAS "RELIEVED."

She stared at the screen for a long while, reflecting on the tragic details. Scarlet had found her answers . . . and her ammo.

☙

At Hawthorne High, Prue stood alone amid the clutter in Dead Ed, scratching her nails down the length of the chalkboard, over and over, still steaming over the code violations dilemma and Charlotte's screw-up.

"I know, let's scare away the buyers," she snipped in a nasal, mocking voice, chastising herself as much as Charlotte for the terrible outcome of the original "haunting."

This little pity party was unlike Prue, but with the new strategy of holding the dance at the house in order to save it, and the whole Midnight Kiss thing, she was sure that Charlotte had driven them all dangerously close to Oblivion. Moreover, she was feeling almost completely powerless to stop it.

"Scare them," Prue said out loud, throwing her hands up in the stagnant air. "What a stupid ide . . . ," She paused mid-thought and went silent.

"Brain is right," Prue stated to herself as she stared at his

empty desk and chair. "I'm going to have to find another way to bring her around."

"There isn't much I can do to *her*," Prue theorized. "But the rest of them . . . ," she said, this time with the certitude of a true believer.

22

Bleeding Heart

The mind has a thousand eyes,
And the heart but one;
Yet the light of a whole life dies,
When love is done.

–Francis W. Bourdillon

We transform in life and we transform in love.

— ✦ ✦ ✦ —

When we transform, we never end. We change. Not completely, but we more or less adapt our new form to our new feelings. The hardest part about this natural process is letting go and allowing it to happen. There is a time and place for everything. A time in life to be someone, and then after that is gone, an opportunity to transform into something else. And, if we're lucky, there is also a time to love someone and, hopefully in Charlotte's case, to transform into someone who is loved.

he great room had been magically transformed into an elaborate, enchanted forest with cool Mexican Day of The Dead skeletons dangling from enormous dead trees that stretched the entire way to the cathedral ceiling, all wrapped in thousands of twinkling lights, mirroring the tiny white star-shaped lilies that Charlotte had tucked throughout her dark head of hair. It was more spectacular than she ever imagined it would be. She couldn't believe that she was actually on the brink of realizing her wildest dreams.

Charlotte walked past the exterior of the haunted house on her way to the dance floor and marveled at the macabre games, like "Pick a Dead Duck" and a dart game with wax replicas of their teachers' heads mounted on the wall as targets. She stopped to watch, thoroughly enjoying herself, as one student threw a dart into a wax Mr. Widget head, piercing the middle

of his good eyeball. Charlotte chuckled as the student was handed a dead baby doll wearing a torn and dirty Hawthorne High sweatshirt as a prize.

She checked out the haunted ride and noticed a girl dressed as a dead prom queen waiting to board. Charlotte watched as she addressed everyone in line, all groping each other and only really interested in getting their dates in the dark.

"Have you seen my crown?" the dead prom queen asked, standing up on the red velvet high-back Gothic chair. "Oh, there it is . . . IN my head!" she screamed as she pressed it down into her head, squirting fake blood in every direction before being thrust into the darkness.

Charlotte was the only one really paying attention. She wanted to enjoy every second of the evening. This was her night and she didn't want to miss a thing. She looked over at the round tables scattered around the perimeter of the black-and-white marble dance floor. Each table had a tower of lush black magic roses stacked tight with ornate black candles throughout.

Across the crowded room, she saw Damen. The heavens opened up and shined upon him, or at least that's how it looked to her. There he sat, dapper and dashing, like a movie star, in a black-and-white tux, just like the one on her screen saver. He was talking to his friend Max and Max's date, leaning over to them so elegantly, like a model in an ad ripped right out of British *Vogue*. She stood there, for quite some time, just taking him in.

"Where is she?" Damen asked, rhetorically, out loud.

"Don't get uptight, she probably entered a Halloween

contest on the way or something," Max whispered as he stood up to leave with his date. "Well, we're headed into the *very dark* haunted house," he said with a wink.

"Yeah, see ya," Damen said, not really paying any attention. He searched the room for a while and suddenly caught Charlotte's eye.

Charlotte gasped when she realized that he was looking right at her—he could see her!—and instinctively swallowed, trying to moisten her throat, which had gotten dry and tight from nervousness. She gave a little wave to acknowledge that she saw him.

Damen smiled and waved back.

Max and his date were just about to enter the ride, but they stopped and looked in Charlotte's direction too.

The music swelled just like a scene out of an old black-and-white Hollywood movie. Charlotte could not believe what was happening.

As she started to walk forward, she noticed that Damen's eyes were not moving along with her. She turned around and saw Scarlet standing behind her. It was Scarlet that his eyes were fixed on.

In fact, all eyes were on Scarlet as she entered, looking like a 1940s starlet, wearing the same dress that Charlotte had picked out of her closet when they met for the first time — a vintage chiffon, tea length, midnight blue dress dripping with Swarovski crystals. Her lips were painted in a classic orange-red matte lipstick and her black hair was swept up in a delicate twist.

Damen's jaw dropped to the floor as Scarlet came into full view, and so did Charlotte's.

Scarlet walked slowly toward Damen and took a seat next to him.

"You look . . . ," Damen said, barely able to speak.

"Normal?" she asked, finishing his sentence.

"No way," he said with a smile on his face.

Charlotte watched them longingly. Her drab vintage dress blended perfectly with the flock wallpaper behind her, making her almost indistinguishable from the background. She looked and felt truly like a wallflower.

"You know, that whole 'across a crowded room' thing isn't so cliché when it's happening to you," Damen said, helping Scarlet into her chair. "So, do you wanna . . . dance?"

"I don't," Scarlet replied, somewhat stunned and over-whelmed.

"Oh, okay," Damen responded, taking it as a rejection.

"No!" Scarlet said. "I mean, I don't really dance."

Damen and Scarlet decided to do something they both liked and made their way to the DJ booth. They crammed themselves into the tight space and chose records, laughing and spinning the whole time. They had a blast, picking lame music from the vinyl selection and mashing it with cool songs from Scarlet's iPod. The place was rocking as mix after mix filled the dance floor.

"You've got skillz!" Damen screamed, feeling every note of Scarlet's set.

After a while, the MC broke through the sound system with his announcement, greeting the sweaty crowd.

"Welcome to Hawthorne High's annual Fall Ball!

"Magic is in the air, so don't you miss . . .

"... the Midnight Kiss!"

Scarlet looked over at her table and saw Charlotte sitting in her seat, waiting patiently for Scarlet to get free.

"I'll be right back," Scarlet said to Damen, interrupting their tandem freestyle spinning session. Scarlet stepped down out of the booth and nodded to Charlotte to follow her.

"Hurry back, or you'll miss my Slim Whitman and The Horrors mash up!" he yelled after her.

"Hmmmm, let's see, wet myself or stick around for Slim?" Scarlet joked, holding her hands out, face up, pretending to weigh each option. "I think I'll pee."

Damen cracked a smile while Scarlet led Charlotte behind one of the creepy dead trees.

"Thank you for doing this," Charlotte said." I can't believe I'm going to get my ... dance."

"Yeah, your ... dance," Scarlet said, putting her hands up to Charlotte to start the process.

Charlotte thought she detected a note of sadness in Scarlet's voice, but Scarlet covered it up with a smile. The possession was completed smoothly and quickly.

"You are really getting good at this," Scarlet complimented, realizing that she had missed the intense feeling of freedom that came with letting go of her body.

"Better late than never," Charlotte answered shyly.

They each smiled and rushed off, Charlotte in control of Scarlet's beautifully dressed body to find Damen, and Scarlet to check out the haunted house.

23

The Ghost of You

When you think the night has seen your mind,

That inside you're twisted and unkind,

Let me stand to show that you are blind.

Please put down your hands cause I see you.

I'll be your mirror.

—Lou Reed

I love you, but I'm not in love with you.

———◆·◆·◆———

This is a false distinction. Completely backward if you think about it. Love is love. What's really meant by being "in love," is obsession, addiction, infatuation, but not actual love. Being "in love" is a statement of your own needs and desires rather than an attempt to fulfill another's. True love, on the other hand, is a bridge between two people. It had taken Charlotte most of her life, and all of her afterlife, to come to this realization.

harlotte was swooning as she made her way across the crowded dance floor and over to Damen in the DJ booth. The exhilarating rush of actually being there, being present in the most memorable moment of her entire life — and now, death — was almost overwhelming. This was everything she lived for and the one and only thing that she died for, and it was all happening right there before her eyes.

"Wanna dance?" Charlotte asked, tapping Damen on the shoulder.

At first Damen laughed, thinking that she was joking, but quickly realized that she wasn't.

"I just cannot figure you out," Damen said, putting on a slow song, turning over control of the turntables to a buddy, and leading her by her delicate hand to the dance floor.

"I think we did a pretty good job with the music," he said, pulling her close to him.

Charlotte changed the subject. The music may have been about Scarlet, but the dance was about her.

"Yeah, but dancing to music is better than just listening to it, don't you think?" she asked.

Damen was confused once again by her schizophrenic behavior, but charmed as well. She put her head on his shoulder and loved that everyone was watching them as they made their way around the dance floor.

"I could die now. . . ." Charlotte sighed.

As they danced, they passed the Wendys, who were watching like hawks from the perimeter of the dance floor. Both girls instantly sent Petula text messages and phone pictures, as much to inform her as to irritate her in that passive-aggressive way that was their specialty. Petula was waiting by her computer, and as she opened each successive message and jpeg, her rage bordered on psychopathic.

"It's on!" Petula texted back to both Wendys simultaneously.

໑

Hoping to avoid seeing Charlotte kiss Damen, Scarlet hopped on an empty car and began a ride through the haunted house. She stopped in front of a bunch of kids who were reenacting a scene from her favorite movie, *Delicatessen.* There was a girl who oddly resembled Scarlet, pretending to be chopping up popular kids into pâté and feeding them to their unsuspecting parents.

"He remembered . . . ," Scarlet said, touched that Damen

went to such lengths to pull this off but also sad that he wasn't there to share it with her.

Suddenly, Scarlet noticed that the breath coming out of the Living kids' noses and mouths was visible, as if it were the dead of winter. The haunted house got eerily silent and deathly cold. Scarlet got a sick feeling as she noticed a peculiar silhouette farther down the track.

∂ಲ

"You know, we never got to have our kiss in the pool . . . ," Charlotte said, watching the clock as it neared midnight.

"Yes, we did, don't you remember?" Damen replied.

"Right . . . but . . . we didn't get to have our other kiss," Charlotte said.

"We've got plenty of time for anything we want," Damen said. "We've got our whole lives ahead of us."

"Right, our whole lives," Charlotte said, sinking her head deeper into his shoulder.

"Come here, Green Eyes," he said, lifting her chin to face him.

"Green?" Charlotte asked.

Just then, Charlotte saw their reflection in a ceiling-high, hand-carved Gothic framed mirror. It was Scarlet, and not she, that Damen saw and was about to kiss.

"This isn't right," she said as she pulled away.

"What do you mean?" Damen asked.

Before she could answer him, screams for help could be heard coming from the haunted house, and they sounded real.

She sensed her friend was in danger, and that could only mean one thing. Prue.

§

Scarlet looked up and saw Prue zeroing in on her. Frozen with fear, she scrunched down and closed her eyes tight.

"Scarlet," Charlotte whispered, departing Scarlet's body in a flash for the haunted house.

Simultaneously, Scarlet returned to her body, jolting it awake, just as Damen was planting a kiss, *the kiss,* on her. Damen liked the jolt, thinking that it was the electricity between them, and pulled her closer to him. Confused and completely disoriented, Scarlet kissed him back. For just a second, every care, every threat, every worry she'd ever had faded away. As their lips separated, Scarlet put her head on his shoulder.

"Was that alright?" Damen asked gently, but Scarlet did not reply.

She shook off the cobwebs and realized that she had just gotten the kiss that Charlotte gave up. And that Charlotte had taken her place in the haunted house.

"Charlotte," she said as she ran for the ride.

"Who?" Damen asked, totally confused, and chased after her.

§

Charlotte was caught in the middle of a nightmare as Prue began bringing the house down — literally. The dolly track and scare stations were upended, and the flimsy pressed-board

walls were buckling under Prue's will. She held Pam and the other Dead kids at bay, leaving Charlotte to face her alone.

"Catfight," Jerry shouted gleefully.

"Let's Get Ready to Rummmmbbbblllllle," Metal Mike yelled like a boxing announcer as Pam, Kim, and CoCo shot them nasty looks, indicating they'd better shut up. Charlotte too was frightened for them as she sensed the mood was about to turn even blacker.

"You think this is funny?" Prue scolded.

"No, sir!" Mike and Jerry gulped.

"Well, let's see what they think," Prue said, pointing to the Living kids who were confused by the invisible forces wreaking havoc all around them.

"This is what you really want, isn't it?" Prue said, staring at Charlotte, as she whisked herself through every one of the Dead kids, jerking each of them to and fro like a deranged puppeteer. One by one, the Dead kids became visible in all their 'gory': bloodied, bruised, mutilated, and decaying. They saw their reflections in the fun house mirrors, and for the first time, the ugliness and finality of their own deaths were revealed to them.

"Prue, NO!" Charlotte wailed an unworldly cry and fell to her knees, sobbing in anguish at her friends' distress.

At first, the Living kids, disoriented and dazed, thought it was some kind of special effect created to scare them, but as the Dead kids began to cry and moan in shame and humiliation, they realized this was no visual trick. They were revolted and shaking with fear.

"Don't do this to them!" Charlotte pleaded.

"Me? You're 'THE ONE' who did this to them! This is the way they will always be remembered, thanks to you!" Prue yelled.

"Why are you doing this?" Charlotte screamed. "What did I ever do to you?"

"You could have helped us save the house, save our souls . . . but you, you only thought of yourself," Prue shrieked. "And now it's all over."

"Prue. Please, don't!" Charlotte begged, trying to buy time for all the Living kids to get out safely. But Prue wouldn't listen. She was hell-bent on causing as much mayhem and destruction as possible.

"This dance is beyond saving now," Prue said. "And thanks to you, so are we."

The dance floor erupted into pandemonium as the kids emerged from the haunted house, running from the awful sights they had seen.

"Panic at the Disco!" a guy yelled on the dance floor.

☙

Scarlet navigated her way through the crowd, bolting toward the haunted house and arriving just as the confrontation between Charlotte and Prue intensified. Damen was still a few paces behind, held up by a crush of kids warning him to run the other way. He momentarily lost sight of Scarlet in the throng.

Scarlet knew that Charlotte had switched places with her to save her, and now she wanted to return the favor. The big

problem was how. Charlotte had closed the door between them, not because she was angry but because she was trying to protect her.

"Charlotte!" Scarlet screamed as she entered the ride, unwittingly attracting the attention of both combatants.

"Scarlet!" Charlotte cried, as much to warn as to acknowledge her friend. Prue sped toward the entranceway with Charlotte close behind.

When Scarlet looked up she saw neither Charlotte nor Prue, but the Dead kids she'd seen when she first went to Hawthorne Manor, ravaged and dangling in midair, their heart-wrenching sobs as disconcerting as an ambulance siren.

Frightened but unable to look away, Scarlet came to a new realization. Dressing up in black nail polish, brothel creepers, and gloomy vintage outfits, listening to obscure indie bands and reading Romantic poetry, that was what she loved. It was her way of defining herself and also a way of making a statement that she wasn't just another preppy Fembot waiting for a party invitation or for some hot guy to validate her. To them, however, this was not a way to express their individuality, to make a statement about not wanting to fit in — this was their reality.

"Care to join them?" Prue asked, motioning to the Dead kids and training her gaze on the scaffolding under the lighting rigs. Little by little, the rigging began to give way.

Damen rushed toward Scarlet as he entered the haunted house, and Charlotte arrived just in time to watch helplessly as her friends' Fate now seemed totally sealed.

"Damen, watch out!" Scarlet yelled, pointing upward.

But it was too late. The scaffolding crashed down before he could react, and he was knocked out cold. The metal, wood, and glass debris pinned Scarlet to the floor right next to him. She could not move her legs, while above her, another set of fixtures and support poles was about to drop.

"I think I know why she's doing this!" Scarlet yelled to Charlotte, hoping to give her ammunition for her showdown. "I read about her death online," Scarlet went on breathlessly. "She was killed in a car accident. He was a rich kid. A track star. Trouble. Everybody warned her to stay away from him, but she didn't listen."

Charlotte's mind was reeling as she listened to Scarlet.

"They were on the way to the dance," Scarlet continued. "*This* dance. And things must have gotten out of control. He left her by the side of the road. She was hit and died in a ditch."

"Prue! He's not like the others! He's different!" Charlotte yelled, now understanding what was at stake.

Prue, meanwhile, was in no mood for such dollar-store psychoanalysis.

"You just don't get it. It's not about him at all, it's about the fact that you've doomed all of us just so that you could have him!" Prue said as she stared Charlotte down. "You've made a mockery of our home," she went on, "of our hopes of moving on."

"I didn't kiss him!" Charlotte blurted out. "You were right. I wasn't 'The One.'"

Prue was visibly stunned by Charlotte's confession. "Why

should I believe you?" she asked, but the truth was, she did believe Charlotte.

The change of expression on her face, from bitterness to relief, was palpable.

"What is it?" Charlotte asked her nemesis.

"I-I think maybe I was wrong," Prue said with surprise.

"You were?" Charlotte asked, her voice rising.

"I thought the only way to save the house, to save us all, was to stop you from getting to the dance," she explained.

"Right. No dance, no kiss," Scarlet mumbled to herself.

"But I guess I really didn't need to stop you after all," Prue concluded.

"You didn't?" Charlotte asked, her voice rising even higher.

"It wasn't me who stopped the kiss. You did that on your own," Prue said, acknowledging Charlotte's selfless act. "You realized who you are," Prue continued, "and where you belong."

"When the time came," Charlotte pondered out loud, "it just felt like the wrong thing to do." Her shoulders relaxed.

"You came through for all of us, Usher," Prue said. "Guess you're not a choker after all."

24

Rest in Popularity

And I thank you for bringing me here
For showing me home
For singing these tears
Finally I've found that I belong here.
—Martin L. Gore

Where do I end and you begin?

We are driven by our wants, needs, wishes, and dreams. When they disappear, so do we. Our success or failure in Life is measured both by what we leave behind and what we carry with us. Charlotte had been in pain for quite some time, afflicted by the only thing more powerful than Death: Love. She learned, with some help, to let go of her life and her love, to allow herself an ending, and with that, for the first time, she held onto herself.

amen slowly came to with absolutely
no memory of what had just transpired.

"I dreamt I was dying," he said to Scarlet,
who'd been gently stroking his face.

"Don't be silly," she said. "You've got so much to live
for. . . . We both do." They dusted off and headed out toward
the ballroom.

Prue's acceptance of Charlotte had a calming, almost nar-
cotic effect, on everything and everyone. The Dead kids,
pleased at Prue and Charlotte's truce, vanished. The Living
kids regained consciousness and left the ride, not sure if they
had been dreaming or drugged.

"That was the best haunted house ever!" a guy yelled.

The guy was right. It *was* the best haunted house ever.

"The art department certainly outdid themselves this year,
didn't they?" Principal Styx said to scattered applause as he

made his way over to the center of the stage. "Well, all that excitement is a tough act to follow, so why don't we just announce the king and queen of Hawthorne High School's Fall Ball," he announced from the microphone.

Everyone gathered at the front of the stage, except for Petula, who'd secretly entered during all of the commotion, standing incognito at the back of the ballroom.

"And this year's king and queen are . . . ," he said, opening the ballot in front of the whole student body. "Damen Dylan and . . . Scarlet Kensington!"

Damen and Scarlet heard their names as they were leaving the haunted house and could barely believe it, their minds were so far away.

"Must have been an amazing hook-up, man," Max said as Damen tucked his shirt in and Scarlet straightened her dress. "I've never seen a building rock like that!"

Damen turned to Max and smacked him upside his head, and the entire football team body-surfed Damen up to the stage.

Scarlet walked up the steps, looking desperately for Charlotte and suddenly saw her backstage. Scarlet ran over, and the two just stood there as they looked at one another. Scarlet immediately put her hands up, fully ready and willing to give herself over this one last time. But Charlotte didn't clasp Scarlet's hands as she always did. She gave Scarlet a big hug instead.

"What are you doing?" Scarlet asked.

"I'm making my choice," Charlotte said. "I can't live through you anymore."

As the red curtain was pulled back, Scarlet and Charlotte walked out together, arm in arm.

"I never understood why you tried so hard to fit in, when you were obviously meant to stand out," Scarlet said as Charlotte nudged her out front and closer to Damen. "But what about 'being seen,' your resolution? You gave me your kiss. You should take the crown," Scarlet said in a last-ditch effort to give the moment to Charlotte.

"It wasn't my kiss to give," Charlotte said as she gently pushed Scarlet into her rightful place, next to Damen.

Just as Scarlet was about to be crowned, Petula popped up with a huge airbrush turbo tanner. She lifted the spray gun and started shooting spray-on tan toward Scarlet.

"Turbo Tan!" the Wendys cheered in unison.

"Fuel-injected for airbrush emergencies," Petula said as she aimed the liquid tanner at Scarlet with a vengeance.

Prue, who had just reentered the ballroom, saw what Petula was planning and grabbed her spraying arm, scaring the living Hell out of her. As she did, Petula's spray missed Scarlet and hit Charlotte instead. The tanning mist settled on her, rendering her visible to the whole school. There was dead silence from the audience.

"Hey, that's the girl who died in school!" some guy yelled from the back of the room.

Petula screamed so intensely, every hair on her body, even the bleached ones over her lip, stood straight up. A Hawthorne High rent-a-cop noticed the erratic behavior and attempted to apprehend her. To his surprise, she jumped in his arms as soon as she saw him.

"I see uncool people!" she kept repeating as the guard escorted her out. As usual, the yearbook photographers were waiting. But this time, her runway moment became a "perp walk." The flashbulbs popped, capturing not her portrait but her mug shot.

A nervous murmur spread through the crowd and some people slowly began to back away from the stage toward the exit.

"Is this part of the haunted house?" a girl yelled from in front of the stage.

"Wait, people!" Scarlet said. "She's the one who pulled this whole dance off."

Everyone in the room stopped and looked at Charlotte, confused.

"Don't be afraid. It's all because of her . . . ," Scarlet said. ". . . All of it."

Scarlet faced Damen and confessed what had been going on all along.

"Remember when you said I acted like two different people? Well . . . I *was*." Scarlet said. "I totally understand if you never want to speak to me again."

Damen stared blankly at Scarlet for a moment, turned away, and then walked silently over to Charlotte. She tilted her head down, not knowing what to expect. He stood there for what seemed forever, just looking at her. Then, gently, Damen moved his hand toward her chin, as if to lift it. Charlotte raised her head slowly until her eyes met his.

"I remember you," he said, reaching down for Charlotte's hand and leading her to the center of the stage.

"This really belongs to you . . . ," Scarlet said, taking off the

crown, brushing Charlotte's hair out of her face and placing it gently on her head.

"You don't have to share this with me," Charlotte said.

"I'm not sharing it with you. It's *yours*," Scarlet said as the crown floated into position.

"That's right," Damen said sternly, "no more sharing!"

Scarlet and Charlotte both tensed up at his harsh tone.

"Unless it's with *me*," he said, eyeing Scarlet and breaking out into a big grin.

"Thanks for all your 'help,'" Damen said to Charlotte as he leaned over and tenderly kissed her cheek. His lips were soft and kind. She closed her eyes and relished every second. It was more than she ever imagined it would be. Much more.

"You're right, he's not like all the others," Prue said as Charlotte ascended above the crowd, shining like a thousand Glo-sticks at a sold-out concert. Her dress transformed into her smoky-gray chiffon dream dress, the one from her screen saver, as she rose up. She looked beautiful.

A round of applause began and became louder and louder as fear and disbelief were replaced by total admiration.

The Dead kids, who were watching the coronation also, started to become visible again, only this time they were wearing graduation caps and gowns. They were all restored, down to CoCo's black, dripping "CC" Chanel necklace, which had morphed into a shiny new gold one.

"She's a resolutionary!" Piccolo Pam trumpeted as she genuinely celebrated Charlotte's moment in the spotlight, the flute sound suddenly gone from her voice.

DJ danced over to the turntables and began spinning a set

of crowd-pleasers; Suzy threw her arms up in time to the beat, ecstatic to see her skin was suddenly scar-free.

"Hey, keep it down!" Mike yelled to DJ's and Suzy's surprise, finally cured of the aural fixation that had plagued him. With everyone's attention returned to Charlotte, Silent Violet remained silent no longer. She yelled for Charlotte and then quickly grabbed her own throat, looking stunned by the fact that she was able to say something.

"I will never gossip again . . . ," Violet said.

Pam and the others were in awe as they finally began to comprehend that Charlotte's journey, the good and the bad of it, was helping them be seen for who they were.

Deadhead Jerry was coyly summoned to dance by a popular Living girl. Now, with his mind totally clear, a new confidence filled him.

"You know what they say, 'once you go dead, you never wanna leave yo' bed,'" Jerry whispered to Mike as he headed out on the dance floor.

"Pray for us, Charlotte!" Wendy Thomas shouted from the audience, crossing herself and trying to capitalize on the "miracle" occurring before her.

"Just because she's dead doesn't mean she's a saint — just like because you're a cheerleader doesn't mean you're a slut," Wendy Anderson snapped.

They both paused, realizing all Hawthorne cheerleaders were indeed sluts.

"Yes, pray for us, Charlotte!" Wendy Anderson pleaded.

"So this is what it's like to be popular," Charlotte said, levitating slightly over the stage.

Everyone burst out into applause as she smiled.

"Way to go, *ghostgirl*," Prue yelled to her new friend.

"Hey, I got a death name!" Charlotte beamed.

"And I got a dance," Prue said, slightly rolling her eyes while dancing. "Guess it turns out you were The One after all."

"Yeah, but I never would have figured it out without you guys." Charlotte smiled. "Or you," she said, turning to Scarlet.

"Way to take a tan for the team," Scarlet said, admiring Charlotte's sunkissed glow. "But I don't understand how some stupid tanner, of all things, made you able to be seen?" Scarlet asked.

"It didn't," Charlotte replied.

"What?" Scarlet asked, confused.

"It was the fact that I was ready to be seen, for who I really am," Charlotte replied as she put her arms around Scarlet.

Scarlet knew this was their goodbye, and a tear fell from her eye, landing on Charlotte's cheek.

"If I'm tan, you're dancing," Charlotte said, pushing Scarlet out on the dance floor with Damen. They stood close and began to sway to the music, awkwardly at first, and then like old pros.

Charlotte felt a sense of calm, like all was right with the world. A sense that her work was done and it was time to move on. Even though it was breaking her heart that she had to leave Scarlet, she couldn't help but smile as she looked at everyone dancing together. She was left out again, just like in Physics Lab, but it wasn't important to her anymore.

Before she could feel too sorry for herself, a ridiculously hot

guy in a suit, looking like he came fresh from his own funeral, appeared next to Charlotte. He was wearing his toe tag around his wrist, just as Charlotte had when she died.

"What's your name?" she asked.

"Uh, I'm not really sure," he answered. "But . . . would you like to dance?"

"Yes, I would," she replied, accepting his invitation.

As they waltzed, Charlotte reassured him that he was okay and that she would explain everything in due time, but for right now, all she wanted to do was dance.

"Look at that, she's already moved on," Damen said while glancing over at Charlotte.

"Aw, are you jealous?" Scarlet asked as Damen pulled her closer.

Damen chuckled and planted a sweet little kiss on Scarlet's cheek.

Cutting in on Charlotte's last dance, Mr. Brain showed up, holding a graduation cap. Charlotte knew immediately that it was time for her, for all of them, to go.

"You'll be needing this now," he said as he took her crown off and replaced it with the cap. "Thanks to you, we'll all be needing one."

Charlotte looked admiringly at Mr. Brain and noticed his beautiful head of white hair, not a brain ridge or skin flap visible.

"Let's bring this to the 'other side,' shall we?" he said sweetly, flipping the tassel over with a huge smile on his face. "Congratulations, Charlotte Usher."

Instantaneously, one of the spotlights rigged on the dance floor started shining so brightly that it was blinding. It was as if a star from the sky had come through the window and was now burning right there inside the ballroom. This was no projector light. Prue grabbed Pam's hand and they instinctively faced it in anticipation, together. All of the Dead kids joined them in a line, holding hands.

"I can't see her anymore."

Damen held Scarlet tightly as she watched her best friend starting to disappear.

"Don't cry because it's over. Smile because it happened," Damen assured her.

"Dr. Seuss," Scarlet said, offering up a grateful smile.

While Damen was comforting Scarlet, Charlotte ran over to join Piccolo Pam.

"Ready to go?" Pam asked.

"Ready, Piccolo Pam," Charlotte said as they embraced.

"It's just Pam again," she said with gratitude.

With Brain guiding them, one by one they walked toward the light, in order of their arrival to Dead Ed. Prue first. Charlotte last. When her turn came, she looked back, satisfied, took off her cap, threw it into the air, and slowly vanished into the welcoming glow.

She was gone.

As Scarlet looked up, she saw the shadow of Charlotte's lone cap flying up to the ceiling. This was a sign from Charlotte, and she immediately knew it meant that she was in a better place. They both were.

Epilogue

There Is a Light

Dreams always come true.
It might not be in your lifetime, but they'll happen. . . .

—JJ

We all like to think the world ends when we do.

The truth is our acquaintances, our friends, and our loved ones all live on, and through them, so do we. It's not about what you had, but what you gave. It's not about how you looked, but how you lived. And it's not just about being remembered. It's about giving people a good reason to remember you.

n early snow fell gently outside of the stained glass windows, blanketing everything from the cold, hard ground to the naked trees in a sea of white. It was hard to believe that a whole season had passed since that Fateful night. It seemed like yesterday that the very same ballroom that hosted the crowning of a Hawthorne legend was now the hottest hangout in town.

Like a game of telephone, the details of what happened that night changed and changed as the days and weeks flew, each person adding a little to the tale, until the story of Charlotte Usher had passed into legend.

The once-decaying Manor was now renovated and restored, and the ballroom where it all went down was a cool café filled with jewel-toned crushed-velvet couches, large dramatic paintings and provocative black-and-white photographs,

floor-to-ceiling drapes, elaborate chandeliers, and dark wooden chairs, tables, and booths.

The Wendys were at their very own mustard-toned velvet booth, dressed in Gothic chic.

"This place is the tits," Wendy Anderson said as she scanned the room to see "who" was there.

"Yeah, I'm glad they used the money they raised from the dance to fix up it up," Wendy Anderson said as she noticed Petula bussing a nearby table. "Isn't that right, Petula?"

"How much more community service do you have to do anyway?" Wendy Thomas inquired as they both laughed at Petula's pathetic-ness.

"Yeah, how much longer will you be rockin' Rubbermaid?" Wendy Thomas asked.

"Very funny," Petula said, grabbing her plastic tray.

"Of course it is — we said it," Wendy Anderson snipped, throwing Petula's words back at her.

In the middle of the room, Scarlet — wearing a tight black sweater over a teal blouse, sleek black work pants, red lipstick, black nail polish, and a vintage apron made from an old '50s curtain — whipped up lattés, cappuccinos, espressos, and an assortment of exotic teas from behind a state-of-the-art coffee bar.

There was a chalkboard behind the bar with all the specials written on it, as well as an advert for a special Saturday night screening of *Delicatessen*. Sam Wolfe sat down at the counter, reading the *Wall Street Journal* and looking completely normal, showing no trace of any disabilities or challenges at all.

"Sam?" Scarlet said skeptically.

As Sam was putting the paper down, Bradley Grayson, his nemesis from the locker room, sauntered by, prompting Sam to immediately act slow and subservient again, offering to get the guy a coffee.

"Make it a hazelnut half-caf with fat-free cream and two Splenda, Wolf-Boy," the guy commanded rudely.

"Wait . . . so you just act retarded?" Scarlet asked.

"Survival of the fitting in," Sam replied with a smirk on his face as he stirred the jock's coffee.

Scarlet threw her dishtowel at him and shook her head in disgust, all the while admiring Sam's ingenuity. As Sam brought the piping hot concoction to the jock's table, the cup was inexplicably forced right out of his hand, falling right into the guy's crotch. The jock screamed in pain and pulled off his pants, running out of the café in embarrassment.

"Cup check!" Sam mouthed involuntarily like a ventriloquist dummy.

"You're dead," the jock yelled back to Sam, who had no idea what had just come over him.

"No, I am," a voice whispered in Scarlet's ear with a laugh.

Scarlet knew instinctively just who the culprit was and smiled just as Damen walked in the door.

"What's so funny?" Damen asked.

"Nothing," Scarlet said, leaping over the counter and into his arms. As she held him tight, she looked above the café doorway at the inscription she had painted like a tattoo with vibrant roses encasing skulls and an angel wing on each side, in memory of Charlotte.

FRIENDS ARE LIKE STARS. YOU DON'T ALWAYS SEE THEM,
BUT YOU KNOW THEY'RE THERE.

"I missed you," she said . . . to both of them.

Scarlet looked Damen in the eyes and gave him a kiss to die for.

The end?

ghostgirl author **Tonya Hurley**'s credits span all platforms of teen entertainment, including: creating, writing, and producing two hit TV series, writing and directing several acclaimed independent films, developing a groundbreaking collection of video games and board games, and creating and providing content for award-winning Web sites. Ms. Hurley lives in New York with her husband and daughter.